A WITCH AND A FISH

SELENE CHARLES

SeleneCharlesPublishing@gmail.com

A WITCH AND A FISH

Welcome to a world of fantasy, fairy tales, and murder most foul...

Never should have been the end of my problems. I should be back on
Grimm. With Hook. Hating Crowley. And working alongside my
partner, the Hatter. But life rarely turns out how I expect. The Sea
Witch, and oh, incidentally my mother, has told me I'm a witch. Not
just any witch either, but one of the biggest bad. I wouldn't believe her,
except I can do magick now. Unfortunately I can't do enough to escape
the predicament I'm in. Hook's dead. Crowley's dead. And I'm alone in
a realm that hates my guts. And there has been a murder. My sister's,
Aquata's. The realm blames me. I didn't do it, but I have no allies
who'll believe me. Worse yet, my father—their King—was injured in
the attack and he's now in a coma. I have days to prove my innocence
before they toss me into the eternal pit of torment. Thankfully, I'll
discover that I'm not as alone as I once feared. But trusting this person
might very well spell the death of me...

UNTITLED

A Witch and a Fish: The Grimm Files
Copyright 2019 Selene Charles
Cover Art by Dan Dos Santos
Formatted by D2D
My super seekrit hangout!

Published in 2019 by Selene Charles, United States of America

CHAPTER 1
ELLE

THE WINDS, how they shrieked. They reminded me of song—of a dirge, more specifically, a lament full of heartache and desperation.

I didn't know if it was just my imagination, or if Grimm literally wept for the birth of something terrible. All I knew was that I was no longer the same. I didn't think I ever would be again.

The waters roared as the doorway to the Under came sliding up like an elevator door opening. The seas were parted, and I all I saw below was the glowing blue of krill and the limp fronds of seaweed curling against the sides of the entryway into my father's water kingdom.

My sister's head appeared just a second later.

Anahita was the beauty of us all, with her impossibly long mane of icy-white hair and eyes the color of tropical waters. Her skin was as fair as porcelain, and her voice sounded like a choir of angels.

Her intelligent eyes were knowing as she studied my form. I saw the tightening around the fine lines and wrinkles of her mouth—the pinching and thinning of her lips let me know her brilliant mind was putting together what had been done tonight.

"Sister," she said in that voice, which had enchanted many leggers in her day. I was mostly human by now, so I was shocked that I did not feel the thrill of her dark magick weaving a spell over me. But I wasn't just human, either. I was something else entirely.

I knew what I must have looked like, my clothing torn and ripped from the fight I'd just been through both on sea and land. My eyes were black as the pools of glimmering obsidian in the east. My body was nicked and scraped, cut by countless lashes of sand and thundering waves. My inky black hair hung in limp strands around my bruised shoulders. There wasn't an inch of me that didn't hurt.

Taking a deep breath, fighting through countless emotions of past and present colliding into one soupy mess, I dipped my head. As the eldest, Anahita had always outranked me, and she was next in line to inherit the throne of the mighty water kingdom. Much as I hated my father and thought ill of most royals, there was still a whisper of fondness within me for my eldest sister.

"Princess of the trenches and the—"

She lifted a gem-encrusted hand. Her fingers were bejeweled with dozens of tiny golden hermit crabs in the shapes of rings. "Stop. This formality, it should never exist between us. No matter what's been done, you are still my sister." She cocked her head, eyeing me strangely. "My sister, who somehow called me to her through wards of father's very own making. A sister who no longer smells of the siren and who reeks of dark magick. So tell me, Arielle, what has happened since we last spoke?"

I snorted. "You always do that." My voice sounded lighter than how I actually felt, and yet, it was actually nice to see her again. It'd been so long since last we'd spoken. I wasn't sure how things would be between us, but it was literally as though nothing at all had ever changed.

Her full red lips curved upward. "I could always read you like a book, little sister. Though"—she paused, eyeing me thoughtfully again —"you don't look so little anymore. You're much changed from that girl I once knew. Let me guess," she said with a soft sigh. "You want safe passage through the Under?"

I clenched my jaw, my back teeth grinding together. I still felt the power trapped within me, the burning darkness that both thrilled and terrified me, but oddly, I also felt mostly the same. It wasn't what I'd expected after letting the blackness consume me. Not what I'd expected at all.

I wet my lips. "Aye. You're not wrong. But I do not seek safe passage only for me."

Uncannily, her eyes zoomed toward Hook's and Crowley's prostrate forms behind me. "I heard he'd come back. He always did have a knack for getting you in trouble." There was an underlying tinge of exasperation in her tone.

I knew immediately who she was talking about. Anahita had never been a fan of Hook. She hated leggers, him most of all. If there was one flaw in my favorite sister, it was her unshakeable belief that all leggers were wicked at their core.

Curling her lip, she shook her head. "Truth is, Arielle, I knew you were coming. We all did, the moment you stepped foot into the Never. I told you to stay away. I warned you. But would you ever listen to me? No, you stubborn, foolish, arrogant girl."

Her words might have come off as cruel to others, but I heard the emotions behind them, the slight telltale quiver of pain threaded through them that only someone who'd known her as long as I had would ever hear. I frowned.

Two things I knew at once. Where I'd been in the dark about my true origins, somehow Anahita had known. More than that, she'd known for a while. And two, something bad had happened.

I swallowed hard, flaring my nostrils. *What?* I asked silently.

She didn't need me to clarify, Anahita had always understood me in a way few others could have. "There's been death in our waters this night, Arielle."

I covered my mouth with my hands, knowing before she ever said it. My middle sister had always been the type to find herself in the middle of trouble without even trying—she'd had a knack for it, in fact. Usually, she found that trouble because of me. And this time... this time would be no different.

Squeezing my eyes shut, I whispered, "Aquata."

At Anahita's sharp intake of breath, I knew I'd guessed correctly. "What hap—"

"She was taking a midnight stroll as was oft her way." She flicked her fingers with a faux-dismissive gesture that I knew was anything but. Her laughter was tight and painful to hear.

I opened my eyes and noted two quicksilver tears sliding down Anahita's left cheek.

"Never saw the blast coming. The Sea Witch is surely back and driven by her vendetta against Father once again. I figured you'd be not to far behind, and my hunch was correct as ever."

There was a hint of disappointment there, and I visibly cringed to hear it, feeling like that same little girl who never ceased to be an overwhelming disappointment to her family, no matter how hard she tried not to be.

"But you should know that Aquata was not our only casualty tonight, Arielle." Her words were soft but fraught with barely checked emotion.

I blinked, going cold all over. Aquata was the sweetest, gentlest little hermit that had ever existed. She'd made even the hardest hearts, hearts like father's, love her, simply because of how pure she'd been. "Father," I said, already knowing by the visible look of weariness and pain shading Anahita's cobalt-blue eyes. "That's why you came to me then. Do you rule now?"

"He is not dead, but he is gravely wounded and in a comatose state. Lethe is seeing to him now."

Lethe was Father's personal doctor, and having him there must have meant that his injuries were bad indeed.

"He would have been so happy to see you, Arielle."

I looked at her strangely, curling my nose. "Right." I scoffed. "Sure. The man who banished me and never looked back. Never—"

"Say another word about him, and I'll drown you myself." Her voice vibrated with fury, and her look was sharp as a blade.

I felt her anger on an almost visceral level. I swallowed hard.

"You know nothing, Arielle. That was always your problem," she snapped. "You thought you did—you thought you knew it all. But you were a simple, foolish, little girl then, and I see very little has changed."

I shook with rage, feeling the stirrings of the darkness within me rise. But Anahita's eyes glittered with tendrils of her own electrified powers—they looked like jagged sparks of lightning rippling through the waters around her. She had truly become the mistress of the deep.

Her smirk was arrogant and waiting.

I curled my hands into tight fists, piercing through the meat of my palm with my sharpened nails

But we only stared at one another. Neither of us, it seemed, were ready to make the first move.

Finally, she inhaled and shook her head. "I have no time for these silly games. If you wish safe harbor for yourself and your pathetic creatures, then fine. It is granted. But we need to make preparations for Aquata's"—at that, she forcibly swallowed and looked away for half a second, but not before I caught the fresh sheen in her eyes. She cleared her throat once and looked back at me, her face once more a mask of composed elegance. "Come or stay. The choice is yours." She shrugged as though she couldn't care less. "But you will be debriefed shortly on what you know about the Sea Witch and why you've released her. After that, the fates will decide." She turned and left.

I just stood there, knowing immediately what that meant. Soon, the council of the Undine would learn that I'd given the witch my soul, that I had indeed given her the power to escape the wards of Never, and by so doing had caused the death of my most beloved sister and possibly even the king of all waters. The result would be bad. That much was certain. I would likely be jailed for it, labeled an accessory to the crime. The death of a royal was never taken lightly in any place, but especially not in Undine. If I stepped through these doors, there was a very good chance that I might never make it back to Grimm.

My sister was giving me the choice. She was letting me know in so many words that once I stepped through, I would be at the mercy of Undine law. Sadly, if I'd had another choice, I would have taken it. But the boys and I wouldn't survive for long in Never without my tail to see us through the turbulent waters.

"Feck me," I muttered. There was an ache spreading, hollow and cold and all the way through me. I'd never meant to bring such harm to my family—we might have been strained, and most of them might not have even missed me, their wayward princess, but we had history that a part of me was still loyal enough that even hearing about my miserable bastard of a father being injured bothered me.

No power on Earth or in the below could get me out of the tribunal, either. Royal decree superseded all rights of Grimm PD. They weren't supposed to, but everyone in Grimm understood how the game worked. I'd quite possibly destroyed a dynasty by my actions, and I would be made an example of because of it.

The darkness within me stirred, and a terrible voice whispered within my soul. *You can do it. You can end them all. We have the power now, daughter...* I shuddered, recognizing that voice instantly.

I knew that whatever was going on, the Sea Witch wasn't actually living inside of me, but when she'd siphoned off part of me, I'd also siphoned part of her. We were mystically bound, she and I. I wasn't sure how, or what that might mean in the future, but we were connected. I didn't know what the limits of my newfound powers were, but I suspected that if I really wanted to, I could make all of Undine burn.

Clenching my jaw and tamping down on that darkness, I snapped my fingers at both Hook and Crowley, stunned when they both actually began floating through the air, linked to me with an invisible tether that I could feel binding all three of us together. They would follow me wherever I led.

Gods, I was powerful. Scary strong. I squeezed my eyes shut and wet my lips in a nervous gesture. Power always came with a price. I wasn't sure what it was yet, but I was sure that I wouldn't like it at all.

Turning toward the yawning waters of the deep, I took the first step down into the abyss.

CHAPTER 2
HATTER

"SHE'S BEEN FOUND!"

My head snapped up at the sound of the excited voice of Rotá, the Valkyrie. My brows rose. I'd not showered in days, and my clothes were untouched—I was still wearing what I had been in when Elle and the ship had gone off-grid.

The sense of overwhelming ineptitude that had flooded me at the thought that I might never again see my partner had nearly crippled me. But I'd stayed the course and charted through maps, building on the very weakest of links to try and trace where the route to Never began. Ichabod had been helpful as well. Together, he and I were sure we'd already pinpointed the exact spot she must have been in Never, doing a type of reverse engineering of sorts on the one thing we still had to use, the blue grains of Never's sands.

I jumped to my feet. "Are you certain?"

"Of-of course."

The smile on Rotà's face fell just an inch. Her lips were tight, the corners of her eyes pinched with forced humor, and my heart sank.

"What's happened? Tell me, godsdammit!" I snapped, barely leashing on to my fires. I felt the invisible burn of flames beginning to ignite upon my sensitized flesh.

I was sleep-deprived. I'd barely eaten a thing in days. My mood was shite, and I knew it. Everyone seemed appalled by my shift in moods, but mostly, they'd given me my space.

Detectives were a different breed of cop. We didn't just solve crimes—we did everything together. We were as tight as siblings, sometimes even tighter.

I'd never intended for what was occurring to happen to me. I never thought I could feel that way again, and I'd tried like hells not to let it be so. For me to attach to anything was dangerous. Attachment was closely tied to my emotions, which I had to leash at all costs, lest I do what I once did, long ago.

I glowered.

She twitched and held up her hands as if to ward off the approach of a mad beast. I felt a prickle of shame but still couldn't seem to contain my behavior.

"She is safe, Maddox. But Elle's been captured."

"Captured?" I snapped and shook my head. *Has the witch taken Elle hostage? Is she broken? Bloody? Crying out for help? Crying out for me?* My skin crawled at the thought, and I flexed my fingers in helpless agitation, staring daggers at Rotá as though she could, in any way, fix the mess that'd been made.

She cleared her throat. "By the acting Queen of the below, Anahita of Undine."

"Her sister?" I asked in confusion. "Then she's safe. Tell me where to fetch her. I'll go find her and—"

"There is to be a tribunal. She is out of our hands right now."

I shook my head, still not sure I fully grasped the situation. "But that's her sister. Surely—"

"The Sea Witch was released, a princess was killed, and the king is in critical condition."

I went cold all over, the fires instantly popped out of existence, and I plopped unceremoniously onto the chair behind me, feeling suddenly weak in the knees as I scrubbed at my unshaven face. "What? What—"

"It doesn't look good for her, but that's all I know. I have to go talk with the Captain. I'm sorry, Maddox. I'm sorry." She did look genuinely sorry. I watched her as she walked toward Bo's office, feeling numb all over.

What can I do now? How can I reach her? There has to be a way. But I still wasn't sure that she wasn't safe. It was her blood. Surely, there was still a bond in there somewhere. But the truth was I knew very little of siren rule.

Squeezing my eyes shut, I wet my lips. She had to get free. She had to. She'd done nothing wrong. *Right? So why couldn't I shake this feeling of doom gripping me so tightly?*

Where there was a will, there was a way. Once, she'd had to fight for me when I wasn't around to defend myself, and I could do no less for her. I didn't know what her situation was, but I wasn't giving up on getting her back, no matter what the cost.

⚜

Elle

I WAS SHOVED NONE TOO GENTLY INTO THE CELL. I HADN'T recognized the guard who'd butted the small of my back with the staff end of his trident, but it'd been some time since I'd last set tail in Undine.

I turned, staring at the golden-haired Adonis with a question burning brightly in my eyes. Being the disgraced daughter of the king would grant me no privileges. Father had seen that my banishment was absolute.

The silence between us grew thick. "What now?" I asked brusquely, sure he would not answer.

His flesh was golden, his hair the brilliant color of morning light, his eyes nearly as electric blue as Anahita's had been. Males and females were sirens, but few actually knew that. We both could enchant, though the females tended to have a little more charm on the whole. Even so, I felt a warm tingle spread between my thighs the longer I looked upon him.

I finally felt the effects of the siren charm as I had not with my sister. His full lips curled into a snarl of disdain, and his voice was heavy and cold as he said, "Jacamoe comes, after that, it is to the tribunal to decide."

Reaching over, he locked the water-resistant steel door. It closed with a deafening squeal and a boom that rang of finality. He swam away only seconds later, his black tail sliding into shadow almost instantly.

I was alone in the darkness of the lowest part of the dungeon keep. Anahita had promised me and mine safe passage, and in her own way, she'd delivered. But her hands were tied, and I knew that. If my actions had caused the death of my sister and possibly their king, I would be made to pay undine justice. I would be held accountable, just as I had been once before. Squeezing my eyes shut, memories began to flood through me of a time not so dissimilar to the current one, when I'd been met with nearly exactly the same fate.

I opened my eyes and stared at the muck growing upon the bone-white coral walls. Because it was nearly as dark as the trenches of the deep, below, the coral actually glowed. I was in water but had been given safe passage and could breathe as easily down here if I'd been wearing my own gills.

My shoulders dropped as the enormity of what had been done to me when the witch came upon me. I was not a siren anymore. I tried calling the change to me, but I had nothing but legs.

I stared at the offending appendages, grimacing as I fought the burn of tears. The curse of being trapped in one of the eternal pools was nothing to the idea that I might never again be able to feel my body in the form it was created to be.

My breath came out in a shudder, and I rolled forward, planting my elbows upon my knees and telling myself to simply breathe and not give in to the pain and panic and fear gnawing away at me.

I kept trying to tell myself that I'd done nothing wrong—I'd been set up, brought out here against my will. And yet, my Hook was only-the-gods-knew-where. He could have been dead—or maybe not. The worst of it was that I might never know what actually became of him.

Crowley was stone, and BS would undoubtedly come searching for him. Everyone knew of our beef, so it would be an easy leap to assume I'd been the one who'd caused him to go missing.

Hatter... I squeezed my eyes shut and shook my head. He would stop at nothing to find me. I knew him well enough to know that. Whoever he really was and whatever he really was no longer mattered to me. The only thing I really wished was that I could assure him somehow that I was safe.

But the truth was, I didn't actually know I was. I'd been given safe harbor, but if the tribunal decided I was guilty, well... I rubbed my temples, I'd been banished once before. I doubted they would make the same mistake again, especially considering that last time I'd only killed a duke, not a royal or their king. I was in shite up to my eyeballs, and I knew it.

I shivered and brought my knees up to my chest, hugging my arms tightly to my body as I rocked and hummed a song beneath my breath. Anahita had once sung it to me—well, more than once, really. As a child, I'd suffered terrible night terrors, and she had sung it to settle me enough that I could rest.

Once, I could have sung the song with magick in it, but now it had become just a haunting little melody upon my very human tongue.

The part of the dungeon we were in was reserved only for the most wicked of offenders: enemies of the state and traitors. I felt heat burn behind my closed eyelids.

How the hells did this happen? Of all the places in all the hundred realms I'd promised myself I would never again return, here I was, drowning in memories past and present, feeling like that same little girl who'd only done as she'd done because everyone had refused to listen.

"So it is true. The prodigal has returned."

I gasped. I'd never heard his approach but recognized his deep voice. Even hidden in shadow, I'd have known the court mage anywhere.

"Jacamoe!" I shot to my feet, clutching at the cage of my cell with cold, nerveless hands. The elder mage stepped into a swath of light in the darkness, and I gasped even as a lopsided grin lifted the corner of my mouth. "It is you."

Dark and swarthy, with eyes and hair as black as night, he moved slowly, painfully. The tip of his cane squealed against the stone floor, and I winced, as I did whenever I saw him.

Once, he must have been a breathtakingly mighty specimen of male flesh, but over the years, his body had become more and more crippled. It was painful to look upon him. His legs were twisted at the knees, his shins bent at a terrible angle. This was worse than I'd ever seen him look before. "What's happened to you, Jacamoe? You look—" I snapped my mouth shut, realizing just how rude that must have sounded, but I hadn't censored myself quickly enough.

His lips thinned, and a garbled sound vibrated through his throat. "I was... caught unawares by the witch's return. It should heal. In time."

I frowned. *He'd fought the witch? Or merely seen her? Had he witnessed what had been done to my sister? My father?* I did not ask him those questions. I doubted he would answer them. Jacamoe had once been my very best friend in the palace. But he'd always been an outsider to everyone else.

He was not a siren. He could not shift as the royals did. In truth, Jacamoe was other. He was a man from a foreign land who did not belong, yet he'd been among us for as long as I could recall.

His upper half was as opposite to his bottom half as could be. Where he was a frightfully twisted nightmare from the waist down, his form atop was almost angelic—it was beautiful, magnificent. His face had been literally chiseled by the gods themselves.

Long before the realms had turned on the gods, we'd lived to serve only them. In turn, they'd gifted us with power, and that power sometimes came in the form of a man.

Jacamoe was from the Eastern realms of Grimm—to be specific, he was a Djinn. Once he'd been tethered to a lamp, but now, he was tethered to Undine. I never knew how it'd been done—I'd never dared to ask, and he'd never shared with me. But I had my suspicions.

I sniffed. "It is good to see you again, old friend," I whispered in a voice grown slightly hoarse.

He moved closer to me. His movements were stiff and awkward—his gait made me want to weep for him. His eyes were clear, his face stoic. He had never wanted my pity, though I'd once made the mistake of giving it to him, and I'd very nearly lost one of the few friends in the under whom I truly cherished.

So I cleared my face of any signs of it and forced a smirk. In seconds, a smile graced his own, full lips. Then he snorted and gave his head a slight shake, and just like that, I felt us sliding right back into familiar roles.

"Only you would say so," he said. "What are you doing back here, Little Fish? I believe I warned you never to return," he chastised.

Often, Crowley had called me a fish, and upon his tongue the name had been an insult. But when Jacamoe used it, I heard only deep affection. I winced at his criticism. "You did, and I'm sorry for it, though I'm sure you've heard why I'm here."

He tipped his head. My people might not have liked or respected him, but he was Father's most trusted mage, and crippled body or no, his power was still formidable. Few would ever try to move against him, though without Father's protection, I wondered what the new dynamic might be for Jacamoe. I was still certain that he could handle himself.

He stopped before my cell, and the flickering lights from a globe of electrified eels cast his handsome profile in a sinister light, filling the hollows of his cheeks with dancing shadow. "You've been marked by her," he said softly.

I stood still as I watched him reach for me.

His hand was warm when it landed upon my chin, and he gripped me firmly but gently, turning my head from side to side and studying me at length before finally releasing his hold and making gruff sounds beneath his breath. "You feel her darkness, don't you?" he asked me softly, gently. But even so, it made me swallow the lump that had worked its way up the back of my throat.

I cast a look over his shoulders, sure that the tribunal most be somewhere behind him in the shadows, waiting to hear me implicate myself. But I sensed that he and I were truly alone.

He shook his head as though anticipating my thoughts. "It is just me. The Sovereign Anahita thought you might be more calm this way."

I snorted and shook my head. "Of course she did," I said, bitterness dripping off my tongue. I hated how well my family still knew me even after decades apart. But I'd changed too. I wouldn't have snapped even if they'd sent Anders's shade to my cell.

Anders—bloody hells, I'd not thought of him in a long time. My brows furrowed, and I shot a troubled look at Jacamoe. "I need to get out of here, Jac. Please." I shook my head, unable to get the rest of the words out. I didn't want to get into the details of it all or relive why I had a target on my back and how much worse it got the longer I remained in Undine.

His hand found mine, and he curled his fingers around my wrist. "You should have stayed away, Little Fish." His fingers, soft and feather light, brushed against my cheek.

I wasn't sure how old Jacamoe was, only that he was older even than Father. I knew he'd seen a lot in his time, and the pain in his eyes as he stared at me almost broke me.

My knees suddenly felt soft and weak. "You know something. Tell me." My voice came out stronger than I felt.

He shook his head. "Nothing is set in stone, little siren. Only rumors and rumors of rumors. Your sister has reached out to Grimm PD."

I pinched my lips, knowing instantly what that meant. The tribunal must have wished for my death, but by reaching out, she'd bought me time. If Grimm was involved, the tribunal tossing me into the abyss without a proper trial would send Grimm PD so far up their arseholes that they wouldn't be able to walk straight for a month.

But my sister had made me no friends by intervening. My position had been weakened in the eyes of my peers. If Undine had hated me before, they would loathe me now.

My lashes fluttered as I tipped my forehead against the cold steel bars and took a deep breath. "And Father?"

I didn't have to explain to him what I meant. He knew instantly. "Still comatose. No better, no worse." His answer was blunt, not cold but not warm, either. I'd never understood the strange dynamic that existed between Father's mage and Father himself, but I would have wagered that it'd never been an overly warm one.

I didn't know why the knowledge that he wasn't dead yet relieved me. I hated my sire, hated the things he'd done to me. He'd always treated me as different from the rest of my family, but damn it all, he was my blood. And that still meant something to me. I shook my head. "So am I to remain down here until they decide my fate?"

He cleared his throat and stepped back, reaching into his long jacket and rifling around in a pocket. "No, I only need a few questions answered and then you are to be released." He pulled out a pair of delicate golden cuffs.

My heart instantly dropped as my gaze landed on the thick cuff on his own wrist. The cuffs cut off our access to our own powers. They were modified so that whoever controlled us could access our magick when needed but otherwise kept us mostly castrated.

I snorted then chuckled. "Of course. They never trusted me. Why should they start now?"

He frowned. "Do not feel sorry for yourself, Arielle. It serves no purpose whatever."

In those words, I heard his own life's motto. If anyone had earned the right to feel upset about their lot in life, it would be Jacamoe, and yet I'd never seen him do or be anything other than a dutiful servant.

"Do what you must. Prove your innocence to the tribunal, and then for the gods' sakes, get the hells out of this place before it destroys you too. Now, what were you doing in Never?"

I shrugged. Pursing my lips tightly before saying, "I was on the hunt for a criminal. Anne Bonny. The Slasher Gang had gotten out of control. Killing..." I paused, nostrils flaring as I thought about the countless innocents who'd perished at the gangs' hands, possibly even Buttons, I sighed, "too many. They killed too many. We were told Anne was leading the gang and that she'd sailed to Never. We followed. But it was a trap. Anne was merely a puppet for the true mastermind, The Sea Witch herself. That's why I was there. That's the *only* reason why I was there."

He nodded. "You should have let Anne Bonny rot. Now slip me your wrists."

His words were harsh but true. Bitterness would get me nowhere, especially not in Undine. I had to behave correctly and be who they wanted me to be if I had any hope of getting the tribunal to free me.

"Who will own my mark?" Only that person would be able to tap into the powers I possessed.

I waited for his answer, but he never gave me one. I suspected it would be my sister, but I had no guarantees. It had been many long years since I'd set foot in this place, and though much seemed as it once had been, much had changed too.

I felt a cold chill of blackness slither like ghostly fingers down my spine—that terrible and frightful darkness tried to consume me, not keen on the idea of cuffs. Maybe it was a good thing that my powers would be muted. I still didn't know who I was or what I was capable of.

I shuddered then slipped my arms between the bars, holding my wrists up to him.

Jacamoe clamped the cuffs onto me, and I felt an instant flare of white-hot heat sizzle through my pores, my blood, and right through my bones. I ground my molars, biting down on my tongue to keep from crying out at the burn. But slowly, the heat melted away like water upon sandy shores. I waited for several heartbeats to feel the terrible weight of the darkness bearing down on me, to hear the voice of the witch snarl within me. But it was blessedly quiet. It was only me in my head now.

When I opened my eyes, I realized I was coated in a sheen of sweat, and while I felt a slight prickle at my wrists, I was not otherwise harmed. Wrinkling my nose, I looked up at him. "And now?"

"And now you have one who wishes to speak with you. Follow me."

The door of my cell opened as though by an invisible hand. The scrape of metal upon metal made me cringe, but I followed him out of the dungeon and up what seemed to be an eternally winding set of staircases. Father always did have a flair for the dramatic, so I was sure he'd built the exit to the dungeon to ramp up the tension and desperation of the guilty as they headed to meet their grim fates.

I didn't know where I was going—perhaps to the tribunal, but I did know that I wasn't going to die today. The cuffs meant they still needed something from me. I would live to see another day, at least.

Hundreds of steps later, we finally reached the lower level of the castle. Jacamoe was moving gingerly. Proud man that he was, he didn't vocalize the pain, but I saw how stiff his shoulders and hips had become.

I began panting dramatically and gasping for breath. "Gods above, but that was exhausting. I've not been forced to use these infernal legs for such a lengthy period of time. I've need of your arm, Jacamoe," I said loudly enough that the kitchen staff prepping the day's meal all heard me.

Their faces were neutral as they looked upon us, but I knew that soon, everyone would hear of Princess Arielle's every word, move, and deed. I was fodder for the rumor mill, the favorite daughter of all their idle tittle tattle. I always had been.

I slid up next to Jacamoe and grabbed hold of his elbow, but instead of giving him my weight, I took his. He looked at me sideways for half a moment, far too intelligent not to understand what I'd done. But I'd kept his pride intact. He was clearly in an immense amount of pain, for he gave me just a bit of his weight. We walked slowly but steadily onward.

Once we'd exited the kitchens, we began walking the long, winding corridors. Every door we passed and every face we spied along the way caused a surge of painful memories. Some were less terrible, like one of me as a little girl racing away from the kitchen matron's evil wooden spoon for the crime of daring to steal two freshly steamed crabs from the pots. I'd been starving, but the crabs had been Triton's own, and if she'd caught me there'd have been hells to pay.

The one that came right after it was worse. I was in chains, forced to swim past a military contingent on my way to face the tribunal's verdict for daring to kill the duke of one of the mightiest houses in all of Undine.

I swallowed hard. I had slaughtered countless men and women, and yet I was fairly sure the only crime anyone gave two shites about was Anders's death.

"After you, Little Fish." Jacamoe's deep, gravelly voice cut through my heavy thoughts, and I twitched back to the present, confused for half a second about where I was.

When I looked up, I saw something I never expected.

Crowley, staring at me with a hard frown, buttoned the last of the buttons on his shirt. His eyes were burning red, and his face looked more animalistic than I remembered.

His hair was clearly freshly washed. His movements were brisk as he tucked the white tail of his shirt into his black slacks. Those weren't the clothes I'd last seen him in.

"I'll see you again, princess," Jacamoe whispered softly. He backed out and gently closed the door.

Only then did Crowley speak. "You look like shit."

I blinked. "What?"

His nostrils flared, and I heard a low rumble barrel through his broad chest. "Nothing. What kind of fucking place doesn't have red meat?" I didn't think he was actually talking to me so much as muttering angrily to himself.

Once he'd finished adjusting his shirt, he picked up a black tie that'd been dangling over the back of a golden-velvet chaise lounge and jerkily began to put it on.

I frowned harder. *Why the hells am I here, watching him dress?* There was only one reason I could think of. "You own my mark, then?" I held up my wrists. My words sounded rough and bitter to my ears, but I wanted to laugh at the absurdity of it all. After all these years, Crowley had finally gotten his way. He might just get to see me hang from the hangman's noose after all—hells, he might even be the one to pull the lever.

The red of his eyes turned nearly black for a split second before he growled, "What the fuck kind of messed up place is this, Detective?"

It wasn't what I expected him to say. "What?" I asked again, knowing I must sound exceedingly simple, but my brain couldn't make sense of any of it. I blinked, and he snorted before finally taking a seat on the edge of the chaise. His shoes were off.

He was fully dressed, yet there was an intimacy to seeing a man like Crowley in socks, resting almost casually against his seat. Shaking his head, he rubbed at the scruff on his face.

He'd been naught but stone when I'd seen him last. "You were dead," I said, not meaning to. And horror of horrors, the words came out full of pain and grit and trembling with sorrow. I was ashamed, instantly assaulted by the feelings and sensations I'd experienced floating upon the waters of Never alone.

I'd been lonely, and that'd been the predominant feeling, followed closely by the weight of failure. Those same feelings came upon me suddenly, crushing me under their weight, taking me right back to the panic and terror of being alone in the Never with Hook and Crowley, not knowing if either of them had survived their encounter. I could taste the adrenaline tang in the back of my throat.

A sound I'd not known I was capable of making slipped off my tongue, and then I was dropping like a stone onto the edge of the unmade bed, my knees suddenly incapable of holding my weight any longer. I hadn't even had a second to process everything, and it was so far from the time to start, yet my damned traitorous body was trying to do just that.

Next thing I knew, I felt the heat of him waft upon me. My lashes fluttered open, and I stared into his hard face, knowing that he was not my friend, yet so desperate for one that I looked to him for any crumb of wisdom.

"Hold your shit together, Elle. You hear me? That's an order."

I wet my lips, feeling the fluttering of nerves and fear in the pit of my stomach. Thousands of questions rose within me, and I felt assaulted by emotion. *Why am I here? Why is he here?* I nodded, recognizing the sage counsel for what it was.

He sighed deeply and glanced over his shoulder. Even from behind, I could tell he was tense and cagey. He flexed and relaxed his fists in what appeared to be an involuntary motion of obvious restlessness.

When he looked back at me, his thick brows were pinched. "I've reached out to the Bureau. Your sister might not like it, but I've got full access to investigate the murder of Princess Aquata." He'd softened his tone. There was no gruffness there anymore, and I was almost sure that I heard something gentle, as though he were silently communicating his condolences to me.

My nostrils flared. I was sure that what I was seeing and feeling was wrong. I was in a bad dream, a terrible nightmare in which Crowley might actually have been a decent being for once.

I glanced to the side, blinking back the heat gathering in the corners of my eyes as the full weight of my sister's death began to settle over me like a shroud.

He cleared his throat. "You're here because I need you to be my partner on this case. You're the only one with any actual Grimm training, so for better or worse, we're just going to have to learn to get along. For now."

I looked back at him, my ire rising to the surface like an angrily whistling teakettle. "You shouldn't even be awake. I saw her curse you. You were stone. What the hells is going on here?"

He flashed that cocky smirk that set my teeth on edge, reminding me once again that no matter how many glimpses into his humanity I had gotten, at the end of the day, he was nothing but a rotten bastard, and that's all he would ever be.

"Get your ass up and be ready to work in five, Detective." Then he stood, turned, and walked into the bathroom, leaving the door slightly ajar.

I had so many questions, but I knew he wouldn't answer any of them. *Where is Hook? If Crowley is awake, shouldn't Hook be too? Had Jacamoe done this? And what about the tribunal? When am I to meet up with them?*

Also, why in the hells is Crowley acting like I'm the only one who can assist him in the investigation? Undine literally had their own police, and any one of them could have been conscripted, which meant he had other reasons for seeking me out this way.

Other than telling me I looked like shite, he hadn't even mentioned my new appearance. There had been such an obvious change in me, and he would have pounced on the chance to rub it in in Grimm. It was proof, he would have said, of my inner dark self coming to the fore. The more I thought about it, the more I began to wonder if he wasn't putting on an act.

I glanced around the room.

Nothing happened at royal compounds that the royals wouldn't eventually find out about. As a BS agent, Crowley knew this.

He was keeping something from them. I looked back at the door he'd left slightly ajar, wondering whether it was possible that he'd given me time to figure this out on my own, believing I was intelligent enough. If so, that meant there was a level of trust being built between us. But that felt impossible. After everything we'd gone through, I found it difficult to believe that a man as hard as Crowley was actually capable of changing his ways.

My opinion of him was morphing, and I wasn't sure I liked it. More times than I could count, I was being confronted with the same hard truth: I might not know as much about the world as I'd once thought. In fact, I was beginning to question everything about myself and those around me.

Protocol said that all royal deaths had to be investigated, even the open-and-shut cases, as an agent of BS Crowley outranked even royal police. It was his case now, and he wanted me as his partner.

Was he, like Anahita, keeping the reaper at bay by whatever means necessary, even by hook or crook? I knew without a doubt that I had enemies on the tribunal who would want nothing more than to see me hang, and if Father died, I had no doubt that's exactly what I would do. But even his living didn't guarantee much. I walked a very delicate line here, and I knew it.

My best bet at getting out of Undine alive might very well have been to trust Agent Crowley. An ironic laugh spilled up the back of my tongue. "Oh, how the mighty have fallen," I whispered.

I was many things, but purposefully stupid wasn't one of them. I knew what I had to do.

I stood and dusted myself off. They'd given him new clothes. My ridiculous cocktail dress the faes had gifted me with was shredded to hells, I'd lost my combat boots in the flooding, and my leather jacket was water logged.

We were in one of the hundreds of bedrooms Father had placed in the castle to entertain travelling dignitaries. I marched over to the massive black-pearl armoire that took up half the wall and opened the doors.

Inside, I found a treasure trove of clothing from all parts of the hundred realms. My people were a bright and colorful bunch—like underwater peacocks, they looked to stand out, which meant that if I wanted to blend in, I would have to be as ostentatious as I'd once been.

I chose a stunning ivory-pearl couture mermaid gown and slipped it on. It would give me the illusion of a tail, so no one who didn't already know would realize I'd lost mine. The bodice was cinched tightly at the waist, and threads of glittering gold and silver ran like eels around my tiny waist and down my legs.

My hair was black as the night instead of the electric blue it'd once been, and I didn't look exactly like a typical siren with my black eyes, but I did still have royal markings upon my forehead. Running my fingers through my hair, I fluffed it out as best I could, making sure to highlight the mark so that anyone who saw me would know I was a siren of not-so-insignificant rank.

I stared at the table beside the dresser, which was laden with pots of face paint, and curled my nose. It'd been so long since I'd dressed that way, and I hated it, but I suspected that if I had any hope of getting out of the tribunal with my head still intact, conformity couldn't hurt.

I quickly painted my face, accentuating my sharp cheekbones and naturally pouty lips. When Crowley stepped out, I looked every inch the arrogant royal he no doubt thought me to be.

His face was a cold, stoic mask as he glared at me, but I saw a glimmer, a spark in his eyes. Whether he hated my guts or not, I was still one of the deadliest and most beautiful creatures in all of Grimm.

"Come," he said simply before shrugging on his black double-breasted jacket. He opened the door, waiting for me to go through first. I felt tension wafting off of him, no doubt matching my own, but we both knew how to play our parts well. I tipped my head and murmured a soft "thank you."

He closed the door behind him. "Where is the garden?"

"This way, Agent Crowley," I said, slipping back into the role I'd once intimately known. When I walked down the long and winding halls, no one paid us any mind. I was a royal—I was feared and respected in these halls, and whoever my suited partner was, he must have been equally important to be so closely associated with me.

In ten minutes, we were outside, under the canvas of black sea stars, walking the quiet gardens lined with yellow crime-scene tape.

I'd felt nothing as we'd made our way here, but the tape reminded me why we were here, why we were investigating anything at all. My beautiful, kind, and gentle sister had died because I'd released the darkest evil upon them all.

I sniffed.

"We will find the bitch that did this, Detective. I swear to you, we will find her."

I gasped, looking over at Crowley. I couldn't possibly have heard him say those words to me. He was stoic and would not look at me, but I saw the muscle in his jaw clench, and I knew that he'd said it.

My heart ached.

But then we arrived, and he was Agent Hardass once more. "Check the perimeter. Look for any traces of the witches' dark magick. Any clues, anything you find. Call me."

That was all he said before turning, lifting the crime-scene tape, and entering. I glanced down, noting the chalk outline of my sister's body still stained into the sea grass beneath. She was cold and dead now, resting in a morgue somewhere. She was nothing but a sack of bones and flesh with no soul to give her life, to give her verve. She was already becoming what we sirens would all return to one day: sea foam. All our deeds, our smiles, and our kindnesses would be forgotten in time by all. All that would remain would be a vague legacy that might not actually resemble the true person at all.

I could feel the heat rising in my belly and blinked away the sting in my eyes. I couldn't do it, break down, lose my shite. I was a royal, trained not to feel such things, at least not in the way that others might have.

So I took a deep breath and reminded myself of my training. If I'd been the one who'd died, they would all be doing the same thing. *Don't think. Don't feel. Just be.*

I smoothed my sweaty palms down the front of my gown as I finally felt my nerves began to settle.

I might not know what was going on or how Crowley had awakened as he had, but I had a job to do, and by damn, I was going to do it right. There would be no more mistakes, no matter what.

Turning on a heel, I walked that perimeter, looking for any signs or clues that the royal police might have missed. An hour later, I found one.

"Crowley, come. Come here," I cried from behind a grove of trees.

When he appeared not even five minutes later, I held up my find, a single grain of dark-blue sand.

"It was her. It was the witch that did this." I squeezed my eyelids together, confronted by the evidence of my own wrongs.

He wrapped his hand around mine, and I felt a pulse of warmth race through me. When he released it and I looked down at my palm, there was nothing there anymore. Somehow, he'd taken the evidence.

"It's been sent to the Bureau for further analysis."

"That's a nifty trick," I said, somewhat awed by how much more impressive the Bureau was than even Grimm PD.

He snorted, and for a brief moment, I saw a glimmer of a smile ghost over his lips before his face was once more a stoic, dispassionate mask. Then he sighed. "I've found something else, Detective. Come with me."

CHAPTER 3
ELLE

I FOLLOWED him as he led me deeper into the gardens, toward the very heart of the giant labyrinth that Aquata had learned as a child long ago. She'd been able to maneuver easily through the twists and turns, never getting lost, often helping my sisters and me find our way out.

Aquata had never been like the rest of us. She'd never wanted the spotlight. In fact, she'd actively shunned it, often refusing to show up to state functions, much to Father's everlasting ire.

Not the prettiest or the cleverest, Aquata had always felt that she lacked in everything, but what she'd never fully grasped or understood was that she'd been the favorite of us all.

There'd never been a need to hide who we really were with her. We'd all told her our deepest, darkest secrets, knowing she would never betray our trust. I was sure even Father had fallen prey to her sweet innocence in the same manner and shared matters of state with no one but her.

She'd learned of my desire for Hook before all the rest of them and of Anahita's desperate love for our house's greatest rival, Ebonia of the House Narina. I wasn't sure if Father even knew that Anahita would never take on a consort. She would never give her hand to any male.

Love between male and male or female and female wasn't forbidden in Undine, save for the royals, whose marriages were more about politics than the heart. We were all to have wed males of Father's choosing so that we might create heirs to strengthen our hold and right to the crown, but only two of us had thus far.

Crowley slowed before stepping to the side.

I felt his curious look upon my face when I glanced down.

It was just a patch of sea grass. The ground looked as though it had been slightly disturbed, but otherwise, I couldn't make sense of what he'd led me there for.

I looked a moment longer, not wanting to admit defeat, until finally I had no choice but to. I turned to him. "What am I looking at here?"

"You don't smell it?"

My heart almost stopped beating when he asked me that. I was a siren, or I had been. I'd helped solve the Charming case by using my affinity to water, sensing the disturbance inside the pond behind their massive estate.

Have I lost my ability to feel change in water too? I blinked, my mouth dry as I asked, "smell what?" I took a long sniff, but I smelled nothing.

In fact, I smelled an absolute absence of anything. Smells were everywhere Even as rudimentary as the human olfactory sense was they could pick up scent, which were the weakest noses of any species in Grimm. But humans could detect the scent of flowers, dirt, freshly shorn grass, and the petrichor upon the land after a good hard rain.

But there was nothing. An absolute blank, in fact. My nostrils flared, and I deepened my frown, sniffing harder and wondering if I'd not only lost my ability to smell as a human but the ability to smell at all. I wet my lips.

"You do smell it." His voice was a rough burr.

"What?" I looked up at him. "I smell nothing."

"Exactly."

I cocked my head, my racing heart beginning to settle down as I once again looked back down at the empty patch. An idea came to me, and I moved two paces to the left and sniffed.

Water. The tang of sea grass. The floral scents of underwater flowers in bloom. Even a thread of tea cakes from the kitchens hundreds of yards behind us.

Pulling my bottom lip between my teeth, I stepped two paces back to the left, to the same spot I'd just left.

Nothing. I lifted my wrist to my nose, knowing I should smell of exotic oils from far off lands. But again, nothing.

Ichabod would have told me to go farther to my left, to zone out the perimeter of just where the smells stopped. So I moved two steps in the opposite direction next and sniffed again.

Nothing. So I took another two steps and smelled everything I had from before: cakes, sea grass, and water.

I took my time walking the circle, but it wasn't a perfect circle, and at one point, the path seemed to pull out toward a wall of water ivy before disappearing completely. With each step I took, if I smelled something, I dragged the toe of my foot inside the sand to create a visible barrier.

When I was done, I stepped to the side. Crowley came up beside me. On the floor of the garden, we saw a perfect circle with a small trail that vanished into the wall of greenery behind.

I glanced at him. His jaw worked from side to side for half a moment before he finally turned to look at me. "So?" He lifted a brow, and I knew what he was really asking. He wanted to know my thoughts.

I wet my lips and stared back at my marking, trying to imagine what could have happened here. "Maybe the witch waited there, inside the circle"—I pointed—"likely for father."

"Maybe," he said, but I heard his doubt.

I turned fully toward him, planting a hand on my hip. "You don't think so?" I knew he wasn't buying my theory.

He shrugged. "I felt that bitch's claws on me, Detective, felt myself get lifted half off the ground. The strength in her body, what she did to you—" He paused. His voice had grown thick and full of grit.

I felt trapped in his predatory gaze, which burned with fire and fury as he obviously recalled our time with the Sea Witch.

But then he blinked, and his eyes no longer burned the red of flame but faded back to their normal brown with mere flecks of red within. He released a deep breath. "That bitch didn't need to hide in that way. She's far more powerful than anything down here—that much is certain. No, she wasn't the one who left the nothingness. I'd bet my soul on it."

"Then who did?"

"Who down here can wield magick?"

"Most if not all of us, especially the royal lineage. You're speaking of sirens. We're very adept at keeping to the shadows to lure our prey away."

"What about the male who brought you to me?"

My lips pressed into a thin line. "Jacamoe? No." I shook my head with absolute certainty.

"You've been gone a long time, Princess. Times change."

I chuckled. "Yes, but there is the not-so-insignificant matter of his golden cuffs. His magick is almost fully suppressed. He can only perform what he's been given leave to perform and no more. My sister owns his mark now. If he used his powers, she'd have known it."

His gaze instantly strayed to my own cuffs.

I smoothed my fingers over my left wrist, pulling my sleeve down as far as it could go to cover the telltale peek of gold.

"So that's what that is?" his voice was grave as his eyes searched mine.

I sniffed even as my cheeks burned and I hid my hands behind my back. "Gonna gloat about it?" I asked him accusingly, waiting for his damnable smirk and the glint of victory in his dark eyes.

Leaning in and invading my space, he quietly growled, "If you must know what I think, I think it's barbaric, *Princess*." He snapped my title as though it was an insult.

I lifted my chin. My spine had gone ramrod straight, but just like before, he confounded me by not pressing his advantage.

"I don't keep with neutering," he said. "If you're gonna kill something, then just kill it. There's no honor in torture."

What does that mean exactly? Does he view me as a wild beast who should be shot and put down for the sake of myself and those around me? Or... is there more that I'm simply not piecing together.

He pulled back, and I almost fell forward. I had to yank myself back. I didn't know I'd been leaning in toward him until the heat of his presence no longer rubbed against my own. He glanced off to the side with a hard and strange look upon his face, and I wondered what he was thinking.

He bit his front teeth together, and suddenly I just knew. Crowley and I weren't friends, and yet, I was as confusing to him as he was to me. Maybe it was the haunted look in his eyes, but I didn't have to ask to know that he was thinking about me handing over my soul to save his.

Truth was, I hadn't done it simply to save him. I'd known that giving the witch that part of me was the only way to get us out of there, so I suppose in a roundabout way, I had tried to save him too. But he'd been more incidental than saving Hook or myself. I didn't want to think about what I might have done if there'd been a way to ensure Hook's and my safety without involving Crowley. I'm not sure I would have bothered with him.

Guilt punched me in the lower gut, but the fact was that Crowley had made my life hells for far too long.

I looked to the side, not wanting to see any more of his thoughts and definitely not wanting him to see mine. What we had going on between us was a tenuous thing at best. My best shot at getting out of Undine intact was Crowley, much as it pained me to acknowledge it. His deep connections in the Bureau would serve us far better than my own paltry ones with Grimm PD.

He sighed.

"So what is this, then? Magick?"

"If it's magick, it doesn't have the taste of it."

I knew exactly what he meant. Magick left its trace. I'd never tasted it, but then I wasn't a shifter, either. I had, however, felt its hair-raising prickle in my time—it was almost like walking through a cloud of ozone just after a lightning strike. Crowley was right. There was none of that there. "It's nothing," I said. "I mean, it's literally nothing."

"Exactly, and what can do that, Detective? In all my decades on the force, I can't think of one single time it's ever been done. And yet"—he jerked his chin at the marking I'd left on the ground—"the evidence is there, right before our eyes. The lack of anything is what makes it so significant."

"So what do we do?"

Licking his front teeth, he shook his head. "We do nothing. We tell no one."

What? I shook my head. That didn't sound like something I'd ever dreamed of hearing Mister Uptight Arsehole ever saying. "But the Bureau?"

He chuckled wolfishly, a low growling sound of dark humor that made my flesh run with goose pimples. "You know as well as I do how much they pander to royals. If we're going to solve this case and get the hells out of here, we trust no one."

I took several deep, long breaths. Crowley, who'd never trusted me a day in his life, was implicating himself in a pretty serious way. He was showing me a level of trust I'd never dreamed of seeing from him. If I reported him to the agency, I could cause him literally to lose his badge for what he was suggesting.

"If not for me, think of Hook, Detective. I don't know what kind of shit I've stepped into here, but I'm sensing it's not good."

All I could hear was the sound of my breathing. Crowley, the agent who'd made my life a living hells for as long as I'd been on the task force, was now the very one asking me to trust him. It didn't make sense. None of it made sense. I felt as though I'd fallen through Alice's rabbit hole and into an alternate reality where I didn't know the rules or the game. "And yet you trust me?" I whispered.

He shrugged. "I always pay my dues, Detective."

"Dues?" I shook my head then realized what he meant. I'd saved his life, so he would save mine. I snorted. "Right. And once we're back to even, you'll go back to making my life hell. That it?" I asked bitterly.

When he didn't answer right away, I looked back at him. There was tension around his eyes and mouth. He shrugged, leaving me to decipher what he meant on my own.

"You really are a heartless bastard, aren't you?" I laughed, but the sound was shrill and full of something even I couldn't quite put my finger on. He owed me nothing. I didn't even know what I wanted to hear him say. I was so messed up from the events unfolding and from the fact that I'd lost my sister, whom I'd not even begun to fully grieve yet. Not to mention the knowledge that the witch had stripped me of the only identity I'd ever known... I was barely hanging on, and he was just a convenient target.

I stopped talking and took two deep breaths, telling myself to stop making everything so godsdamned personal. Fact was, Crowley was my best chance at going free. And if we were at each other's throats after that, it would be status quo.

"You're not the only one on trial. I am too," he said in a near growl, leaning in until his nose was mere inches from mine. "And don't imagine for one moment that BSI won't hesitate to give my ass up if that's what's best for them." He poked at his chest even as he straightened.

I wasn't ashamed to admit that Crowley was an intimidating guy when he cared to be. I cracked my neck before speaking. My tone was purposefully neutral. "It doesn't matter. Solving this case won't save us. You have to understand that. If the tribunal decides we're guilty, we're done for. That's how shit works on Grimm. You know this, and I know this. How many times do we have to see an innocent swing before it sinks in?"

His smile was nothing but sharp teeth. "You think I don't know that? Of course solving this case won't save our asses, but what it does do is buy us time. Time that we desperately need, Fish."

My spine tightened and my fists curled when I heard that damnable word slip off his tongue. But in seconds, my brain registered that he hadn't used it as a slur. There'd been something else this time, a softness that I was sure I must be misinterpreting. My brows puckered, but I relaxed my grip infinitesimally.

I shook my head. "Time for what, though? Who is going to step in to help us out here?" I laughed darkly. "If you think I've got allies who are suddenly going to swoop in and save us from the dark abyss, you're sorely mistaken. The people of Undine might actually hate me more than you do."

He pursed his lips. "I don't hate you, Elle."

Then he turned and walked back toward the scene, leaving me to gape at his back like a slack-jawed fish on a hook. Somewhere, pigs were flying.

CHAPTER 4
ELLE

I DON'T KNOW why I followed him. I should have gone back to my room or investigated more on my own. A few years ago, that's exactly what I would have done, but I'd spent too long as a partner, and I found to my everlasting shame that I liked being half of a dynamic duo —"dynamic" obviously being the key word. But Crowley was turning out to be as keen minded as my own partner had been.

Thinking of him brought on a fresh onslaught of questions and worries. Hatter must have been climbing the walls, panicking, wondering. I squeezed my eyes shut for half a second, swallowing my own sense of panic at knowing how badly he must be taking things. He hadn't wanted me to do it in the first place, and I knew him well enough to know that he probably suspected foul play on Crowley's part. There hadn't been, but he wouldn't know it—or maybe he would, if he got a vision of the past. I hoped he would, if for no other reason than to give him some peace of mind.

My only hope was that Anahita had already reached out to Grimm PD to at least let them know I was alive.

Even if they knew, they wouldn't be able to enter Undine without the king's—or, given the circumstances, the acting queen's—implicit okay. Unlike in other realms, there was no way to force one's way into

Undine unless one was a water spirit or a witch with some high level magick. Otherwise, one needed the queen's okay to breathe down there.

But at least if Hatter knew I was okay, he might be able to calm himself enough to figure out why none of us had anticipated the truth of the matter. His visions had shown us the witch—I knew that in hindsight, as he surely must have too.

Even so, neither of us had expected it to be anyone other than Bonny herself. I sighed, shoving my hands deep into the hidden pockets of the very expensive and ostentatious gown I was forced to endure wearing while in Undine.

Crowley grunted, pulling my thoughts away from my partner back home. He'd slowed his pace to match mine. I must have been lagging behind.

I shook my head, an automatic apology resting on the tip of my tongue, but I realized I had nothing to apologize for and simply sighed, staring over at him and waiting to see if he might have something to say to me.

We had moved into the corridor that led directly toward the main dining hall. For reasons I couldn't quite fathom, I reached toward his elbow, latched on, and stopped him when he still hadn't said a word.

He looked at me with a hard, quizzical frown. That's when what I'd done dawned on me. I snatched my hand back, flexing it and shaking my head softly, but the less inclined he was to talk about it, the more crazed I became. I needed to know how the impossible had been made possible. "How did you come back? What's happened to Hook? You never did explain any of that."

His stance was cold, his visage frosty and aloof. I half expected him not to answer, of if he did say something, to snap at me and threaten to rip my limbs off and beat me blue with them for daring to touch him in so familiar a manner.

But once again, he surprised me. It was his turn to latch onto my elbow and pull me toward a shadow as one of Father's countless servants swam by. I noticed the male's cursory and curious glance in our direction, but he was a well-trained staff member and didn't linger.

Still, I was sure I'd be hearing the gossip about my "forbidden and vile tryst with a legger" at some point later.

"I'll tell you everything. But..." His jaw muscle twitched before he leaned over me, invading my bubble with his heat and lowering his mouth to my ear. "Not here. These walls have ears."

I lowered my brows. There were no more listeners than in any other castle in any other realm, but he was acting cagey, even more odd than usual.

"Tonight, in the gardens. When the sun's set. We'll talk."

"But we were just—"

"Tonight, Detective." He said it with such finality that I knew I would get nothing more out of him.

Then he turned and walked away, not waiting for me, making it even more clear that we were not continuing the conversation. I didn't doubt that my presence would be far from welcomed now.

I watched him go, wondering all over again what in the twin hells kind of reality I'd found myself in. It was a world in which my only ally in my own home was a male who'd wanted nothing more than to see me dead at one point in our not-so-distant history. Maybe things had changed, but I couldn't help but think that maybe they hadn't.

But I was no helpless damsel in distress. Whether I still had friends here or not, it had once been my ancestral home. Still was, I supposed. And since I was here, I might as well take advantage of it.

Turning on my heel, I headed for the hidden stairwell blanketed by one of Jacamoe's wards. If anyone but a royal tried to use these particular stairs, they would be burnt to a cinder immediately. I felt a tingle ripple through my body when I stepped through. Outcast though I might have been, my blood was still pure, and the veil of magick parted reluctantly for me. Jacamoe's brand of magick was almost tangible—I could literally feel the spell's fury at being denied a meal.

I climbed the steps toward Father's private chambers, my lungs feeling strong even though my legs were weak. I was startled to note several eels popping their heads out of small crevices above me—the veil that charmed the place had also been a deterrent against sea life, or so I'd thought. Maybe Jacamoe's magick was growing weaker since Father had been injured.

I took another step, and my knee buckled. "Holy hells," I muttered through clenched teeth, wondering what the devil was happening to me. I'd been just fine out in the gardens with Crowley.

It wasn't as if I wasn't used to using legs. I wore them often enough when on a case, so I was sure the fatigue stemmed more from my fight with the Sea Witch rather than any true weariness of limbs. But by the time I reached the top of the stairs, I was quite literally clinging to the walls just to ease the shaking of my inner thighs.

Just how much damned magick had the witch taken from me? It almost felt like it had decades before, when I'd first been cursed to use that foreign form. Taking two quick breaths, I shook my shoulders to loosen the kinks in them, staring at the heavy drift wood door that separated me from Father's chambers.

Memories came flooding through me. None of us were ever allowed within the chambers of Father's most private study. Our tutors would yank us away by the ears should they ever find us within, but I'd proven adept at not getting caught, finding small enough nooks and crannies that I could hide in.

Mother's massive portrait hung upon his wall. It was the only one that didn't look faked and forced. In it she was smiling, her eyes practically glowing. I'd been young when she died, and most of my memories of her had faded with time, so the portrait was how I'd remembered her. When I felt the memories slipping away, I would hide away for hours, just staring at her, looking for myself in any part of her, and sometimes seeing it in our smiles—but never in our features.

My heart sank. Clenching my jaw, I gently rapped at the door.

"Come in, sister," Anahita's voice sounded muffled through the wood.

My lips thinned even as I turned the knob. The inside of the study hadn't changed one iota from how I remembered it. There were miniature seahorse carousels on every shelf and one resting on the floor was nearly the height of Father himself. Mother had been obsessed with them, and he had been extravagant in his presents, gifting her one each year on the anniversary of their marriage. We girls had probably been more excited than Mother to see each year's token.

I swallowed a lump in my throat. The seahorses were carved of ebony and pearl and had shimmering inlays of abalone shell and gold. Their eyes burned like hell flame—I'd always found the beasts terrifying as a little siren. Now, they looked fake to me. They weren't the terrors of the deep I'd once fancied them as. They were just carvings with no life in them whatsoever.

I lowered my brows, blinked away the memory, and glanced at my sister, who peered up at me from over the edge of her wire-rimmed spectacles. She had sheaves of paperwork in front of her. "I'm going over Father's ledgers. What do you need, Arielle?"

I couldn't hide my momentary flinch at the aloofness of her tone. She and I had once been close. I grinned to cover for my strange feelings. "How'd you know it was me? Developed new powers in my absence, have you? Can see through walls now? Should I call you 'Sister' or 'Super—'"

She snorted. "Father installed seeing eels a few years back." She pointed to a row of monitors I hadn't yet noticed, masquerading as volcanic rock within the walls.

That would explain the eels I'd seen. They weren't real after all, though they'd looked incredibly lifelike. I immediately frowned. "But why? The stairwell is warded. Doesn't that seem a little paranoid?"

She shrugged. "You know Father."

I wanted to tell her that no, I didn't know father at all—not anymore and maybe not ever—but that would surely lead to an argument I didn't want nor had the energy to deal with at all. So I swallowed my words and studied her instead.

She wore a cape of glittering glowworms that even in the light of day cast her smooth, ivory-colored flesh in tones of blue bioluminescence, giving her an otherworldly quality. It was all she wore. Her rose-tipped breasts were bared proudly, and upon her head, she wore the heart of the sea. It had once been Mother's crown. Its center was a geode of crystals that burned with the colors of amber, sea green, and rich ultramarine blue. It was the only stone of its kind and therefore very precious to the grand history of our peoples.

To see it upon her head forced another lump to work its way up my throat. Fisting my hands tightly by my sides, I forced myself to take two deep breaths. I hated feeling that way, stirring up all those damned memories. The sooner I figured out a way out of here, the better. "Why do you look as though you'll be ready to receive dignitaries?"

She'd gone back to poring over the ledgers, but at my words, she sighed deeply, as though I was an annoyance she was too polite to tell to feck off. "Surely, you've not forgotten that tomorrow is our sister's song, no? It's a matter of state, Arielle. All major houses will be arriving today."

"Narina too?"

Her nostrils flared, and I knew my hunch had been correct. "To be sure," she muttered, feigning sudden interest in the parchment before her.

"They are father's greatest rival, or they were when last I lived here," I said coyly, knowing full well why she was actually hosting them.

She scoffed, but her look was full of pain and sorrow. "Be that as it may, I hope that we can broker some kind of peace to honor our late sister's passing. It's the least the houses could do, considering how important Aquata was to us all."

I felt a stab of guilt for trying to needle my sister about Ebonia. I was petty, and I would readily admit that. But there was also something depressingly sad about the fact that Ebonia and my sister still were tiptoeing around what were obviously deep feelings for one another.

I should have apologized to her for that, but I'd never really been any good at it. Instead, I rolled my wrist and said, "I'm just saying, not all rules are good ones, Anahita. And you're in charge now. No one can deny that Ebonia is—"

"None of your business, that's what she is." She stood upon her tail, glaring over me.

I'd forgotten how much more imposing our tails made us when we stood to our full height. As a pathetic legger, I felt sorely underwhelming.

"Do you imagine for one moment that just because father is ill and unconscious I would abuse my authority in such a manner? He is still king down here!" She practically vibrated with fury, and even the waters around us had warmed significantly from her wrath.

The under responded to my sister in a way it never had for any of the rest of us, save for Father. The very land itself chose its successor. It was clear to me that Anahita had been born to rule. It was also obvious that my sister harbored more powerful feelings of resentment toward me than I'd first imagined. I held up my hands and took a step back. "I didn't come here to argue with you."

"Then why have you come?" She bristled but slowly sat back down. All of the fight in her deflated, and though she was still stunning, I could again note the strains of weariness eating at her.

She might never believe me, but I'd only ever wished her joy. I'd loved Anahita in a way I'd loved few others, and I'd begun to see that those feelings had never waned. I might have moved on with my life and they with theirs, but I loved her still and always would.

That knowledge, rather than making me glad, made me feel the opposite. Even my beloved sister did not want me here anymore. Whatever bond we'd once shared was no more. I was a stranger in a strange land, and I would do well to remember that. I wet my lips. "I've come to ask if it's you who holds my wards?" I held up my wrists, shaking the golden cuffs at her.

She lifted a brow, acknowledging without words that she was.

"Then I would ask you to give me leave to speak with Jacamoe about a matter concerning my powers now?"

"Already I've given much and yet you still ask for more. Greedy as ever, Arielle."

I scowled. "What the devil do you mean by that?" My words came out waspish because I was suddenly feeling highly offended. I'd not asked her for a damned thing since coming here.

She thinned her lips. "Are you not walking free? Do you not work a case with your Agent friend? Why do you think you are not locked up? Or has that question never even entered your mind?"

I blinked. Suddenly realizing that she was right. By rights I should be locked away in that dungeon still. The crime I was being charged for was a very grave and serious offense. The fact that I was free to work on Crowley's case alongside him meant she must have intervened, she was also right that until just now the thought had never entered my mind.

Wetting my lips, I glanced off toward the side. Gods, I hated this feeling of indebtedness, and yet I knew that I was. But I also knew that I had no choice but to train with Jacamoe, not if I had any hope of learning to control this sudden darkness that now lived in me.

"And what kind of powers have you, baby sister?" she asked softly but with a hint of wary intellect, as though she'd read my thoughts of just a moment ago. I looked up at her, and gave my head a slight shake.

Funny to me how my sister still seemed to just know me. We'd often been accused of being twins because of how well we'd been able to read one another. Our bond had been that strong. I rubbed at my aching chest.

It hurt to imagine that she might not love me as well as she once did. Though she'd be well within her rights not to, considering all that I'd done in the intervening years to father and in some small way to her, too. Deciding to be completely honest and transparent with her, I said, "I don't know."

She snorted inelegantly, and I almost chuckled, doubting very much that my prim-and-proper sister would ever break character that way in front of others. It gave me hope that maybe she didn't hate me quite as much as it seemed.

I rolled my wrists. "I'm serious. I don't know, Anahita. And it worries me that I don't. I don't know what I can do now or even who I am anymore." The last came out in a shame-filled squeak of sound. "All my life, I was a siren. A siren with some fragment of soul, who tried to become better than she'd been made to be. But now..." I threw out my arms and shrugged. "I don't know who I am, what I can do, or even why the Sea Witch said all that she did to me."

She winced just slightly. "Don't... don't tell me more about your time with the Sea Witch. I shouldn't know more than I already do. The tribunal should be the first to hear your testimony."

I nodded solemnly. If father did lose his battle, then Anahita would be crowned queen, and the last thing she needed was the scandal of her sister's run-in with the bogey monster. No doubt the tribunal meant to keep Anahita far away from any association with me in court. I released a long, slow breath. "Of course. But if you hold my mark, I need your permission to—"

"If you think it will help you, Arielle," she whispered, "then you've got my blessing."

I felt a pulse of warmth rush through me at her words. The cuffs recognized her authority, and I would be able to learn the true depths of what I'd lost or gained from my time with the witch. I nodded. "Thank you." I turned to leave.

"Arielle," she said faintly but with authority.

I looked at her over my shoulder.

Her hand was outstretched, and there was a strange look, almost a little like yearning, upon her face. But she quickly smoothed it. "I've followed your exploits on Grimm."

I waited to hear if she would say more, but she was silent for several moments. Her jaw flexed, and the muscles in her throat worked. I could tell she wanted to say more about it, and yet she didn't. "What have you learned about our sister?" she asked instead.

I blinked, needing a second to adjust my frame of mind to the sudden shift in topic. "Er." I cleared my throat then turned fully around. I opened my mouth, ready to tell her about the nothingness Crowley and I had found, but then I remembered his words of caution, and though I didn't have a damned clue why I was actually going to take his warning to heart, I did . "Nothing yet," I said, feeling only the slightest twinge of shame at the deception. "We plan to go back out tonight to double-check and see if we've overlooked anything. Of course, I'll inform you right away if we find anything."

Her brows furrowed, and I plastered on a smile so tight that I knew must have looked like plastic on my face.

She nodded. "Fine. Tell me the moment you learn of anything. Be careful, Arielle, Undine is not what you remembered." With those cryptic words, she turned her attention back to the sheaves before her, and I knew that our moment of bonding was done.

What in the hells did she mean by that? I couldn't help but wonder if my sister was hiding a secret just as I was.

It dawned on me as I began to turn that I'd not asked her about Hook. In all the drama, I'd almost forgotten that he was being kept here. I almost didn't ask, doubtful that she'd tell me much. But at least if he was alive, I would gain some measure of peace.

Before I could talk myself out of it, I loudly cleared my throat.

Anahita's brow twitched and she looked up slowly. "Is there something you still need?"

Don't fidget, I told myself sternly, even as I began picking at my nails. For the life of me, I could never understand why being in Undine always made me feel more like a child than the intelligent woman I was. Giving myself a slight shake, I straightened my shoulders and lifted my chin. "I only wondered if you knew anything about Hook?"

If anyone in Undine did, it would be the acting queen, but I'd worded my question as politely as I could.

Her lips had thinned. Anahita had never been a fan of his. Feeling heat rise in my neck, I quickly stammered, "I-It's only that when I last saw him, I wasn't sure if he'd survived, and I'm anxious to learn—"

"The legger lives."

My heart almost lurched out of my chest, beating like a fist against my ribs, and my knees turned to jelly. I had to brace myself against the wall beside me. "H-He lives? Is he awa—"

"The legger is not your concern. Not anymore." There was true anger in her tone, which helped me to realize that how she'd been just seconds before had actually been more of an act that anything. She had always despised Hook, and it seemed that her feelings hadn't shifted in the slightest. "Now." She jerked her chin toward the door in a clear directive that it was past time for me to take my leave of her.

My nostrils flared. Hope and disappointment warred within me like rival factions, tearing and clawing my innards. He lived. But to what extent, I wasn't sure. Perhaps Jacamoe had him. I could go see, check in. He might be more forthcoming than my sister.

With a swift nod that she did not see, I turned on my heel and marched slowly toward the door. But before I left, I looked up at the massive portrait of my mother, with her vivid red hair and sparkling green eyes, her skin as bone-white as Anahita's own, and her beauty as equally legendary. I could see bits of each of my sisters in my mother's face.

But I was not in there. I never had been, and I wondered all over again if the Sea Witch had told me the truth of my parentage. I *was* a witch—I could feel the power of the darkness curling like smoke within me. But I was also siren, and whether I had the powers or not, she couldn't strip my identity from me. The only problem was that I didn't know which part of me was more real, the siren I'd been or the new person I'd been fashioned into. I knew absolutely nothing about what had happened, but it felt more and more real as time moved on.

My palms began to tingle as the swirls of dark magick were nulled by the cuffs on my wrists, making me grit my teeth. All that power had no place else to go but back inside of me.

Sweat trickled down my spine as the waves of magick settled down once more. I took a trembling breath and straightened my shoulders. Swallowing hard, I opened the door and left without a backwards glance.

CHAPTER 5
ELLE

IN NO TIME, I found myself returning to the section of the castle that only a select few were given access to, the left wing, where Father could escape when the crown he wore grew too heavy. Mother had most often been found there, usually in one of her dozen or so solariums, warming herself in the rays of the Undine sun as she read a book or drank some seaweed tea.

I actually had a few fond memories here. Adella and Adrina, the most artistic of my sisters, would put on massive productions for sirens as young as they had been, with much help from the staff, to be sure. But Adella would paint the entire set and sing with a voice that could make anyone willingly fall to their death, just so long as they could hear her a little bit longer.

Both of them had been darker of complexion, like Father, but with Mother's piercing jewel-green eyes. Adella wasn't as beautiful as Anahita but had been the first of us to marry into a strong siren house.

I didn't realize I'd been staring into the library, replaying visions of yesteryear until a voice spoke over my shoulder. Instantly, the visions scattered like chaff on the wind.

"I assume you have come all this way to speak with me, Little Fish." Jacamoe's exotic accent sounded amused and a touch curious, even as he studied me with dark eyes tinged with curiosity and a smidge of concern.

Clearing my throat, I brushed my hands down the front of my gown with nervous fingers and gave him a crooked smile. "Are you the only one who still maintains a residence here?"

"I like being solitary," he said by way of explanation.

I nodded. "I always did know that about you. I'd swear, if I didn't know better, I'd say you were more my father than my own dad has been."

He laughed robustly. It was rare to hear Jacamoe let loose in that way, though I'd gotten him to do it a time or two in my day. "Would not that be miraculous. I believe if I had, my peers would have taken me back long ago, if for no other reason than to gawk at the curiosity."

It was well known that Djinn were created sterile. That way, there was no chance of ever passing that much power through one family tree. It effectively cut off any ability for them to create an uprising against their puppet masters. I wasn't quite sure who had crafted the Djinn, mostly because Jacamoe would never share it with me, but I reckoned it had to have been someone or something of exceedingly great power. Definitely a god, but I didn't have a clue which one.

Jacamoe was quickly stuffing an oblong-shaped item into his pocket. I frowned, and catching my look, he said, "Anahita summoned me to retrieve her spy glass." He patted his pocket.

I snorted. "Do you mean to tell me that my straight-laced sister who never, ever breaks the rules means to spy? Scandalous."

His face was long and serious as he said, "Go easy on her, Little Fish. Your sister does her very best in these most trying times."

His reminder was as good as throwing a bucket of ice on my face. Twisting my lips, I nodded. "Do they all blame me, then?"

Normally, I wouldn't have cared. Once upon a time, I hadn't cared if all of Undine had known that I'd been the one to violently butcher Anders. In truth, I still didn't care. The perverted bastard had deserved his fate.

But for some damned reason, I found myself caring all of a sudden, and I suspected I knew why. Much as I'd told myself I no longer needed these people, the crown, the title, or the wealth, the truth was that being here and recalling my past was reminding me that not all of it had been bad. The material things could go hang, but my family, well, I'd missed them more than I'd imagined. It was like a wound in my heart I hadn't realized until my return. And it throbbed, all day and all night. I gently skimmed my fingers over my breastbone.

"Truth?" he simply asked.

My heart sank, but I snorted. "You don't have to say more, Jacamoe. You've already said enough."

He spread his hands as though in apology, but I shook my head and latched onto his fingers. "It's okay, my friend. I think I would blame me too if I were them. I am, after all, a *traitor*."

We stood in contemplative silence for a moment longer before he cleared his throat and gestured for me to walk with him.

I did with a grateful nod in return.

"Tell me, Little Fish, did you come all this way simply to visit an old man?"

I chuckled softly. "You're not an old man, Jacamoe. That's a silly notion. Why, if I didn't look at you practically as my own father, I might even be tempted to—"

He laughed and held up his hand. "My heart cannot take such flatteries, but truth, tell me what I can do for you."

He thought I lied, but I hadn't. I'd always found Jacamoe strangely beautiful and appealing in a forbidden way, but Djinn weren't just sterile—they were eunuchs capable of platonic love but not Eros love.

I'd once walked in on Jacamoe while he'd been in his private chambers, and it revealed a truth I would never forget seeing, one forever burned into my heart and mind. Not only had his berries been taken, but his twig had been terribly disfigured as well, serving only to be used for the most basic of human functions.

He'd simply stood there in the center of his room, his legs bowed and withered, his sex monstrously disfigured, and he had stared at me with dark and broken eyes. What I recalled most was that he didn't shout at me to go away or scream that I'd violated a sacred trust by entering his private chambers with the zeal of a silly ten-year-old who'd only wanted to share a happy moment with her friend. I'd seen humiliation, pain, and pride burning in his eyes. He hadn't wanted my pity, and even as a vain little girl, I'd known it. All I remembered was murmuring nonsensical words before I'd promptly run away, vowing to myself that I would never, ever mention it to him. And I never had, though we both knew what I'd seen. There'd been an unspoken pact crafted between us that day.

I lifted my cuffed wrists. "I came to you because you're the only one who can help me figure out what's been done to me."

He glanced at my wrists with a softly furrowed brow. "The witch, you mean?"

"Aye." I nodded. "I need to know what I'm capable of, how far she's changed me, or if she's even changed me at all."

"You would need Princess Anahita's—"

"I've gotten her approval."

He nodded then stepped into my space and took my wrists in his hands. He bowed his head, and my pulse quickened. He smelled of jasmine, myrrh, and frankincense, lush scents that always made me think of the glittering jewel of East Grimm.

The East was as different from the West as could possibly have been imagined. I'd been sent on a case there once. The sights, sounds, and smells had all made me think painfully of my friend and how much he must have missed it. There were flying carpets and women dressed in pants crafted of rich silks and bursting with every color of the rainbow. It'd been like walking through a garden—not of flowers, but of people. Their skin had been as dark and rich as gleaming mahogany, with hair as thick as roped vines and accents that were strangely sensual and erotic.

I'd loved it there, mostly because it'd made me think of my beloved friend. I'd almost sent him a letter detailing my exotic travels, but though I'd gotten as far as writing it, I'd never actually sent it. I told myself it was because Father's spies would never have delivered it to him, but I think the truth was more that I was too chicken to crack open his wounds, which had only begun to heal.

"There is a dark magick within you," he said, cutting me off from my thoughts.

I quickly yanked my hands out of his, still feeling the electric currents of his warm magical pulses rush through me. Mine had made me feel pain back in Father's study, but Jacamoe's magick felt like soothing waters. I rubbed my fingers together, trying to shake off the last of the tingles. "A lot? A little?"

He looked straight into my eyes, and I knew before he even spoke that it wasn't good. His eyes gleamed. "It is vast and it is very wild. Dark. Very dark, Little Fish."

I shivered and hugged my arms to my chest. "So even if the tribunal decides I'm not guilty of being an accessory to my sister's murder, I'm still going to hang for having such black magick coursing through my soul."

He shook his head then cupped my left cheek with his warm hand, patting gently, and the memories of all the other countless times he'd done so when he'd been proud of me—or even put out with me—blasted right through my mind.

I was exhausted by all the memories that continued to pour through me, but they wouldn't stop. They just kept coming and coming. I should have stepped away from him and refused his tender touch, but it'd been too long since I'd felt anything quite so pure, so I stayed, squeezing my eyes shut, fighting the strange urge to fling myself at him and hug him tightly as I wept like a little girl for all that I'd lost.

"I never said that it cannot be tamed or controlled, Arielle. The wellspring of the magick is dark, but even a dark mage once had the choice whether to walk the black path or stay to the light. Did you not know that my own power was once as dark as yours?"

My mouth parted just a little, and I leaned away from his touch enough that I could look at his face without being forced to cross my eyes. "It is? I thought that—"

"I am bound to a lamp, Princess, and therefore to a master who controls me in all ways. I cannot do more than I am allowed. My own powers are birthed of darkness, but if a Djinn is fortunate enough to know and feel love... Well"—he looked at me deeply—"there is hope for us all."

I didn't have to ask him what he meant. I felt the truth of his words in his touch, in his gentleness toward me, and I knew he loved me just as I loved him. I pressed my lips together, fighting their trembling so he would not witness my shame.

With one last pat of my cheek, he stepped back. "I must deliver the spyglass to your sister, and then if you would like, you could meet me in your mother's solarium tonight so that we might begin to learn the true scope of your powers."

I almost agreed until I remembered that I was supposed to meet Crowley in the gardens again. I sniffed and pretended to scratch an itch on my neck. "Tonight, I cannot, old friend. I must meet with Agent Crowley to—"

"The crime scene, of course. Although your father's people scoured the grounds, they said it was cut and dry. The witch killed poor Aquata."

I knew he was as curious as the rest of them, but though I loved Jacamoe, my training kicked in all the same. "I'm so sorry. I wish I could tell you something, but my hands are tied. I'm assisting what is now a top-level case. If you wish to know anything you'll have to go through Agent Crowley."

"Ah"—he batted my words away—"forget I asked. Of course, I understand how the law works. It is only that what's been done was so shocking to us all. She was a good girl, your sister. She did not deserve what was done to her." He took a deep breath.

I heard the overwhelming note of sympathy and misery in his voice. Jacamoe had always taken a keen interest in me, but he'd cared for my sisters, too, in his own way. Most of them had viewed him less as a friend and more as a servant, but Aquata had been kind to him. It'd been her way. She'd never had a mean bone in her body.

It was my turn to pat his cheek. "Do not blame yourself for what was done to her, old friend."

He blinked, forcing a tight smile onto his face. "If only I could have saved her." He stared hard at his wrists, where the same tools to squelch his own not-so-insignificant powers were visible.

I would have bet that a Djinn versus a dark witch would have been a showdown for the ages. They both had infinite power, but it could have been very possible that Jacamoe would have won such a trial. We would never know, though, because his powers were as limited as a baby mage's for as long as he was forced to wear the cuffs.

"Tomorrow, then?" I asked him.

"Yes, Princess. Tomorrow."

I smiled stiffly. "Not anymore, Jacamoe."

"You will always be a princess to me, Little Fish. Now, I must—"

I grabbed hold of his elbow, stalling his exit just a little longer. "I did come here for one other reason."

"Ah, the truth finally wins out." He smiled warmly before nodding for me to continue. "What can I do for you, Arielle?"

I took a deep breath to steady my nerves. "I came here with two men. Agent Crowley and *my*"—I coughed, catching my slipup a second too late—"*er*, that is to say—"

"Your Hook." He finished my thought.

I winced but nodded anyway because the truth was the truth. After what Hook and I had done in the ship, he wasn't just another man to me. The old fire, the old love... it was still there.

He shook his head. "No, my dear. I do not have him. But I have heard that he is being kept in the east tower."

I winced again. Nothing good ever happened in the east tower. It was where Father had stored his prisoners of war, keeping them chained until their executions, or worse, their public humiliations. Father had been a benevolent king as equally as he'd been a cruel and terrifying tyrant. It simply depended on whom one asked.

I took a deep breath and hugged my chest. "What are they doing to him?"

Jacamoe's eyes looked worried. "I do not know, Princess, but if you would like, I could look in on him. I could at least do that for you."

It wasn't much, and we both knew it. Jacamoe would be as helpless as I was to stop Hook's tortures, if that was indeed what Anahita had ordered. But knowing something was better than knowing nothing at all.

I glanced at Jacamoe's pocket where he'd hidden the spyglass, wondering for a split second if I could convince him to let me borrow it.

As though he sensed exactly where my thoughts were, he covered the pocket with his hand. I looked at his stern face. "This goes to your sister now."

I heard the warning. *Don't steal. Don't be stupid and give the tribunal anymore opportunities to convict me.* My hands curled into fists at my side, and my lips thinned, but I didn't move. I didn't make a grab for it. I just looked at him.

He executed a nearly perfect bow, which must have been extremely painful for him, then elegantly turned and walked slowly down the hall toward my sister's wing of the castle.

I watched him fade into nothingness before I slowly turned and stared at the hallway full of portraits of Undine heritage that felt as foreign to me as they always had.

Much as I wanted that spyglass, I knew he was right. Damn him to the twin hells, he was right. I was on shaky ground. I had to watch my p's and q's, for whoever was chosen to head the tribunal I could almost bet my weight in gold would be no friends of mine. Something as simple as stealing the king's spyglass, which now belonged to my sister, could have been all they would need to convict me, should the greater crime miraculously be absolved. Father had murdered others for less. My people were a bloodthirsty lot.

I kicked at the wall hard enough with my bare foot to make my toes throb miserably when I'd finished. I had to get out of here—I had to get us all out of here. I might have been walking around freely, but I was far from free, and I knew it. The feeling of claustrophobia, as if I was being squeezed in on all sides, was overwhelming. I wasn't used to sitting still, to not always being busy.

If I had been in Grimm, I would have had so many things to do: cases to solve, people to speak with. But in Undine, I felt like a burden, mostly forgotten by all, with nothing to occupy my mind or time.

I had hours yet before I could meet up with Crowley. I was no princess. I would not be expected to greet any of the incoming dignitaries. I literally had nothing to do.

Lowering my head, I rubbed at my aching temples and muttered, "what am I gonna do now?"

I needed to focus and create an action plan, just as Hatter would have done.

Hatter. I sighed. I hoped he was all right, wherever he was.

CHAPTER 6
HATTER

As I RODE the elevator to the top floor of my flat, I heaved a weary sigh as I rolled my neck from side to side. It was nighttime in Grimm, and the moon was at its zenith. Outside I could hear the murmurs of the midnight bar crowd. I was tempted to go find a place to sit a spell.

I'd been at work for the past thirteen hours, until Bo had returned and caught me still wearing the same clothes as when she'd left me eight hours earlier. After that, she'd kicked me out with a sternly worded command not to return for at least eight more.

Knowing Elle was relatively unharmed hadn't lessened my anxiety for her in the slightest. I'd spent the day learning just what an Undinian tribunal entailed. It was some nasty, dirty stuff. There was no jury, no assumption of innocence until proven guilty. She would be tried by randomly selected elders of rival houses and if found guilty would be tossed into the eternal pit of the damned.

I knew a little of Elle's past, at least enough to know that she was not entirely liked in her realm. She was a true outcast in every sense of the word.

The elevator stopped suddenly, and I glanced up, wondering if I could be at my floor, the fiftieth, already. It'd been quite fast.

But when the fae-enchanted-oak doors parted, I didn't recognize the floor at all. In fact, it was like nothing I'd ever seen inside of the Whispering Willows. I'd chosen the flat because of its similarities to Wonderlandian workmanship. I enjoyed the seamless merging of nature and the urban sensibilities of Grimm.

Never had I seen a floor with such an aquatic flair, though. The floors gleamed like mother-of-pearl, the walls themselves looked carved from bone-white coral, and—I blinked, wondering whether that had been the fin of an electrified eel rounding the corner.

Scratching the back of my head, I stared at the empty space. It literally seemed to ripple like the invisible bands of water currents.

I took a deep breath, reflexively more than anything, halfway wondering if I might soon lose all ability to breathe if that was really water before me. But even though my heart banged in my chest at the thought of drowning in my elevator, I didn't actually seem to be in danger of losing my air supply.

I blinked, wondering if it was the work of fae craftsmanship or—I glanced down at my arms. *Am I having some sort of strange vision?* But I saw no glow of light and knew in a moment that whatever it was, it was very real.

"Hello?" I asked, glancing around, considering if perhaps someone was out there, waiting to enter. When no one responded, I automatically said, "Going up?"

But when there was still no answer, my anxiety only increased. *What the bloody hells is going on here?*

I glanced over at the glowing button for the fiftieth floor. I pressed it once more, wondering if there had been a malfunction. But nothing happened. The doors remained opened, and when I looked back, I definitely saw a fish swim by.

"Bloody hells," I muttered, even as the water began to swirl and ripple faster before me. That was definitely water out there, which meant that whatever was happening was of a magickal nature.

In my gut, I knew it was related to Elle.

Then a shimmer began to take shape in front of me, a loose image that was vaguely human but veiled in a bioluminescent glow.

"Elle?" I whispered.

"Not Elle," a deep masculine voice replied.

I scooted back on my heels, immediately hearing the growling tones of Crowley's rasp. "Agent Crowley?"

"Aye," he said. "I do not have long. Seconds at best. But you are Arielle's partner, no?"

I lowered my brows as the glowing smoky image shifted closer toward me. Crowley's glow was so bright that I could not make out his features, but it was definitely his voice I was hearing. Still, he knew that I was Elle's partner, so the only thing I could figure was that he was being purposefully secretive.

"Yes," I snapped as my pent-up tensions came pouring out of me. "How is she? Where is she? Can I speak with—"

"No time. I am not a magick user. As it is, I am depleting what reserves I have left from the agency. Listen to me carefully, Constable Hatter—"

My spine went taut to hear him refer to me as such. Not that there was any shame in in being a constable, but he knew damned well I'd advanced a year ago. I wondered if it was some sort of backhanded slight.

I clenched my jaw, quieting the hum of anger burning like a caged, angry thing inside of me, and focused my energies instead on simply listening. Crowley had reached out to me for a reason.

"—it does not look good for Arielle right now. The tribunal is desperate to lay the blame somewhere. The King is gravely injured, and a princess has been killed by the willful releasing of the Sea Witch."

"I'm sure that if Elle did so, her reasons were—"

"—immaterial," Crowley cut me off.

I fisted my hands by my sides. Glad to see the bastard hadn't changed at all since I'd last seen him. "The law is the law, Agent. She deserves a fair and honest trial." I pled to his law-enforcement side— surely, he could see what was obvious to me. Blaming Elle for the death of her sister and her father's injuries was unjust.

The laugh he gave sent chills straight through me. "You are the biggest godsdamned fool if you believe that, Detective. They need a scapegoat, and Arielle is it. She will be sentenced to die for this—make no mistake."

"How do you know this?" I snarled, fury making me forget myself. My vision was turning bright with spots as I felt my inner flames began to roil and churn at the thought of Elle alone and unprotected down there.

"I have worked amongst the royals long enough to know how these matters work themselves out. I tell you all of this because we need an ally in the above whom we can trust to work alongside of us and not against us. Secrecy is the key here, Detective. You must tell no one what I am about to share with you. Do you understand?"

I nodded.

"Do you understand?" He snapped with the sharp edge of a growl to it.

My brows gathered into a sharp vee. "I understand what you're suggesting I do, Crowley: go against my damned precinct, my captain, and any and all authority. Now you do you understand how bloody awful this can go for me if they find out I worked behind their backs?"

He grunted. "It's a chance you will have to take if you want her back alive."

"What the hells does that even mean?" I snapped, taking a step forward as my fists began to burn with flame. The waters outside the doors started to sizzle, filling my elevator with steam as the heat from my hands hit its wall. *Is he implying that she is in danger from him as well? Knowing the bastard, I don't doubt it.*

"Is she what matters most to you?"

I hissed, shaking my head reflexively. I didn't trust Crowley in the slightest, and a confession might free her from the tribunal's clutches but could land us both in a different kettle of fish when she came back home.

"Well, is she?!" he snapped, and I didn't think.

"Yes, godsdammit, she's everything to me. Now you—"

"Good. That is good." The obvious note of relief in his voice shut me up instantly.

Confusion circled like water around a drain in my head. *Why does he sound so pleased by that? Crowley has always had it out for Elle, but this doesn't seem like the Crowley I remember.*

"No matter what happens, Arielle must survive this. Do you hear me, Detective?" he asked, cutting through my musings.

"Of course," I answered honestly.

"She must survive this," he expressed once more with an urgency that infected my own soul. *Just what in the hells had happened to them in the Never?*

"Now, listen to me, and listen closely," he said. "There is a chance, a way to turn the tribunal's focus elsewhere. The answers begin in a tavern in Grimm, a place called *Bârân*."

"In the Persiannous district?"

"Aye, the very one. You must go there and speak to one known only as the Tinkerer."

"What?" I shook my head, noticing that the image was becoming more and more insubstantial. His voice was growing weaker. "I need to save Detective Elle. I don't need to go to the—"

"If you wish to save her, as I do, you will do exactly as I have told you. In three hours, you must go find the one they call the Tinkerer, Detective, and let her know that it is the agent who has sent you."

None of it made sense. The conversation had only raised a thousand more questions. "I don't understand. How can going there be of help any to you?" I didn't get a chance to finish my thoughts before his ghostly vision vanished and the floor was water no more, but a verdant garden of perpetual flowers in bloom.

I stared dumbly around me for several moments, feeling oddly as if I'd found my way back to Wonderland, given the surrealistic nature of my predicament. But when nothing else happened, I riffled my fingers through my hair and scooted back on my heels until my back hit the wall of the lift, watching with detachment as the doors slid silently shut. Once more, I felt the rocketing movement of the lift rising.

What the hells just happened? Why had Crowley seemed so strange? Why had there been such an urgency in his voice?

"Elle," I said aloud, closing my eyes as my skin shivered with electrical currents. *What the hells happened in the Never to have made Crowley make such an about-face? How much danger are they really in?*

Moments later, the lift came to a stop, and the doors parted to reveal my own one-bedroom flat down the hall.

Would I go to the Eastern district and not tell my Captain why, on nothing but a vague command that I should?

The answer was simple. I would have sold my golden soul to save my partner. I would return to my Hel. And I'd go to the damned tavern to speak to the Tinkerer, if it meant bringing her home. I would do anything.

Anything.

⚕️

Elle

IT WAS FINALLY TIME TO MEET UP WITH CROWLEY. HE'D MENTIONED the gardens, and that was the direction I was headed. I'd spent the past couple of hours reading in the library, learning what I could about all of Undine and specifically father's rule while I'd been exiled.

That hadn't been all that exciting, in truth. Life had seemed to grow dull after my absence, if the histories were to be believed. Perhaps I had brought on much of the calamity in that land with my antics, after all, just as father had once accused me of having done.

I was just rounding a corner when I bumped into a large and sturdy chest. "Oh!" I cried, instantly reaching up to shove back the curl of hair that'd slipped over my eye. "I'm so sor—"

But the second I realized it was Crowley, I snapped my mouth shut and shook my head. "What? How?" I squeaked, more surprised than anything to see him in this wing of the castle.

I blinked. "How the hells did you find your way toward the private section of the castle? Did they give you leave to just wander about in this manner?" I winced a little the second I heard how uppity it sounded, though I hadn't intended it to be—he had surprised me.

But rather than take me to task as he once would have, Crowley merely glowered, took me by the elbow, and said nothing as he guided me down a set of stairs that were usually accessed only by the wait staff. His footsteps were sure and steady as he marched us through the kitchens, past the cold storage pantries, and out of one of the castle's many hidden doorways that headed directly and unerringly toward the start of the labyrinth.

Someone had been learning the lay of the land on his downtime. My flesh prickled, half in wonderment, half in curiosity. He was thorough, but he was also kind of intensely single-minded, like a dog with a bone in the very literal sense.

It made sense, considering our history. I was seeing firsthand just how obsessive Crowley truly was when on a case.

I said nothing until we were well and truly out of earshot, but the moment we were, I ripped my arm out of his grasp and twirled on him, stabbing a finger into his chest. "You navigated my ancestral home like you'd lived there your whole life. I saw you skulking about a section off limits to all but those of noble birth. What the hells were you doing up there? How did you get through the wards of the stairwell? That should have killed you."

His eyes glowed red like a dog's in the moonlight as he riffled his thick fingers through his unruly mane, causing it to poke up in all directions, reminding me even further of his shifter heritage. Any second, I half expected him to explode from his flesh and turn full into wolf mode.

His eyes were bloodshot, his skin looked pale even in the night, and there was a tense weariness to his shoulders. "I know you have questions, Detective, and I'll answer them all. But you've got to trust me." He gestured with his hand toward the entrance of the trail.

The meaning was clear: *It is not safe here. Let's keep walking.*

Crowley was acting cagey as all hells, but something on his face and in his eyes made me bite my tongue and decide to trust the strange and tenuous bond being forged between us.

"I'm a bloody fool," I muttered beneath my breath, but then I turned and began to walk.

"Join the club," he grunted softly behind me, which caused my lips to twitch. He sounded as put out by the prospect of being my ally as I was being his.

The old adage, "keep your friends close but your enemies closer" suddenly took on a whole new meaning to me. We walked in strained silence for what felt like another hour, which was highly probable, considering where the sea moon rested in the underwater sky.

By the time we'd stopped, I'd thought for sure we'd circled back toward the scene of the crime, but we hadn't. We were in a completely different section of the garden. I frowned and took a small half step forward.

There was a bloody house there—not a large one by any stretch, but most definitely a home, though it looked just big enough to host one of Wonderland's anthropomorphic creatures, maybe a skink or badger. Made to look like seaweed and sea ivy, its siding of leaves swayed gently in the slowly moving current, but I could definitely see that a portion of its wall had been recently disturbed.

I took another three or four steps until I was at its side, and then I knelt to run my hand over the damaged section that revealed the truth of what was in there. I felt the warm snapping of magick wash against my fingertips.

I yanked my hand back, but my fingertips still tingled from its sting. "What the ruddy hells is this, Agent?" I asked, glancing back at him over my shoulder.

His face looked grim, and his strange eyes glowed deep red wherever the moonlight bounced off of them. He was dressed in a different outfit than the one he'd been in earlier, one that looked less refined and more urban. With that black leather jacket, he looked far more imposing and more like the Crowley I was familiar with, though I had no clue where he'd found the jacket, considering that Undine was not known for tanning its animal skins, a barbarous trait my people thought to be one solely of the legger lands.

"You wanted to speak. This is as private a place to talk as I could find in that whole godsdamned castle," he said in his familiar gruff tone.

I was still a bit in shock about how differently he acted with me. He was surly—I could see it in the tension of his shoulders and the stiffness of his movements—but somehow, I'd broken through a barrier I never thought could be possible to crack.

He wasn't the same male I'd known for the past several decades. It was discombobulating, to say the least, and made it difficult for me to focus on anything other than the fact that I seemed to be his ally all of a sudden—of a sort, anyhow.

"Bench," Crowley spoke, and suddenly, the wall of seaweed and sea ivy began to roll like a wave crashing onto a beach. The vines crept along like tentacles and began to form a bench.

My jaw dropped. I must have looked like a stupefied baboon—I was stumped by the sudden turn of events.

Crowley sat on the edge of the bench that looked big and sturdy enough to sit three full grown adults easily.

"How did you—"

He shrugged. "I know things. It's what I do. What I'm best at. Solving the unsolvable."

I was impressed, but I was also hella uneasy about it. Yes, Crowley was a shifter, but the way he was learning my birth home and the hidden accesses of the place made him far more dangerous than I'd ever credited him with being before.

His lips thinned.

"What?" I asked when he still didn't say anything, continuing to press me with that unnerving look of his.

He shook his head and sighed. "Well, you've answered one of my questions just now. Because if you knew, you'd be badgering me relentlessly about it."

"What the hells are you jabbering on about?" I grumped, crossing my arms, ready to roll my eyes as I felt that familiar ire start to rise up in me.

"You do not scent the trace of your sister here, do you?" he asked softly.

The gentleness of his response obliterated my bluster. I frowned. "My sister?"

There was no jeering leer, no snarl or arrogant hubris painted upon his face. Crowley, the big bad wolf who'd dogged my steps for so long, was nothing more than a man. My shoulders slumped a little.

"Aquata," he said. "It's faint, but she's been here. Many times."

"How can you tell all this?"

He tapped the side of his nose. "I'm a shifter, Detective. Surely, you already know this about me."

I recalled the image of him with the Sea Witch, how he'd fought and battled against her impressive will, even beginning to shift as he'd fought to escape her. The blackness of his fur, the magma-like red of his eyes, the length of his muzzle, and those terribly sharp fangs felt indelible in my mind. I rubbed my upper arms, smoothing down the goose pimples that had suddenly sprouted. "Of course, I know who you are."

His lips stretched up at one corner into a halfway familiar smirk, but there was no heat behind it. "You've never seen me shift, though. I don't like to do it often. Hurts when I do," he said, snapping a leaf off of the bench and idly playing with the edge of it as though he had nervous energy.

We were entering foreign territory, one neither he nor I had likely ever imagined to be possible.

I decided then that trusting him hadn't come back to bite me on the arse just yet. And considering he was my only true ally down here, well... I took the steps that led me to my corner of the bench and lightly sat upon it, eyeing him warily.

We sat in tense silence for several seconds before he gave a deep and hearty chuckle and shook his head. "Godsdamn, this is awkward."

Hearing him say exactly what I'd been thinking had me snorting, which quickly turned into a chuckle and then a laugh that he shared in too.

Laughter was magick, in its own way. The moment we'd finished and stared at each other, I knew in my gut that our paths had been irrevocably changed. I looked back at the little shape of the house. "Did you look inside it?"

He answered instantly, "Couldn't. You felt that pulse of magick yourself. Something's warding the door."

"What a strange little thing to find here in the middle of nothing. But it might not even be a house. I mean, it could just be a mirage. Right?" I turned, looking toward him only to find that he'd already been looking at me. I swallowed hard at the intensity of is stare.

He shrugged. "It's a house."

I thinned my lips. "How can you be certain?"

"Because I smell death inside there."

That wasn't at all what I'd been imagining he might say. Turning on my behind, I looked back at the wall and tilted roof and frowned, trying as hard as I could to peer through the leaves and twigs to what had to have lain beneath. If it was a house, there should be windows and an obvious door, signs of... well, something. But none of that existed. It looked mostly like a lean-to. *A wall and roof covered in thick waves of magick,* my inner voice reminded me. But when I'd first seen it, I'd thought of it as a house, which was strange because I'd had no cause to think of it like that. "Great magick rests upon it. Thick bars of it. Like someone or something—"

"—is trying to keep it hidden," he said, finishing what I was thinking.

I looked back at him over my shoulder, catching his eye once again, this time more prepared for the heavy intensity of his gaze.

"*Mmm,*" he mumbled in agreement.

"You don't cover something unless you're trying to hide it." I frowned and looked back at the mysterious section of wall and roof. "And you say you smell death in there? Aquata may—"

"No," he said softly. "No. It is other. Unique. Mammalian, I believe."

Again, I studied him curiously, surprised that he was still talking to me as a peer. I remembered the hells he'd given me when I'd been solving Alice's case... Or even the bloody fit he'd thrown when I'd dared to release Aladdin from holding.

Crowley and I were not friends. We never had been, and I doubted we ever would be. We'd simply been thrown into a situation so far outside the realm of normal for us that neither of us seemed sure how to navigate these strange waters, though I applauded the fact that he was obviously trying.

He kicked out a long leg and leaned his elbow upon his knee, moving into the thinker's pose as he rested his strong chin on his fist and stared straight ahead without blinking. His stance looked at ease, even easy. But I'd been on the wrong side of the man for many years and knew that he could wind tighter than a spring coil in an instant.

"I..." he said softly, his word trailing off as he stared unblinkingly out at the night full of drifting sea stars and the lighted blue phosphorous of dancing krill. Blowing out a heavy breath, he continued. "I know you have questions, hundreds of them, no doubt. But I have questions too, and I won't answer a damned one until you answer mine."

"There's the arsehole I know and love," I snipped, but there was an edge of rough humor to it too.

He chuckled and snorted. "You're such a royal bitch. You drive me fucking mad, Fish," he snipped right back, and though his words rolled with a growl, I could also hear the relief coursing through them. It wasn't easy for him, and hearing that relieved me greatly.

Not overthinking things, I finally extended the olive branch and shoulder bumped him.

He inhaled sharply before relaxing just a second later and scrubbing at his jaw with his long, blunt fingers. "Fucking hells," he muttered softly. "You saved me," he said more loudly. "Or tried to, anyhow."

I frowned. "Tried? What do you mean?"

The muscles in his cheeks were tense and rigid, and I could tell he was biting down on his molars as he looked over at me, his nostrils flared and he began scenting the air—scenting me.

I shivered beneath his heavy-lidded gaze.

"I"—he licked his teeth—"I... did... die." His large rib cage flexed and, it was as though a great burden had been taken off his shoulders with those words. Groaning, he squeezed his eyes shut and rubbed at his eyes with long, slow strokes.

"Wait. What? No, you didn't. You're right here." I rolled my wrist, gesturing at him though he couldn't see because he still had his eyes closed.

Finally, after several more seconds of rubbing, he opened them. The whites were bloodshot, and his irises were nearly pure black. "I did die, Detective. But I remember what you did for me. What you tried to do, anyway. Ah, fucking hells." He sat up and leaned back, staring straight ahead with a hard glare at nothing in particular, as though he was looking not at the present but at the past, recalling all he'd seen and heard. "That sea hag turned me to stone. I did die. Fucking hurt like all hells too. Why in the twin hells did you give her your godsdamned soul? I told you not to!"

He sounded legitimately angry, and I leaned back a little, feeling my own ire rise in challenge to his. "You stupid prick!" I snapped without thinking. "I did it to save your sorry arse. Had I known you were impossible to kill, believe me, I'd have let you suffer. You insufferable bast—"

At first, he'd looked furious with me, but after a second, I began to see his lips twitch and his nostrils widen, and then he tipped his head back and barked with laughter. "Godsdamn, it's good to see you again, Detective. Thought for a second we were about to have a fucking heart-to-heart." He curled his lip with disdain, but I heard the impossible humor behind it, and I was so damned confused that all I could do was clamp my lips shut and stare at him as though he'd suddenly sprouted a second head.

He slapped his hand onto the bench between us, sat up, and rolled his neck from side to side again, not saying anything. But oddly, after our spat, the mood weirdly seemed more mellow than it had before.

"You hate me?" I asked before I thought better of it, mostly out of curiosity and because I was terribly confused everything that was happening.

He didn't answer me for half a beat, long enough that I thought maybe he hadn't heard me. But he was part shifter, so of course he'd heard me. He shook his head. "I should, but I can't. Not anymore."

"Because I saved you?" I laughed lightly, feeling too high-strung and weirdly emotional all of sudden. "I'd have done the same for anyone else." I lashed out because that's what I did when I felt things going weird on me.

He turned to look at me with a dark brow raised and a hard set to his jaw. "Maybe." He shrugged. "Or maybe not."

I wet my lips, turning to look straight ahead and shifting my knees just a little.

He snorted. "Nine lives, Detective." He said the words so softly that they were almost a whisper.

I barely heard him. "Huh?" I was forced to look at him, cringing at the vulnerability so clearly exposed on his face.

"I've got nine lives."

My brows gathered into a tight V. "That's a feline thing, not a canine one," I corrected, sure that he was playing a prank on me for some reason. Playing jokes didn't fit with Crowley's normally taciturn character, but I was still feeling edgy and prickly.

He sniffed, and it was his turn to stare straight ahead. "You know very little about me, Detective, but you know more about me now than almost anyone else in my life."

"That can't be true," I said with a light laugh, but when he didn't join in, continuing to stare unblinkingly ahead, I had a sinking feeling that he wasn't actually pulling my string.

I shook my head. "Are you serious?"

He didn't answer.

"How many have you used?"

Licking his canines, he gave me a bold and assessing look. "That was unlucky number seven."

I softly gasped. "How... old are you?"

He chuckled, and the sound reminded me of rolling gravel. "One hundred and fifty three godsdamned years young." He sounded angry about it.

I didn't know Crowley well enough to understand it all, but I thought that maybe he wasn't altogether happy about whatever had been done to him. Shifters were not as long-lived as other Grimm species. They didn't age as quickly as their nonshifter mammal counterparts, but their years were more accelerated than an average human's. The lifespan of a typical shifter was anywhere between forty-five to fifty years.

"How?" I asked.

Leaning back on his hands, he crossed his long legs in front of himself, still staring straight ahead with hard look.

"I grew up in a time where the government wasn't quite as regulated as it is today. Human experiments were the norm then, and those who met a certain genetic disposition for a trait the government wished to exploit were packed up and shipped off, no questions asked." He glanced at me.

Crowley was much older—even older than me, and my species was long-lived— than I'd ever imagined. Though, to be fair, I'd never actually given him much thought. Other than the fact that he'd been a giant pain in my arse, I'd never cared enough for the man to take the time to learn anything of value about him. "Seven lives... So you've only got one left? Or do you have full use of the ninth life as well?"

He shook his head. "From all I know, I've got full use of the ninth."

"And after that?"

"It's an eternal dirt nap for me." He chuckled bitterly.

I didn't have a clue what to say. It wasn't as though Crowley and I were good enough friends that I could offer him sympathy that he might actually accept. I shivered.

A second later I, felt the ghostly press of a finger over mine, but when I looked up, his hand was already gone. "Just two more lives, Princess, and I'll be out of your hair forever." He said it as though I should be happy about it.

But I didn't know what I was feeling: some combination of sadness, sympathy, and confusion. So I said nothing, because I had no reply to such a macabre thought. "Yay!" or "That'll be the day" felt wrong, so I pretended instead to have something in my throat and cleared it loudly, giving myself a couple of seconds to think about what to say next.

"So you died. Okay. I'm sorry I couldn't help you after all. I-I did try," I said weakly, figuring that if he could open up to me, I should at least try to return the favor.

"I guess I had an unfair advantage. I should have warned you about my ability, but I—"

"—didn't trust me." I finished his thought, knowing exactly what he would say.

He shrugged unapologetically, and I knew I'd guessed correctly.

"No, I get it. Believe me. I know all about secrets." I sighed and thought about my own. "Why did you give me Hook on that ship? You didn't have to, you know. I know that the agency planned to sacrifice him to the Sea Witch."

He snorted. "Yeah, and then you had to go and fuck it up to twin hells by being so bloody godsdamned noble."

He sounded put out, and I laughed. The temporary truce between us felt so strange, and yet, I sort of liked it. "I guess even an old dog like you can still be surprised."

He chuffed, a strange sound that was half chuckle and half huff, before shaking his head. "Aye, I reckon I still can be. Mind you, this doesn't make us friends." He gestured between us with one long finger.

"Oh, heaven forbid, old timer."

"Fucking hells," he grumped.

I shoulder checked him, having way more fun than I thought I could with him. For so long, Agent Crowley had been my own personal boogeyman, and I wondered what Hatter would think if he could see us.

Hatter. My laughter ceased as I thought of him. My heart hurt whenever my mind strayed toward my partner.

Crowley cleared his throat. "I released Hook because it was the right thing to do," he said. He sat up. "Anyway." His tone was no-nonsense again, and I understood that he didn't wish to get any deeper into icky feelings so I respected his right to move on. "Anyhow, I tried looking for Hook today, just to see where they were holding him and what they were doing to him, but I had no luck. Sorry, Fish."

Once, when he'd used that term, it had made me want to rake his eyes with my claws. Now, not so much. I shrugged. "I know he lives, and I've got an inside man helping me out."

He turned his body partially toward me. "Who?"

"Someone you'd hate." I chuckled.

"I've got a pretty good idea, so just spit it out," he shot back.

I shrugged, deciding to test him. "Jacamoe, my father's mage."

"The enslaved Djinn? The one who I'm pretty sure knows more than he's telling us. That one? Godsdammit, Elle, I thought you were smarter than that. I already warned you about him. I don't trust that bastard. Not one bit," he said in a sharp growl.

I laughed because there he was, the real Crowley. It was good to see him again. His eyes were glowing in an almost-heated-looking red.

"He's the eyes and ears of the castle, Crowley. Anything you want to know about anybody, he likely already does, or he can learn it soon enough. Father used to call him 'the whisperer.' He's a good ally to have. Trust me." I winked.

"He's always skulking about with a shifty look in his eyes," Crowley persisted, pointing to his own eyes. "And trusting you will happen the day the twin hells freeze over."

"Ha!" I laughed, and it was a real one that he soon reluctantly joined in on.

"Gods, you're such a bitch," he growled, but the insult lacked any real heat. It sort of felt like two detectives taking the piss with each other, it was familiar; it was even kind of... nice. I rolled my eyes, playing his game and laughed again before saying, "Well, I guess it takes one to know one. And don't think I've forgotten, fyi."

"Forgotten what?" he asked with a slight shake of his head as he scrubbed at his jaw with his long fingers.

"You never did answer me. How the hells did you get onto the noble floor? You do know that anyone not of royal blood or given regulated permissions is allowed to be up there, and yet there you were, la-de-da, without a care in the world." I flicked my fingers for emphasis.

His smile was only half-formed, his eyes full of secrets. "Wouldn't you like to know, Princess Fish?"

I shook my head. "You're such a bloody bastard, Crowley. Anyone ever tell you that?"

"A time or twenty." He smirked. "Now, some of my secrets are mine, as they pose no danger to you or others. I'd say that's fair. Wouldn't you?"

I found my fascination with getting to know who the real Crowley really was only beginning to grow deeper, like a child who was suddenly interested in a toy that she'd ignored before. I narrowed my eyes. "I'll figure you out someday, rest assured."

He tipped his head back and gave a full belly chuckle, and holy twin hells, my body exploded with a riot of sensations as I watched him dissolve into a spate of true laughter.

Crowley had always been an attractive male, but it had been hard to admire his beauty because he was always doing douchebag things to remind everyone what a giant dick he was. But he wasn't behaving that way anymore, not at all.

I clutched at my throat with cold fingers and forced myself to take two deep breaths. I might not have been a siren true anymore, but my body still felt the effects of it sometimes. When he finally stopped laughing, I had to look down at my feet and get my riotous emotions under control.

It was Crowley. Not my friend, and definitely not my lover. I had enough problems to juggle, anyway, with Hatter and Hook. I definitely didn't need to add more to my already full plate.

Many sirens take on a harem, a small obnoxious voice in my head suddenly said loudly and clearly. I glowered and gave myself a small shake. *What the effing hells was that?*

I am a one-man woman, I reminded myself sternly, but Hook had obviously changed me.

I cleared my throat, embarrassed by the thoughts rolling through my head. Thank the gods he couldn't read minds, because Crowley would never let me live it down. *It's the stress of all that'd happened getting to me now,* I thought. *That and this constant forced proximity.*

So I thought of him as he truly was: chasing me, hounding me, and up my arse for everything. I remembered his constant threats and his bullying, and that was enough to douse whatever temporary insanity had been about to grip me. I was stressed out and knew that sex would help. It was biological—Ichabod had taught me that. But I would die before I bedded this beast.

"How'd you find this wall?" I asked, needing desperately to switch the subject.

When I looked over at him, Crowley wore an uneasy look that reflected how I felt, and I had to wonder what he could have been thinking about. He shrugged and ran his fingers over his chin. "I've had a lot of time on my hands, and with only one case to work on and a smallish perimeter to boot, well, I've been climbing the walls and obsessing a bit." His grin was sheepish.

"Me too." I chuckled softly then frowned and shook my head again. *Stop that,* I mentally castigated myself. I needed to keep a professional distance. Once Crowley and I left this place, we would fall right back into our old routines as bitter and sworn enemies at odds constantly. What was happening was nothing more than a temporary truce. Period.

"How'd you know that this area would respond to your wishes as it did?" I asked, referencing his ability to command the seaweed and ivy to turn into a bench for us.

Scratching the side of his nose with the edge of his thumb, he gestured with his chin toward the hedgerow and the smallish lean-to peeking out from the damaged section. "My ability to smell isn't merely limited to smell alone, if that makes sense. If the trace of a scent is strong enough, I can see faint, almost ghostlike images of what's occurred. Of course, the image has to be one that's been created so often or with such a powerful desire behind it that it's been practically burned into the DNA of the object. In this case, the sea ivy itself stored part of the memories."

First had been Hatter's ability to see the past and future, and now, Crowley was saying he too had a strange ability. "Is that why you were chosen for the agency?" I asked, suddenly realizing that it must have been that ability or one very similar to it that had given him the edge over so many other applicants.

I'd applied to be part of the agency almost a decade before and had been soundly turned away. I'd thought my credentials should have been enough to get me through the door at least, but I'd never even made it to boot camp. There hadn't been many water elementals then, and there still weren't, but even I could admit that if Crowley really did have that ability, it made him incredibly valuable—maybe even more valuable than a cast-out princess of the deep.

This new knowledge also answered many of the questions I'd had about how he always seemed to have a sixth sense about what I was up to.

He nodded slowly. "One of," he simply said.

My feelers went way up. "One of" could mean a whole host of different things. But I reminded myself for the hundredth time that I wasn't there to shoot the breeze. We were actually working a case, one that was far more personal to me than any other I'd ever worked.

"I won't pretend that I understand you at all, Crowley, because I don't. I won't even pretend that it isn't driving me mad with desire to learn all I can about you. You're far more interesting than I'd have ever thought possible. But that's not what this is about. My sister is being buried in two days—I have no doubt the tribunal will give us that long before they call our hearing, which means we have to work quickly but accurately. So if you know anything at all that can help us solve my sister's case, please, help me." The last of my words came out as a breathy plea. I fluttered my long lashes as I glanced down at my feet.

I'd humbled myself. I'd revealed to him just how much it mattered to me and how much I needed him to be not my enemy but my ally. I bridged my fingers and idly rubbed hard circles on the backs of my hands with my thumbs.

He inhaled deeply. "I brought you here, Princess—"

"I'm not a princess," I corrected.

"You will always be a princess," he said simply and without rancor, glancing at me from his periphery with his hands clasped gently in front of him as he leaned forward. "I know you're a witch now. I saw what the Sea Witch did to you. I heard what she said."

Immediately, I tensed, wondering where he might be going with this. Our past was such that it wouldn't be a far stretch to imagine him following those words with threats of reporting my unique and potentially deadly status to the agency. I could still wind up on all-points bulletin.

"I brought you here, Detective, because this is all I can do," Crowley said. "I can tell you that I smell death, but I can't pass those wards."

I blinked, still mightily confused but trying to act as though I wasn't. "And you think I can?" I chuckled, holding up my cuffed wrists. "I'm as good as neutered with these on. Not to mention the little fact that I don't have the first clue how to be a witch. I've only ever been a siren. That is who I am. That is what I'm good at."

Even I heard the hint of longing in my words. I hadn't had a chance yet to consider what might happen to me and who I might become if I never took my powers back from the witch. The thought that I might never again swim the waters or feel the sluicing wetness of a mighty wave massaging every inch of my body as I cut cleanly through it made my heart tremble in the cage of my chest. There was the twinge of a small fracture in my soul.

He stood, and I felt the heated press of his stare looking down at the crown of my head. I turned toward him, glancing up, curious about the look on his face.

"We're not born to be just one thing or another, Detective.

Remember that." Thrusting his hands into his pockets, he turned and made his way back toward the castle, leaving me to stare at the spot where he'd left me with hundreds of new and different thoughts milling around in my head. *Just who is the real Crowley?* I wasn't sure there was an easy answer anymore.

I glanced back at the lean-to, someone's home but with the smell of death inside it. Standing, I dusted off my legs.

Jacamoe had said he would start to train me whenever I wanted, and that was as good a place as any to begin.

CHAPTER 7
HATTER

I'D NOT HEARD BACK from Agent Crowley's specter since the incident hours before, but I'd been climbing the walls of my flat with worry. I'd even gone down to the precinct, debating about whether to alert Bo to what had happened.

But the echo of Crowley's warning to me still rang in my ears, making me hesitant and cagey, a fact that the others noticed. Bo had eventually emerged from her back office—alerted by someone, no doubt—and promptly sent me home. She'd told me not to come back for at least eight hours after that, cautioning me that if I couldn't get my act together, they would consider a longer leave of absence for me. which I couldn't have, not when I needed the department's resources. Also, going home would mean being alone, and I hated being alone. I hadn't always been that way, but I knew no one in Grimm Central on a personal level other than Elle, which left me stuck in my one-room apartment alone and with nothing to keep my mind occupied.

I didn't trust Agent Crowley as far as I could throw the man, but he was likely Elle's only ally in Undine, and he had seemed adamant that Elle be protected at all costs.

I felt useless, adrift, and consumed by hundreds of worries and questions, but at least I knew that I could turn the mania into some-thing useful.

I rubbed my neck, wondering what in the hells she was going through. I leaned against the back wall of my flat and stared out the window at the flickering lights of downtown. The neon buzzed and glowed.

It'd been almost three hours since I'd had that chat with the agent in the lift. The time to act was coming hot and fast. I could either trust the word of a man who had never given Elle or me reason to and hope that he was being honest, or I could try to find her on my own.

I already knew the second option was not only unlikely—it was impossible because of where she was being held.

Rubbing the bridge of my nose, I blew out a heavy breath. It would have been so much easier if I could just speak with her and see for myself that she was okay, that my fears were nothing but unrealistic anxiety.

Disreputables were starting to crawl out from under their rocks, leaving the dark shelter of their daylight hours to crowd the sidewalks and corners. I frowned, rubbing at my devil's marking that'd been burning like hellfire all day. But no glow meant no sight, and I couldn't understand why, other than maybe stress. I knew my gift was trying to show me something, but I felt magically constipated. No matter how much I felt the need to *see,* nothing was happening other than my arm feeling scorched to holy hells.

I hissed as another hard bolt of fiery energy tingled and sizzled through my pores, but just as before, all I saw was a blank canvas of darkness. It was the past being shown me, or at least trying to be shown, but I knew there was more to the darkness than what I saw, I also know deep in my heart and soul that it all centered around Elle.

When I'd been pair bonded to Alice and we'd had our child... A muscle in my cheek clenched and I glared at nothing in particular, forcing myself to stop focusing on Mariposa and to think of anything else. Finally, slowly, the thought of the March Hare's devotion to haloshrooms caused me to grin and helped calm the riot in my mind. My visions and flashes had been centering more and more on my family, and I didn't like it, although it wasn't surprising. My emotions were deeply entwined with every other aspect of my nature—I simply felt things on a greater and deeper level than most, which was why I always knew the moment when those closest to me needed me or were in trouble.

I opened my eyes and looked out once more into the sea of life thriving and buzzing down below. I had to get out in it. I knew I couldn't tell Bo anything yet, though I should. But if I told her, she would only take me off this case or, worse yet, tell me I was too emotionally invested and force me to go speak to IA. She might even split Elle and me up.

I worried my bottom lip. I had to do it alone, and not because I trusted Crowley—I didn't. But she was down there, ready to face a tribunal of peers who were incapable of remaining unbiased in matters concerning her. I would be damned if I let my partner down again, and...

Taking a deep breath, I swallowed forcefully. Just because. That was why.

I kicked off the wall with my bare feet and padded silently toward the door to find my shoes. I hadn't changed out of my work clothes. I slipped on my shoes then grabbed my keys, wallet, and badge. Technically, I was off duty, and I knew I shouldn't be abusing my authority like this, but I would kick down whatever doors needed kicking to get her back, safe and sound and in once piece.

I slipped out then shut and locked the door behind me and headed toward the Persiannous district. I would find the damned Tinkerer even if it killed me.

๛

Elle

A SHORT WHILE LATER, I FINALLY FOUND JACAMOE IN HIS STUDY. HE was bent over a long desk with a pair of spectacles perched jauntily on the tip of his nose, muttering beneath his breath as he read aloud from the open book in front of him. The words sounded strange—they were in his native tongue, lyrical and beautiful and full of power. Every fine hair on my body stood on edge each time he uttered a new sound.

"Gawking is rude, Little Fish. I do believe I taught you better than to spy." He peeked at me over the rim of his glasses with a knowing gleam in his intelligent eyes.

I jumped, feeling like the little child he'd always castigated for lingering in doorways. Clearing my throat as the heat of a blush formed on my cheeks, I gave him a tight-lipped smile, though he'd long since returned to his task. "I wished to know if we could have our lessons now," I mumbled pathetically. I sometimes felt that no matter how many years lay between me and this place, there were moments where I was not an adult but a child again, especially in instances when gave the look he was giving me now. His lips were pressed tightly together, and one eyebrow was raised high, his displeasure stamped clearly upon his face.

I smiled with teeth, letting my lips thin to nearly nothing. Why he made me so nervous, I had never understood, so I merely smiled wider. "I-I wasn't snooping. I promise."

He harrumphed but said nothing.

"What were you reading? Sounded beautiful," I said.

He snorted and slowly shook his head before gently closing the massive tome and snapping his fingers so that it vanished. "And she says she was not snooping."

My grin turned lopsided, and I gave him a one-shouldered shrug. "Well, I guess I was, a little. But I honestly came here to see if you'd train me."

The wards on Jacamoe's room were very specific: it was the only place in the castle where he could still use his magick at its fullest potential. As Father's personal mage, Jacamoe was required to create potions and spells for him, but because Father was the uptight bastard that he was, Jacamoe was strictly regulated regarding when and where and for how long.

From the moment Jacamoe entered the room, a timed cycle of two hours on and four hours off was set off. That meant he could perform magick for eight hours out of a twenty-four-hour cycle. Jacamoe himself had been instrumental in setting up his wards—on Father's command, of course.

He rubbed at his uncuffed wrists, which seemed more a habitual gesture than anything else.

I held up my own hands. "I'd really love to have these off me, old friend," I whispered with obvious entreaty in my voice.

Sniffing, he shuffled painfully over to me before leaning his hip against the desk and gesturing at me with both hands. "Give them to me," he said.

I rolled my wrists upward and breathed a sigh of relief once he'd released me from their venomous clasp. Already, I could feel the release of power, which the cuffs had dampened almost to the point of nonexistence before, roiling deep inside of me. But with its return, I felt the rise and stir of the darkness that had been nullified as well. I bit the inside of my cheek. I wasn't sure whether it was better to have no magick or to have it and be forced to fight off that damnable voice inside my head.

Resting my weight on the desk, I hung my head and felt my back muscles spasm and pop as I tried to acclimate myself to the waves of power so much stronger than before.

"It always feels that way at first," he said gently. "I liken it to a stoppered steam valve. Give it a second, Little Fish, it will pass. Breathe," he commanded.

When I did, I inhaled the scent of lush and exotic spices deep into my lungs.

When next I opened my eyes, I noticed a small smoking brazier in his hands. The smoke relaxed me. The tightness in my back and the tension in my stomach had eased a bit.

After another breath, I felt almost normal again, apart from a low buzz that was quickly receding in the back of my mind and the echoing scream of that dark voice. I shivered. "Holy hells, does that always happen to you?" I asked a second later.

His response was to press his lips together, which was answer enough.

"I'm sorry," I whispered.

"You get used to it. Now, we only have an hour left to use our magick here, so we have no time to dawdle." His eyes were intensely serious, and his manner brooked no arguments.

I nodded, as excited to learn about my newfound powers as he seemed eager to teach them to me.

"Now, let us see the extent of your potential, Elle. I need you to focus your will."

I recalled trying to do just that while stuck in the Never's endless pool, sure that I would die along with Hook and Crowley as I'd sought to tap into powers I'd never known existed. "What does that mean, exactly?" I asked with a tinge of exasperation. Focusing on my will seemed like such a useless waste of the very short and preciously valuable time.

"I am a Djinn. My powers are like breathing air to me. I cannot do one without doing the other." To demonstrate, he snapped his fingers, taking a deep breath as he did. A ball of brilliant lime-green fire rested on his overturned palm.

I sucked in a little breath, in awe of how easily he'd been able to do that and wondering if I was capable of it myself. I was a creature of water—I always had been—but I was drawn to something different now, something edgier and slightly darker.

I reached out and tried to trace my fingers through the light, but he quickly snatched his hand away. My confusion was instant. "What? Why?"

He shook his head. "You cannot touch this, Arielle. This is the manifestation of my magick. It responds only to me. Yes, it is a beautiful light, but it is also quite deadly. If you learn to harness your powers into a ball of your own making, then you can manipulate it to suit your needs."

He demonstrated by placing the tiny ball upon the top of the workbench. But the ball of green light began to twist and turn in on itself, stretching in places and undulating like a snake's body in others, until it was no longer a mere ball but a small dragon. Jacamoe held out his hand to it, and the dragon scampered up his arm, winding and curling its way up his body until it came to rest upon his shoulder, clinging tightly to Jacamoe's neck with a small clawed hand.

I grinned, bending down so that I could stare the magnificently formed creature in the eye. "What is this?" I asked.

Glancing down at the little beast with an almost affectionate grin, Jacamoe petted its head. The miniature dragon made a purring, grunting sound that caused its throat pouch to inflate like a balloon. "This is a mage's familiar."

I frowned. "How did I never know that mages had familiars too?"

"How many mages are you friendly with?" He grinned, his eyes twinkling with obvious mirth.

I snorted. "Far too few." I shook my head, a sudden sadness gripping me unexpectedly. I tried to shake it off, not wanting him to see it. But Jacamoe had always been far too observant.

He gripped my shoulder, patting it affectionately. "You will learn this, Arielle. I have never met a pupil more able than you."

Rubbing my thigh absentmindedly, I sighed. "The world has changed for me, old friend. It's turned from something I knew, from something I was good at... Now, I feel like a child being forced to relearn everything. I ache for my true form. I hate these damnable legs. I hate being forced to remain in this body and not having a clue who or even what I am anymore."

"You are a witch," he said simply.

"But I don't want to be!" I hissed, pounding my fist upon the table. I'd held it in for so long, but the resentment of what had happened with the witch, with Hook, Crowley, myself, my sister, even my damned bloody sire was starting to make itself manifest to me.

"Did you ever wonder why my legs are bowed as they are?" he asked softly, cutting through my pity party of one.

Sniffing, I swiped at my nose before shaking my head roughly. "I thought you were injured."

He chuckled, but the sound was full of hurt and pain and venom. "I am not a creature of the land, just as you are not. When your father captured me and made me his manservant, I was forced to endure a trial for which I was unprepared. My body bows because I was not made to walk this world, Arielle. But that is merely physical. My spirit is strong. It is free."

As he said it, the wee dragon on his shoulder glowed like a brilliantly cut jewel in flame. Its legs were no longer resting upon Jacamoe's shoulders but upon the ground. Its body was growing, filling the room, hinting at something grander and bigger, something much more frightening. I gasped then cringed as I saw it near me, thinking its girth would soon devour me in its rapid evolution. I squeezed my eyes shut, so shocked by the sudden turn of events that I didn't even have a chance to beg Jacamoe to stop it. But though I felt the heat of the familiar brush up against me, when I opened my eyes again, he was naught but a tiny dragon perched upon his mage's shoulder.

"What?" I breathed.

"Familiars," he said simply, "are not bound by the rules of our lands, only by the scope of your imagination and strength. Now, we have wasted far too much time. Show me what you can do." He grabbed my wrist and turned it so that my palm lay open before him.

I knew what he wanted me to do, so I focused on my hand.

Instantly, the same energy I'd felt in the Never pool flooded through me, more easily since I seemed aware of it inside of me. Recalling how it had felt to manipulate that kind of power, I closed my eyes and focused all my will on my palm. A tremulous grin of hope and excitement tipped the corners of my face as I called the fire to me. Jacamoe's wee dragon chirped as if he sensed that soon he might have a playmate. And I chanced a quick glance at him.

Jac's familiar was silent and no longer watching me. In fact, he was ignoring me altogether before he casually winged off Jacamoe's shoulder toward a hidden rafter above us.

I frowned, staring down at my hand, feeling as though I had a great deal of energy roiling and gathering within me, but... Nothing. I saw nothing, not even the heat-wave shimmer that I sometimes saw with Hatter when his anger was too close to the surface. I suddenly wondered whether he was a mage too—I'd seen him manipulate fire.

"Concentrate, Arielle," Jacamoe said softly. I twitched, realizing I'd been losing focus, thinking about my partner's mysterious origins.

Giving a low growl, silently reminding myself just how important it was, I squeezed my eyes shut even more tightly, imagining that manifestation of fire, practically willing it to fill my palm as it had Jacamoe's.

For cripes sake I'd been able to drag Hook and Crowley's body behind me with magick when I'd first entered Undine. I'd used the power effortlessly then.

But no matter how much I willed it, how much I pleaded with my powers to reveal themselves, there was simply nothing. My arms were trembling, my legs were shaking, and I had rivulets of sweat sliding down my back. And the voice was back: *Unleash me. Use me. Together, we can topple it all. Together, we can make the world our own...*

I shuddered and grabbed the desk with a white-knuckled grip. My breathing was hard and erratic. "Jacamoe, I-I can't—"

"You can," he assured, placing his warm hands beneath mine. I felt his strength merge with my own. He was much more powerful than I ever could have imagined. His touch was a shock to my senses. It felt sort of like trying to grab hold of lightning, burning but seductive. I wanted more of it.

"There is such darkness in you. Your mother's voice is too loud. It is drowning out your own." He released me slowly.

I opened my eyes, watching him look at me with gleaming narrowed eyes. "I think I know how to fix your problem, if you will allow me liberties."

I frowned. "What liberties?"

"In the transference between you and your mother, it appears that she left behind too much of herself."

"What does that mean?" I leaned back on my heels, my mouth turning down into a frown.

He grinned at me.

I realized how I must have looked. I relaxed my stance a little.

"It's nothing terrible, Arielle. At least not for you, though she must be extremely weakened now, especially after her attacks on your sister and father."

I cocked my head, studying his guileless features. "Are you implying... What now? That she might still be in the realm somewhere, lying low?"

Shrugging one shoulder, he rolled his wrists. "I could not say. I can say that she would be vastly depleted at this point. Perhaps she attacked your family in order to steal back some power for herself."

My brows furrowed. "But they have no magick. What would be the purpose?"

"Royal blood has great potential as a power source." He shrugged. "I am not claiming that is what she did, only that there's a possibility that she became desperate enough after that transference with you. She gave too much, and now you are brimming over with it. She suffers from a lack of power, and you from too much. There needs to be a balance to everything."

I sighed. "So how do I get balanced?"

At first, he said nothing, but then he pressed his lips into a tight line and jerked his chin in my direction. "If you would allow it, I could siphon off just a portion of that power, just the bits that are trying to overwhelm you."

"What happens to me if you do?"

"Nothing," he waved his fingers, "other than you no longer feeling attacked by her powers."

That sounded good, but I knew so little of magick that I had to wonder whether there could be consequences. "And the power that you'll siphon off, what of that? Where does it go?"

"Without a bodily source to lay claim to, the power will inevitably weaken until it eventually ceases to be altogether."

It all sounded like Greek to me. And yet, I wouldn't lie and say it didn't also sound tempting. I couldn't see any harm in allowing him to help me achieve balance. "Fine," I said resolutely. "Let's do it."

With a clipped nod, he stepped to me, and in the next instant, his hands were upon my cheeks. In a flash, I felt the heat of his power course through me like a hot surge, and that terribly ungodly voice inside of me screamed. It felt like claws raking down my innards.

I grunted and stiffened, my neck went taught, and a dark plume of ebony smoke coiled out of me. I knew instantly it was the witch's power. As it slid out, the voice in my head grew dimmer and dimmer until there was blessed silence.

I shuddered. He dropped his hands instantly, and then there was a clear vial in his palm. The plume of smoke curled like a cobra down the small shaft. I frowned but said nothing until the last tail of smoke sank down into it. He put a stopper in the mouth of the vial.

I shook my head. "I thought we were going to let it dissipate?"

"I am a scholar, Arielle. Having access to study such power is a great boon. Now, when your mother returns to finish what she has started, I will be able to stop her. She will never harm another one of us again."

My stomach curled with apprehension, not because I didn't believe him—I did. But it seemed strange to save chaos magick when the potential for great harm was still very present. He was far more learned than me, though, and if he said he could use it safely, then I had to trust him. I gave him a tight smile. "I understand."

He vanished the vial with a flick of his wrist. "And how do you feel now?"

I rolled my shoulders, waiting to feel the heavy presence of the witch's mind, but there was nothing in my head other than my own thoughts. "Great, actually."

"Good. Then let us try this again, shall we? Give me your hands."

I did as he asked. He cupped them gently in his, and I suddenly felt a massive roiling of the great power of the two of us combined. His power was just as heavy and dark as my own but more mature, like a gleaming fruit at the peak of ripeness, ready to be plucked and consumed. It was perfect power, perfect magick.

He closed his eyes, and I saw his brows knit in consternation. "Hm," was all he said.

I frowned. "Hm? Hm, what? What now?"

Without opening his eyes, he spoke to me. His fingers rubbed against my own, as though to comfort and relax me. "I am looking for the witch's flame inside of you but I do not sense it. Instead, there appears to be a wellspring of darkness."

I pulled my bottom lip between my teeth and bit down sharply enough to make myself wince. "I felt that in the eternal pool at Never, too, as I floated. I felt something dark and twisted and wrong in me."

He shook his head, his dark eyes snapping open and holding mine with an intensity that made me lose my breath. There was a lick of flame at the center of his black pupils. "Not wrong or twisted. Dark, yes. It simply means you draw your energy from a deeper, more ancient source of untapped power, from the very zenith of its wellspring. But just because you draw magick from the beginning of all energies does not mean that you must be bad. Magick is neither good nor bad, my dear one. It simply is. It is the user who shapes its destiny. Look."

I sucked in a sharp breath the instant I looked down, unable to believe my own eyes. I shook my my head even as I felt a big smile cut across my face—there was a ball of intensely black floating power in my hand. It wasn't fire—it didn't burn. It moved like curls of winding campfire smoke, twisting and turning to form an indigo, ebony, and steel colored baby otter.

"It is beautiful, my Little Fish," he whispered, and I looked up at him, my eyes suddenly full of heat.

"That is your power, Arielle. That is it. Not evil, you see. It just is. You determine who this little one will become."

"C-Can I touch it?" I asked him in timid little girl's voice.

He chuckled. "She belongs to you."

"She?"

He nodded. "She is the physical embodiment of your most inner self, your very personal and private truth. Your little familiar knows you as no other shall. It will sense your desires long before you even know them yourself. It will rise up to protect you one day, shield you, be all that you need or could ever want. She is you, Arielle."

He slid his hands out from under mine.

It was ridiculous how bonded I felt to the wee beastie already, but I brought my hands close to my face and cooed nonsensical words to the little thing. I felt love as I never quite had for anything else. It wasn't the love of a woman for her partner, but more like the love of a mother for her child.

I looked at her perfect little otter face and her smoky, silky fur. A soft, gleaming glow emanated from within her tiny body, and the only thing I wanted in that moment was to protect her and always keep her safe.

It was the most ridiculous thing, but she felt like my child already. It was as if my entire life had been leading me to this very moment, this instant when I would fall in love so completely and knew I would do anything to protect her.

She blinked her big brown eyes back at me, and I was sure she smiled. I reached a finger toward her, wanting to touch her fur and to hug her. But she faded, just like that, and without warning, she was gone.

"No!" I hissed, jerking my hands and staring frantically at Jacamoe. "What's happened? Where did she go?"

"She was tired, Arielle. She is but a babe yet. You must grow in your control, and then she will grow stronger herself. But this was a brilliant start. Not many witches can manifest their familiars so quickly and easily. You are strong, Little One. Stronger than even you believe."

I felt the dampening cuffs clamped onto my wrists just a second later, and I hiccupped a strange sound that was half sob and half denial. "What? Why—"

"Our hour is at an end. To try and perform any more magick now could kill us. But next time I will teach you to create a bubble. You would like that, I think."

I snorted, even as the effects of the cuffs began to manifest. "I'm not ten, Jacamoe."

He chuckled, but I couldn't focus on the conversation any longer. I squeezed my eyes shut.

The heat of those dampening cuffs rushed through me like a geyser, almost knocking me to my knees. I shook my head as I gripped the workbench, my knuckles turning bone white from the force. My muscles strained and trembled.

"Breathe, Little One. It gets easier each time you do it."

I didn't want to have to get used to it. It was unfair. I didn't ask to become a witch. If I couldn't learn to control my new powers, they might very well control me, and putting me in cuffs was the very opposite of allowing me to learn to regulate myself. But I didn't tell him any of that because there wasn't a damned thing Jacamoe could do about it. More than that, he'd suffered the indignity far longer than I had. Once the pain had passed and my muscles unclenched, I blew out a strangled breath and gave a short bark of laughter.

He said nothing in reply, but I knew he understood.

❧

Maddox

BOTH MY ARMS BURNED. I RUBBED THEM FORCEFULLY AS I STARED UP at the glowing marquee sign. The stylized letters read *Bârân*.

I'd been asking around, befriending those loitering on the street corners, including beggars, petty pickpockets, and soiled doves. At first, none had a clue who the Tinkerer was, but as I neared the Persiannous district I got far fewer blank looks and more knowing but furtive looks.

Finally, a female troll with large, brightly painted purple lips and dark olive-green skin covered in boils and pustules pointed me in the direction of a club.

The bitch—for that was what she would be called in troll society —was a beauty of her species, and I compensated her well, handing her my last business card. "If you ever have need of me, female, call this number." I closed my hand around her slightly smaller, hairier one.

She quickly snatched the card out of her hand and tucked it into the crevice between her fleshy triple breasts, glancing around furtively to make sure no one stared at us.

No doubt she had a pimp or madam who owned her. It pained me that she should, but sadly, life was far from perfect, and often there were injustices in the world that I would remain forever helpless to stop. I wasn't necessarily against being a madam or a pimp—Alice was one, but she treated her employees fairly. She never raised a hand to any of them, would never dream of letting them walk the dirty, rough streets of the capital at night, and compensated them exceedingly well. It made her a rare treasure in the industry.

Sex was not amoral, at least not to me—it was simply a matter of biology and if both or more parties were willing participants, I saw nothing inherently wrong with sex work—but the seedy, dirty version of that world had always bothered me immensely.

I gave the bitch a tense, smallish smile.

For anyone in this side of town to be seen carrying anything associated with the law was not a good look, but having a detective's contact info was as good as gold too. It meant that no matter what, she had at least one get-out-of-jail-free pass, which she would no doubt need sooner rather than later.

The club stuck out compared to the other buildings surrounding it. Where everything else was done in a standard-brick-and mortar layout, it was all stucco and golden overlays everywhere. The building was a creamy white, with a domed golden roof upon it that gleamed blue and red from the neon that hung off the sides of the other buildings.

There was a sultry, sensual style of music filtering out from underneath the heavy looking door. And even from where I stood, I could smell hookah smoke and exotic perfumes from another land.

It was times like these that made me miss my partner. Usually, we would walk to a door, where she would distract them with the power of her sheer and overwhelming siren's beauty while I got them to divulge whatever secrets I could in the interim.

Though it wasn't just her beauty that opened doors for us. Elle had been working in Grimm for decades, she was an established cog in the wheel, and the citizens inherently trusted her, or at the very least knew of her.

Fixing my cravat with nerveless fingers, I watched as a group of youths, who couldn't have been a day older than eighteen, knocked rapidly on the big door three times, followed by two slower knocks.

It opened on soundless hinges just a moment later. A big mountain of a male stood intimately beside it. As he turned, a face that bore no eyes, no mouth, and no nose tilted down at them, and it was easy enough to imagine that if he could, he would be glaring at the boys.

My angel brand burned like the devil upon my arm at the sight of him, and I clenched my molars together, biting down on the hiss that threatened to spill off my tongue.

I knew his species almost immediately. He was demon bred, lower caste, nothing major. Though he looked intimidating, as far as demons went, the Alû was not much to concern oneself with.

The boys never even glanced up. They'd clearly been there many times. They laughed amongst themselves as they sailed through.

I looked at my hands and at the clothes that I wore, wondering if I should have chosen something different but realizing there was no time to worry about it. But I couldn't help but wonder what kind of a club dropped tens of thousands of pounds a year on hiring a demon bouncer—low caste or not, his power would still be considerable.

Realizing I didn't have much time to make up my mind, I squared my shoulders and decided there wasn't a choice or time to waste. Crossing the street, I reached the door and knocked out the same sequence the boys had used.

Years of perfecting a stonewall mask didn't mean that I didn't feel nerves—I still did. Every time I entered someplace new, especially a potentially hostile one. My hands balled into tight fists when the door was whisked open by the same Alû as before.

But unlike before, when he'd merely glanced down at the boys, his large hand immediately shot out and slammed against the cage of my chest. His entire frame bristled, and I knew that if he could grow, he would. Just because he had no mouth or teeth didn't mean he couldn't rend me limb from limb.

But I was no mere mortal man, either. I glanced down at his hand, and a small smirk tilted the corners of my lips.

"You know what I am," I said softly but with a deadly undercurrent. "Good. That also means you know you can do nothing to stop me, should I choose to make an issue of this."

The beast trembled. He had no ears, but I knew he'd heard me just fine. And I knew so much more than that about his kind.

I licked my teeth, feeling the burn of my incisors wishing to drop and the heat of raw fire beginning to spark within me. "Now don't be a fool, Alû. You cannot win this against me. So tell me where the Tinkerer is, and I will leave you be. Aye?"

I stilled, lifting a brow, daring him to do other than what I'd just bade him do. Some still thought to test me once they realized the taste of me was not the usual. But most knew they didn't stand a chance in the twin hells against something like me. I was tamed, but who I was—who I really was—had never left me. The Alû must have come to the same conclusion, for he released his hold on me and pointed over his shoulder with his thumb to indicate that the Tinkerer would be back that way.

With a nod of thanks I knew he would never see, I dusted the wrinkles out of my jacket and walked around him. The sooner I found the Tinkerer, the sooner I could leave and hopefully bring my partner back home, safe and in one piece.

CHAPTER 8
ELLE

I SENSED Crowley's presence behind me. He was sitting, and his posture was relaxed, but I knew the truth of him. How he could be loose one second and a feral wolf the next. I'd been on the wrong side of Crowley for long enough to know it was fact. One wrong move, and the male would turn into the darker version of himself.

He'd asked to come and watch my studies with Jacamoe early the following morning. His words had seemed innocent enough. He wanted me to believe it'd been nothing more than happenstance that'd found him at my door at the exact hour I'd planned to sneak off to train.

The next six-hour cycle had begun, and though Jacamoe hadn't seemed overly excited to see me at his door at such an ungodly hour, he had grudgingly let me in.

The fact that Crowley seemed to have been waiting outside my door at midnight so that he could conveniently tag along, aka stalk me, hadn't escaped my notice. He took an eager interest in my studies, though I wasn't sure why. Maybe he wanted to know all there was to know about me so that he could maintain the upper hand when we get out of here. If we ever did, that was.

"Focus, Arielle," Jacamoe whispered. "Our time is nearly at an end."

"I'm trying," I hissed, scowling at him, knowing that I must look like a hot mess. My long black hair was sticking to the back of my neck like octopus tentacles, I was covered in sweat, and my breathing was ragged. I'd never dreamed that learning to use magick would feel like running a marathon. Every witch I'd ever encountered had always made it looked so easy.

"It is not hard," he said, and again I detected a note of aggravation. Maybe I shouldn't have come at midnight. Clearly, Jacamoe wasn't a night owl like I was. "You have merely to focus to bring her back."

The small ball of shadow in my hand, nothing more than a slight bit of steam at the moment, fizzled out. There was no doubt that my frustration wasn't helping. I clenched my fist and growled. "Dammit! I brought her to me today. Why can't I bring her back again?"

Jacamoe snapped his fingers, and instantly two steaming mugs of jasmine scented tea appeared, the lovely smell filling the room. "Drink," he commanded with an imperious point toward the delicate bone-white China mug.

Twisting my lips and feeling thoroughly ashamed of my performance, I grudgingly reached for it and took a sip. It was scalding and burned the back of my tongue, but already I could feel my limbs growing looser, and a pleasant feeling of warmth filled my belly. The effect almost reminded me of witches' brew coffee, to which I was completely addicted.

I sighed and squeezed my eyes shut as I continued to sip.

"Her will is stronger than yours yet," he said slowly.

"What does that mean?" I asked, but I suspected I already knew. I just didn't like the answer.

He gave me a one-shouldered shrug. "She does not yet recognize your authority over her. You are a baby witch. Your familiar may look innocent and tiny, but what lives inside of her is an immense wellspring of ancient tribal magick. You are now part of a very select and unusual group. But do not assume that means you will reach my level of mastery with just a few training sessions." He snorted as if the idea was laughable.

It made me instantly surly with him. "I never did assume that," I snapped. "You're the one assigning that emotion to me."

"And yet you are the one upset that you cannot control her," Jacamoe said softly.

Crowley snorted with laughter, and I glared hotly at him, wishing I could smack that smirk off his handsome face. I felt a little as though he and I were back to our old, familiar antagonistic ways again.

Rolling my eyes, I looked to Jacamoe. "I'm frustrated because I have no control over anything at present. No one will tell me when the tribunal will decide my fate, and no one will talk to me. So yes, I'm frustrated, but this frustration goes much deeper than being unable to control a rebellious familiar!" I said the last with a pound of my fist upon the workbench.

Finally, the humor faded from Jacamoe's eyes, and he rubbed the bridge of his nose with his long, mahogany-colored fingers. "Forgive me, Arielle. You are, of course, correct. You are under an immense amount of strain at the moment. I forget myself."

Blowing out a heavy breath, I looked at the empty space where my familiar had winked in and out of existence just a moment ago and shrugged. "I think we all are. Tomorrow is Aquata's life song, and I—" My throat squeezed shut, and I took several deep breaths, trying to settle myself. I'd thought very little about why I was here today, but when the dawn came, I hoped my reason for being trapped in the Undine would make itself very clear.

Tomorrow would be the final night that we all got to see my sweet, sweet sister. We—and by "we," I no longer really even meant myself— would sing her soul back to us. As a creature of the under, Aquata's spirit now rested in the bosom of the water mother, who would gift her back to us for a few hours at the witching hour. She would not be corporeal, and she would not be able to talk, but she would be able to give us an opportunity to say our goodbyes.

She had been a royal, and she would be honored. There would be a celebration of her life, a party where we all sat and swapped stories about her and how much she meant to us all.

Of course, usually these affairs were naught but an excuse for a good time, a large party full of drink, and a reason to let loose. But I rather thought that the festivities the next day might be different. Though I'd been outcast decades before, I was still of noble blood and could not be barred from my sister's song. But I dreaded the thought of it too. No one would be happy to see me there, and with these damned cuffs on me everyone would know why I still remained.

Speaking of the cuffs, I felt their terrible pressure suddenly being clamped back onto me and knew that our two hours was at an end.

I stared at Jacamoe, miserable to my very core.

His face was stoic. "Get some rest, Princess. Tomorrow will be a busy day."

I missed my sister very much, but I didn't want to go to her song. Still, I knew I could not get out of it. "Can we train tomorrow?"

He shook his head. "I must make preparations. I will be gone the whole of the day. We resume our studies the following day. Should you be free, that is."

The reminder felt like a bucket of ice water thrown on my face. I frowned. "Can I at least use your room to train without you?"

He glanced around, and I could sense his uneasiness at allowing me in here without him.

"If there was another room in this bloody castle for me to train in, you know I would, Jacamoe."

Wetting his lips, he nodded forcefully. "Yes, I know it. Of course, you are welcome. Only please lock up after you are gone."

I nodded. "Thank you."

Then looking over at Crowley, I lifted my brows in a silent gesture saying that we should leave now.

I was tired. My body hurt from all over from the plugging up of my magick. Mentally, I was drained. And yet, I was also wired and wide awake. I needed sleep, but I knew there would be none for me tonight.

My footsteps were slow when Crowley and I entered the hall. Neither of us spoke for several seconds as the tension grew and grew.

In fact, we didn't even speak until we'd turned down into our wing of the castle. "Are you well?" he asked gently.

I didn't mean to, but I snapped, "What the hells do you think!" I glared at him as I planted my hands on my hips. My chest heaved up and down with my heavy breaths.

He stilled, and I could see the glow of the animal rise in his eyes. Even his upper lip pulled back, and the air tingled with the sudden rush of his raw energy. For a brief second, I wondered whether he meant to attack me, and for another brief second, I was pretty sure I would have welcomed a good, knock-down, drag-out brawl. I welcomed anything to help me not think about what tomorrow would bring.

But then he swallowed, and I felt the energy evaporate as quickly as it'd appeared.

Moving as only a beast could, his hand was suddenly on my chin, and he was turning my face, looking at me intensely. "How long since you've slept?"

Since last I'd lain with Hook aboard the ship, I thought and then shuddered. Feeling so old and decrypt of a sudden. Extricating my chin from his grip, I rubbed my arms with my hands and sighed.

"You need sleep, Detective."

I snorted. "Easy for you to say."

"It's not easy for me to say. Do you think I've slept a damned wink out here? To answer my own question, no. But I'm fucking tired. And I know you are too. You might be whatever the hells you are now"—he gestured at me with a finger wave—"but I'll wager that you need rest just like all the rest of us. Elle, fuck—don't forget all that we did before we even got here."

He was right, of course. But I didn't want to hear it. I was pissed off and ready to rage, and he just happened to be there.

Laughing almost maniacally, I glared at him. "My sister is dead because of me. My father might very well be joining her soon. My lover? Dead, come back, and maybe dead again." I laughed again, but it was more shrill and higher pitched than before. "No one will talk to me. I might very well die in a few days myself. I look like a fecking monster now. I don't even know who I am or what I am. No fecking surprise that I'm as messed up as I am right now, and you have the nerve to tell me that I need to—"

"Godsdammit," he growled and grabbed me by the shoulders, shaking me roughly and making my teeth rattle. "Stop this shit," he growled, the wolf in his words. "You don't get to feel bad for yourself,

Detective, you hear me? You don't get to do this! You're a fucking Grimm PD detective. You pull your shit together before I make you."

I laughed even harder, feeling an uncontrollable urge to slap his face. But thankfully, recognizing how out of line that would be, I instead drove my clawlike nails into my palms until I felt them pierce my flesh. The pain cleared my head a little, just enough to know I was losing my head. The moment I did, I felt the fight leave me, and I suddenly had very little strength left. I felt my body sway and my knees grow weak, and my back suddenly pressed up against the wall behind me.

"Whoa, there," he said gently, but still with an edge of the beast in his tone. Then his hands were on me, and he was helping me walk the rest of the way back to my room as I fought not to cry, not to show him how messed up I was feeling. That anger had been nothing more than a mask hiding the fact that I'd screwed up royally. And because of it, I had to say the last goodbye to the gentlest heart I'd ever known.

I didn't know when we'd entered my room or even how we'd ended up sitting on my bed, but when I blinked again, we were there, he was looking at me, and I needed someone to confide in. I couldn't stop. "I don't know who I am anymore. I'm a stranger in this place." I sucked in a trembly breath as the tears started to fall in waves.

I poured out my soul, and Crowley just listened, saying nothing and not touching me. But he was there, fully present, and for once, I was grateful that it was him and not anyone else. I knew he would not give me hopeless platitudes, like Hook would or Hatter might. Crowley was as practical as I was. And when I'd finally unburdened myself and had no more tears to shed, I looked down at the mattress and shuddered.

His warm hand found mine just a few seconds later, grounding me in the present and making me feel tethered and weirdly safe. "Look at me," he said softly.

I did.

His handsome face was stoic, but his eyes roamed mine with a heavy sincerity in them. "I know Hook lives."

I nodded, knowing he was right. Because even after all this time, my bond to Hook was as strong as ever. If he'd died again, I'd have known it, just as I had the first time.

"And *we* will get him out of here." He gestured between us.

I shook my head. "You maybe, but I screwed up b—"

He growled deeply in his chest and I clamped my lips shut.

"You had your chance to speak. Now, it's my turn," he said in a no-nonsense tone. "Do you think I lose, Detective? At anything?" He didn't give me a chance to answer, because he answered himself. "I don't lose. I never do. It's not why I got into this business. I'm good at what I do. The fucking best. And so are you. You hear me?"

I nodded, and he responded in kind.

"That's right. What we did, we did because we had to. That Sea Witch was a monster who needed stopping, and if we had to do it again, we would. I'm not letting this tribunal do shit to you, Elle, and I need you to believe and trust in me. Just as you would your own partner."

So rare was it for him to call me by my gods-given name that it stuck out like a sore thumb to me when he did. And a strange warmth rolled through me at the sound of it.

His thumb scraped repeatedly over the top of my hand in a soothing back-and-forth motion. "And until that tribunal convenes for us, we have work to do. We're the only ones who know that your sister in all likelihood was murdered. Now, I don't know much about the Undine world, but I know what the song ritual is, and I know that Aquata will return one last time."

I shook my head. "She is only a spirit, Crowley. She cannot speak to tell me what was done to her."

The corner of his lip twitched.

I was struck all over again by how strangely fascinating his facial dimensions were. He was really quite interesting to look at.

"Maybe not," he said, "but I've been around enough murdered spirits to know that they all act the same, no matter their species. Everyone will look for her appearance tomorrow in the gardens, where she was killed. But you and I both know that it is to the place that they felt safest at in life that they return to in death."

"The house in the hedgerow."

He nodded. "We could sneak off and wait for her. No one will think to look for her there, which means we'll have a few minutes with her, and who knows what secrets we could learn then?"

My stomach felt jittery, as though razor-tipped butterfly wings flapped inside it. I was scared to hope, scared to believe that something positive could actually come out of the pain I would feel when I confronted her loss, but I did hope. Damn him. I burned with hope, which was dangerous. I bit my top lip before saying, "You think she'll show us something?"

"I've got a hunch, Detective. That's all. But I'm rarely wrong about them—or have you forgotten who was always there to thwart your ass?"

I laughed, but the sound was choked. "Aye, I've not forgotten. Damn bastard."

It was his turn to chuckle, and his thumb scraped more slowly, more gently, almost tenderly across the soft flesh of my wrist.

As if suddenly aware that I knew just how intimate a touch that had been, he stilled and looked down at where we were joined hand in hand. He released me slowly, gently, almost like prey backing away from a predator. Then he sniffed and cleared his throat. "You need sleep. You look like shit."

I barked with laughter, needing his tough brand of whatever the hell he was doing more than he could possibly know. Any bit of tenderness from him would likely have had me sobbing again, but all I felt was weary and surprisingly ready for bed. "Likewise," I sassed him back, and his full lips twitched.

Standing, he rolled his thick neck from side to side until even I could hear its crack. I cringed, but he didn't seem fazed by it at all. "I've still a few things left to do," he said.

I cocked my head. "What in the devil are you doing skulking about this castle as you are? You do understand that if you get caught, you're likely to wind up in clamps, just like me." I held up my wrists, jiggling them at him.

He smirked. "I never get caught, Detective. I thought we'd already established that." With a wink, he turned and crept from my room so stealthily that even though I saw him doing it with my own eyes, I didn't hear his movements at all.

I stared at the empty room, which seemed much smaller without him in it, wondering why it was that I suddenly felt the way I did. But it was also a feeling I had no desire to explore any further.

I was still in my gown. *I should change. I should strip. I should do something, wash my face, at least.* I forgot everything until the sun rose bright and early the next day.

CHAPTER 9
MADDOX

I WAS LED to a back room. Everything about Bârân was meant to entice. Much like Alice's crown and thorns, it was just another den of sexual pleasures, but with a decidedly Eastern theme.

A contemplation pool was at the center of the room with lotus flowers floating upon it and brightly colored koi fish swimming within it. Lush and exotic smells, oils and perfumes from far-off lands, were everywhere.

The room itself was a wonderous mixture of indoors and out, with walls covered in crawling vines bursting with flowers and chitinous beetles that flew colorfully through the air like wheeling fairyflies.

Pressed against one wall was a pile of brightly textured sitting pillows. As far as traps went, it wasn't exactly pinging my radar. Wherever Crowley had sent me, it didn't seem to be a snare, yet it made no sense to me, either.

But maybe as an agent of Grimm rather than a mere detective, he had access to places and people I could barely even dream of.

Taking a seat on a mound of surprisingly comfortable pillows, I picked up a meditation stone and rubbed its smooth surface for several seconds. But as the seconds ticked by and still no one else joined me, I grew worried that maybe I had stepped into an elaborate scheme of some sort, or worse yet, a terrible prank. It seemed entirely out of character for Crowley's serious nature, but I couldn't explain why he'd sent me here any other way.

Twisting my lips, wondering how I'd explain it to Bo, I tossed the stone into the pool. It landed with a soft *plop* before slowly sinking from sight. Counting the ripples of the pool preoccupied my time as I waited and waited and waited.

Finally, when I was sure I would have to actually fight my way out, the door opened.

I looked up and frowned.

I wasn't sure what I expected to see, but an elderly woman with wheels for legs and metallic pincers for hands wasn't it. I cocked my head even as I instantly jumped to my feet.

I'd not expected to find a cyborg—it was the only way I could describe her—meeting me, but good breeding was good breeding. I bowed deeply toward the matron, who had unusually kind and expressive eyes.

She chortled, a sound that seemed to come easily and often to her. She held up one pincered hand. "It's been many a moon since I've been bowed to, son, though you've made this old woman's heart glad for it." She tipped her head gracefully back to me.

I couldn't help but wonder how it was that she'd been turned into an amalgam of woman and metal, but whatever had caused the transformation must have been violent.

She wheeled over toward a cabinet. "Drink?" Her manner seemed easygoing, and it instantly put me at ease.

"Fire water, if you have it," I automatically said.

"Ah, a Landian. You aren't very common here in Grimm Central, though I should have known by the fine cut of your coat. You all do tend toward the peacock, don't you?" she lightly teased.

Taken off guard by the woman, I gave her a sheepish grin. *Why had Crowley sent me to find her in particular? What was she to him?* She seemed harmless and far too pure to be tangled up in his web. But then... I knew better than most how often appearances could be deceiving.

I cleared my throat as I accepted the crystal tumbler full of green fluid. Fire water was thick and stripped the flesh going down, leaving a trace of burnt cherries behind. I'd always had a taste for the foul stuff, much to Elle's chagrin. She'd likened it to cough syrup and "the bad kind at that," she'd often teased. I slammed it back then handed the Tinkerer the empty tumbler, refusing a refill.

She took a shot of something clear before finally looking back to me. "Now," she said, and instantly I sensed the shift in her. She went from matronly grandmother to a shrewd businesswoman in a blink.

That's when I knew that Crowley hadn't been lying to me. Whoever this women was, she was interesting, to say the least.

"—who sent you? Not just anyone knows my true name."

"I was sent by Agent Crowley."

"Who?" She asked instantly, and her shoulders tensed. Her openness of just seconds earlier had vanished, replaced by an implacable curiosity, and I suddenly had the sense that this was not a woman to be trifled with.

I cleared my throat, trying to remember how the agent had worded his directive. Many times, when we in law enforcement were talking to our informants, we spoke in code, so that if our communiqué were intercepted, they couldn't be decrypted.

"Ah"—I cleared my throat—"he referred to himself as 'agent.' That's it."

The distrustful gleam in her dark eyes hadn't relented, but she slowly cocked her head to the side. "I heard you the first time. And I assumed that was who you'd meant. Why has he sent you to me? Why did he not come himself?"

I thought about how I'd seen Crowley, and to be honest, I still couldn't make sense of it. I couldn't figure out how had the agent had chanced upon such powerful magick. Shifters were not inherently practitioners. Their magick rested within their very nature, but it was instinctual and not something that could grow to be more, not in the way a witch or a mage could.

My brows lowered. "He is currently being kept in the under. The case is classified, but I can assure you that I was sent on his behalf." Reaching into my coat pocket, I extracted my badge, flashing it at her.

"Detective Maddox Hatter," she said softly, raising a gentle brow before shaking her head and her pincers. "Put that away. I believe you, though I fear you do not know what you've stepped into or just what your *agent* friend truly is." She snorted. "No matter. The sooner I give you what you need, the sooner you can get on your way."

Hearing the soft whirring of a metallic panel pulling apart, I glanced over my shoulder, expecting to see the door opening. But instead it wasn't the door behind me that had opened—rather, the Tinkerer herself had reached inside of her own chest cavity with one of her pincered hands and withdrew a small and very unusual looking timepiece.

It had no hands, and its face was nothing but metallic gears and cranks. Gently, she handed the trinket to me. "Do not, for any reason drop this. It is the only one of its kind and can never be replicated again. It can only be used once."

"What is it?" I asked, curling my hands over the cool glass surface.

"It is called a wave amplifier noise device, or WAND for short."

I snorted. "Of course it is."

She shrugged. "Don't shoot the messenger. I didn't name it."

"What does it do?"

"Exactly as the name implies, it disrupts sound waves by shifting the normal pattern into a higher frequency that can scramble even the most unbreakable bonds."

"He's planning to break them out of there," I muttered under my breath.

"What was that?" she asked.

I shook my head before quickly pocketing the piece. "Nothing." My pulse rocketed in my chest. *Elle might soon be free of her cage, at least.* I still wasn't sure how Crowley planned to escape the undersea world, but I was glad to see that he had a plan. One thing was certain: I would have to alert the captain. We had to figure out a way through the proper channels down there. Surely, Undine would have to recognize our authority on the matter if we had a warrant in hand.

"Thank you, Madam Tinkerer," I said with sincerity, moving to stand before I could bow a farewell to her. "You do not know how much I—"

There was an uneasiness around her eyes before she quickly hissed, "Do not be deceived, Detective. You do not know the agent as I do.

He is not a good man, though he plays the game well. For all our sakes, I beg you not to release him. Let him rot down there."

My skin shivered with ice, and I stared at her intensely. "If he rots, so does she. And I can't allow that. I won't allow that."

"I won't ask you who you mean. I doubt you'd share, anyway." Her words sounded so defeated. She twisted her lips. "It was he who turned me into this thing I am today. He who banished me from my lands to this stinking cesspool of rot and decay. He is a monster, Detective. And if your friend's life depends on retrieving this, then may the gods have mercy on her soul."

❧

Elle

"Come."

I glanced up from my studies. I'd not been able to bring my baby otter back for longer than even a second that day, and my thoughts were scattered, my concentration absolute shite. I was in desperate need of a break that I had no wish to actually take. I clutched at the desk with nerveless fingers, feeling stretched thin and nearing my breaking point.

"Detective, come," Crowley said again softly, more gently.

I sniffed and wiped at my nose with my sleeved arm. I was dressed in the gaudiest, stupidest gown of all time, black silk taffeta that in the light shifted from purple to blue, encrusted with gems. My black hair was pulled up and pinned in place with golden hermit crabs. My face was painted like a harlot's, and I wore false eyelashes that were so damn long I couldn't stop blinking—it felt as if I had bugs trying to crawl into my eyeballs.

"You'll smear your face, Elle," he whispered slowly, taking my wrists in his and massaging gently, his thumbs scraping my tender flesh and making me shiver despite myself.

I shuddered. "I can't do this."

"Forget about magick for now, Detective," he whispered, rubbing at my jaw with his thumbs, which I could assume was because I'd badly smeared the pancake face paint. "I promise that you'll want to see what I've found." He dropped his hand to his side.

I frowned at his cryptic comment. "What?"

Shaking his head, he placed a finger over his mouth, the universal sign of shut the hells up already. I almost laughed at his growly and frustrated look, but his eyes were glowing red, and I thought that maybe he was in as good a mood as I was.

Sighing, I tried to withdraw my hands from his, but he jerked with his chin toward Jacamoe's workbench. "Your cuffs. I'll be fucking pissed if you blow yourself up by walking out of this room without them."

I snorted. "You'd only be pissed because you'd die with me."

"You're damn right," he growled before clamping my locks back into place with a finality that stole my breath.

I was getting better at adjusting to the sudden dampening of my powers, but I still swayed, and my stomach still roiled for a second. "Gods, I hate how much you must be enjoying this," I said between gritted teeth.

Once the dizziness had passed I opened my eyes, only to note an odd shape lying beneath a pile of scattered sheaves. Frowning, I reached for it. I wasn't sure what made me do it, but when I shoved the sheaves aside I frowned. Hard. As I stared down at the looking glass I'd seen Jacamoe taking to my sister days ago.

I picked it up.

"What are you doing, Detective? I've something to show you."

I shook my head and tipped the looking glass toward him. "Don't you know what this is?"

"It's a looking glass, obviously. Why are you playing with it?"

I rolled my eyes and snorted. "I'm not playing, idiot. And this is much more than a mere looking glass, it's actually a spy glass. It's quite powerful really, it can see for miles in any direction, in fact there is no limit to how far you can look through it. And nothing is hidden from you, you can look through walls, rock, metal."

His brows rose high. "Royals are such fucking bastards."

"Hey," I elbowed him in the ribs and chuckled, quite forgetting my irritation of just seconds ago in the ease of our banter. "It's much more useful than simply spying on someone. With this I could even find Hook, I've merely to—" I started to place the glass to my eyes, but Crowley gently shoved it away and shook his head.

"Put it back, Detective. We've no need of it."

"What? But I need to find him, Crowley. I've told you that since getting here. I need to know that he's okay."

He chuckled below his breath, plucked the glass out of my hand and replaced it, covering it back up with the sheaves just as it had been when I'd found it. "Just follow me, Fish," he said.

"I think you love bossing me around. Sadist," I teased, but with an edge of annoyance in there now too.

He only snorted, but didn't bother denying it either.

Considering that I was absolutely useless with my magick and wanted to do anything other than think about the fact that my sister's song was only a mere hour away, I finally capitulated. It wasn't like I had anything else to do right now.

I'd managed to keep myself occupied today by doing stupid work, helping in the kitchen, though my services hadn't been appreciated in the slightest, the constant gossip that none of them tried to censor around me about me let me know soon enough I should go. But I'd gone from that to then forcing myself to go through the rituals of bathing and becoming the castle's gilded lily once again. At one point, I'd even caught sight of my middle sister, Adella.

She was a great artist, so I shouldn't have been too shocked to see her in such an ostentatious, over-the-top ball gown, but I was. She literally looked as though she wore the waves of Undine wrapped around her body. There were even deep-sea fish trapped within its folds, swimming and jockeying for each other's positions. Sea kelp in strategically placed locations covered her important bits. I'd felt a moment of aching, desperate sadness when I caught sight of her lavender-and-teal tail—I missed my own golden one desperately.

I'd stood there like a guppy, watching her, knowing eventually I'd be spotted. And I had been. I'd raised a hand in greeting, but she'd never returned it. She'd only glared at me and if it looks could kill, well... there'd have been no need for a tribunal.

With a snarl she'd turned, never having said one word to me but the look was enough to let me know she blamed me for all that happened to Aquata. Possibly even to father. Once, she might have been happy to see me, but I knew I could not expect a warm welcome from any of my sisters after that. Not even my beloved Anahita had time for me anymore.

Tonight was going to be the death of me. I just knew it.

I frowned when Crowley suddenly turned down yet another one of our secret stairwells, shocked to see one I'd never even known about. It must have been constructed after I'd been expelled.

I blinked, staring at his back. "And where are we going? Did you say?"

He chuckled darkly. "You know damned well I didn't say, and just keep quiet, Fish, if you know what's good for you."

I rolled my eyes and crossed my arms, but I was curious, so I would play the game. The stairwell twisted and turned, going down and down and down into what felt like the very bowels of Hel itself. Every so often, Crowley would stop and flick aside a trick stone in the wall that would open up a small looking hole for us to see through. But just as quickly, he would growl, shake his head, and move on.

"Forgotten already?" I couldn't help but goad him after the fifth time.

His eyes glowed like ruby fire in the darkness when he turned to me. With a low growl, he said, "They keep moving things around. But I can smell it, so I know we're close."

"That sounds disgusting. Smell what, by the way?" I asked curiously.

He snapped his teeth at me, and I knew the big bad wolf would give me no more.

I didn't have to wait long, though. Not even ten minutes later, he peeked once more, and then a low, rumble of approval vibrated through his chest. "C'mon then, Fish. Come see your surprise."

Honestly curious all of a sudden, I tossed him a furrowed glance, and he shook his head, merely pointing to the peeking hole.

Deciding to trust him, I walked over, noticing how close beside me he stayed—so close, in fact, that his head and my own seemed to merge into one. My flesh prickled from the contact when I finally placed my eye to the hole and looked through.

When I did it felt as if all the breath left my body and I'd been sucker punched.

"Hook," I said breathily, gripping the walls with suddenly nerveless fingers as my breathing trembled from out my lungs.

I caressed the walls with the pads of my fingers, imagining it was his face I held. The stairwell stood well above where he was floating below us. He was in a room full of brightly glowing coral and flickering blue phosphorescent lights.

He didn't have any scratches on him anymore. His eyes were tightly shut, but his jaw was relaxed, as though he was sleeping. They'd changed his clothes—he was in his black leathers. I don't know who'd found them, or where they'd come from, but seeing him was like a punch to the gut. He looked just like my old Hook, the one I'd fallen in love with back when I'd still been a child, when I hadn't been so jaded and bitter.

"What is this?" I breathed, my voice cracking as I fought the sudden swell of powerful emotions rising up in me.

"I'd hoped you'd enlighten me with that answer. Doesn't look like any holding cell I've ever seen." Crowley's voice was hard and gritty and seemed too close to me all of a sudden.

I shook my head, shifting on my heels just enough to make me feel like he wasn't caging me in. "No. It doesn't."

His look was knowing and his lips tight, but he said nothing. The air felt charged with static. He glanced over my shoulder, toward the peephole I knew he couldn't look through with my body in his line of sight.

Swallowing hard, I turned back to the hole, focusing on Hook and how it was that he was suspended that way. There were no wires, no pulleys. It was magick, pure and simple. Even though I'd lived here all my young life, I couldn't think of a single moment I'd had cause to find my way into this part of the castle, and now it was Crowley showing it to me for the first time.

I looked at Hook's face. His chest rose and fell in repetitive fashion. I felt the energy that surrounded him on a visceral, almost tangible level. My skin tingled with the rush of his invisible energy, as if someone had driven a spear of light through me. "It's definitely magick."

"No shit, Sherlock," he snapped, but there was an edge of dark humor to it.

I rolled my eyes, fighting a grin. Crowley was like no one I'd worked with before. Ich had always been diplomatic in his responses to me, and Hatter always had a gentle way of saying and conveying everything. It took a lot to make him snap. Crowley, on the other hand, seemed to thrive on calling bullshit on just about everything I said or did. It made him both frustrating and surprisingly refreshing. "You're such an arsehole, Agent. What I meant was that I don't think the magick is simply there to suspend him in air. It's doing something to him."

I didn't know if the magick was forcefully keeping him alive—he hadn't been breathing when he'd floated with me on the Never Sea—or if they'd figured out another way to keep his vital organs going.

He looked peaceful, though. My fingers dug into the naturally pitted grooves of the stone wall, and I wished I could touch him again, hold him, and reassure him even in his sleep that I was there and not going anywhere ever again.

I placed my forehead against the cold stone. "Is there a way in from here?"

"I've found a section of wall that moves. But it's only large enough to fit a small child, which means"—I felt his hard look—"you should have no problem fitting through."

I snorted but chose to ignore his taunt. "Show me." I started to move, but he grabbed my elbow as I made to glide past, stopping me in my tracks.

"I don't think it's safe to go traipsing around down there, Detective. I've seen nurses and doctors come in and out at random. If you get caught—"

Shoving away from the wall, I turned and glared up at him. The prick didn't have the sense to back up. My nose practically crashed into his stupidly square jaw. "I'm a princess."

"Which means you're a dipshit!" he snapped, straightening to his full height, towering over me.

If he thought that was enough to intimidate me, he had another think coming. I snarled.

So did he, taking a menacing step toward me, and I wasn't sure, but it seemed that his muscles might be literally swelling right before my very eyes. I almost laughed. I had to be pissing him off something terrible to make his shifter side flare so brightly and so quickly.

"Considering," he said, in a deep, raspy growl, "the fact that you weren't granted access to see him yet, you might want to ask yourself why, Fish. Why is that, huh?" His eyes gleamed like hell fire. "Well?" he snapped when I didn't answer. "C'mon, use that head for something other than a hat rack. Show me that you're more than just tits and ass."

I raised my hand, offended to my very depths by his sudden high-handedness. "You sonofabit—"

He grabbed my wrist in a steely grip, and his eyes glowed the red of heated magma as he glared back at me. "Don't even think it."

Our chests brushed together, our breaths were heavy and hard, his eyes still burned, and I could feel my own sirens markings start to glow. I would kill him for daring to touch me. And no, it wasn't the darkness whispering that to me—it was me alone. The old hate and animosity between us came rising up like an angry kraken from its cave. My smile was nothing but teeth, and neither was his. I opened my mouth to speak, but the hushed tone of someone new broke through our standoff.

"How is he?"

With a small rush of air, I yanked my elbow from Crowley's grip and turned. I stared back through the peephole, and my mind instantly went blank when I saw the faces of the woman and the man below us.

It was Anahita, dressed in royal funeral garb, all in indigo with veins of glittering mother-of-pearl throughout. She wore armor plating upon her shoulders and across her chest. On her head she wore not a crown, but a plated helmet. Some of the many falsehoods perpetuated about my kind included that we were soft, lazy, and simple. But none of those were true. We were a warring people. Most of us trained from our infancy to learn how to fight with a staff or trident. She looked like a knight of old, dressed in her most ceremonial garb to finally lay my sister to rest.

Beside her stood Jacamoe. His dark, stormy gaze rested on Hook's comatose form.

My jaw opened, and the air suddenly felt thick and soupy. I couldn't breathe correctly. *What are they doing together?* My sister could barely spare a moment for me, and my friend had promised that the second he found Hook's whereabouts, he would let me know about it. It made no sense.

"No change," he said softly. "Not even any activity. He lives, but he is not there."

I rubbed at my chest, feeling Hook's soul burning with the heat of a candle's flame within me.

Anahita turned her electric-blue eyes toward my one-time lover, and my heart squelched as I saw her swim nearer to Hook. She reached out with a hand, looking as if she would caress his temple.

"No," I whimpered, hating to see her hand on him. I knew her deep-seated hatred toward him.

Beside me, Crowley growled and knocked his hip into mine, causing me almost to trip. Hissing, I glared at him. But he merely placed a finger over his mouth and shook his head, giving me a silent reminder that I needed to keep quiet.

Pissed as hells at him but also realizing he was right—the bastard— I scrubbed a hand down my face and shuddered as she began to speak.

"Daddy warned me about him. He warned me, and still I did nothing. I said nothing to her until it was too late and she'd already screwed her life up to hells. I will not make that mistake again. I don't care what you have to do to activate him, Jacamoe, you do it. He knows what that murderous bitch was up to, and I'll be damned if I don't get those answers soon. I fear this nightmare has only just begun."

I frowned, wondering why she would imagine that Hook knew anything. Grimm Central had only just learned that truth a few days before, and so far as I knew, Anahita wasn't privy to anything Grimm Central knew. *Right?*

"As my queen wishes." My friend bowed deeply, almost reverently, before unstoppering a vial that had suddenly appeared in his hand. I almost gasped but at the last second remembered the need for silence.

I would recognize the smoky black power anywhere. It was what he'd taken from me in the practice room. *Why does he have my essence?*

I shook my head as a fog bank surrounded Hook. Then I trembled as I saw his flesh begin to absorb it.

"That sonofabitch." It wasn't me who said it. "Fucking prick. Of course." Crowley snarled softly beside me but with enough heat that it made my ears burn.

I knew instantly what Crowley was thinking, that Jacamoe must have taken my power purposefully for this very reason. But Crowley was a jaded bastard. I was looking toward my sister, the pleased smirk on her face, and the way her eyes glittered.

It was completely her doing. But I didn't know why. Hook was no witch, and he wouldn't be able to tap into that wellspring of dark magick. I had no clue what it would do to him, though I very much wished I did. I looked back at Jacamoe in confusion, unsure what I was seeing.

"How much longer?" Anahita asked, glancing over her tense, tight shoulder. She looked almost as if she was worried about getting caught, which made no sense—she was the acting regent, and her word was the law, at least for the time being. Maybe what they were doing broke a sacred pact.

My heart squeezed, and I gripped the stone tightly, feeling impotent and annoyed that I couldn't go down there and stop them.

"Not much longer now, my Queen," Jac said.

"Good. The sooner I can learn what needs learning, the sooner I can make use of his newfound loyalty."

"Yes, my Queen."

I cocked my head, wondering why he seemed so deferential to her when I knew how much he secretly despised his role in this castle.

Maybe I had been wrong, and he had never hated my family. Maybe it had just been me who he'd feigned an interest in. And I couldn't figure out what exactly Anahita meant, the bitch, or if she was speaking of the Sea Witch. I couldn't understand any of it, least of all where the witch had gone. She must have passed through there—Anahita had so much as said that the Sea Witch had been responsible for Aquata's death and Father's state of stupor, and Jacamoe had basically corroborated her story. But he had also added the not-so-insignificant detail of her being weakened after she'd killed my sister and nearly murdered my father, which meant she couldn't have gone far. She had to be lurking in Undine somewhere, at least until she gathered enough strength to leave.

Right? Again, I felt myself asking that question over and over. *Why does nothing make sense anymore? Why do I have a sick feeling that I'm overlooking something vitally important?* It felt as though the pieces of the puzzle were lying right in front of me, but I couldn't make heads or tails of any of it.

"I will check on Daddy now," she said, beginning to swim off before pausing and glancing at Jacamoe over her shoulder. "How goes Elle's training?"

My heart lurched, and I leaned up on tiptoe.

He shook his head. "She is weak. There is nothing of significance in her now, my Queen. She poses no threat to the kingdom. She is a waste of our time. Our focus lies elsewhere."

My sister flinched, and I clutched at my breast, my ears ringing at the stinging criticism from a man I'd once idolized. I was nothing. I had no real power. And I was a waste of his time.

That was why he'd never told me about Hook—it had to be. I'd only been a pawn to them. And Jacamoe had been their trusted ally, a man my sister would have known I trusted enough to let my guard down with.

I pushed away from the wall, feeling as though I was sinking into an existential quagmire. *No wonder he hadn't wanted to train me today. No wonder he hadn't told me the truth of Hook.*

Hugging myself, I swallowed hard, trying to suck down the ball of bitter bile that'd suddenly come flooding up the back of my tongue. All the shite I'd been through for the past few days was suddenly surging up in me: the trauma of losing my sirens magick, of losing my Hook, of knowing I might never again see the upper lands, of never again feeling Hatter's warm arms around me. I felt sick.

I squeezed my eyes shut, thinking about how pointless and stupid and useless the entirety of my life had been. Crowley had so much as told me that I was nothing. *All these wasted years, and for what? An ignoble death at the end of it all?* Crowley had been right all along. He'd been the only one honest enough to at least tell me that.

He breathed, and I heard the shiver of the beast in his tone. "Hey."

I looked up, suddenly feeling cold all over and frowning because I'd not even heard him move toward me.

"Hey," he said again more gently. He placed his warm palm on my elbow and squeezed. "Look at me."

I blinked but did as he commanded.

His other hand was on my jaw, and he was tenderly holding my face in his. "He's full of shit."

My brows furrowed.

Crowley shook his head. His eyes were a mixture of the darkness of night and fiery embers. "He's full of shit, Elle. You hear me?"

I licked my lips, still feeling numb all over and like I wanted nothing more than to lie down and sleep forever. I was fooling myself, imagining that anything I did down here could actually help my cause. I was imprisoned. And the tribunal were going to do whatever it took to rid themselves of me once and for all. It was their chance to pay me back in full for all the hells I'd caused them years ago.

"I feel it. I smell it. You're the real thing, Elle."

"What?" I finally spoke, trying to regain some sense of order through the chaos rolling around in my head. "What?" I asked again, not sure what in the hells he was getting at.

"I don't know why that damned Djinn said what he said, but he's a fucking liar." He growled and stepped even closer to me, so close that he had to spread his legs wide so as not to fall on top of me.

I looked up at his roughly hewn face, at the scruff of beard covering his sharp jawline, at the bridge of his nose that was slightly too crooked to have not been broken at least once. "What are you talking about?"

"That fucking bullshit you and I both heard down there. You know it's not true. You created a familiar, Elle. I may not know a lot of shit about magick, but I know this: you need to be pretty damned powerful to make one come to you."

I snorted and tried to shove him off me, but instead I found my hands spread widely on his massive chest, my nails digging into his shirt almost like hooks to hold him still. "Yeah, and it doesn't obey me. It's a baby. It's pathetic. I'm pathetic." My laugh was bitter.

His growl was a hair-raising rumble of sound that vibrated so forcefully through his thick chest that I felt it against my own. "You're new. You're learning. But I smell that power in you. And more to the point, who gives a fuck anyway if he's right? You don't need magick to be a damn good detective. You weren't swimming away from me, Elle. You were outmaneuvering me, every fucking damn step of the way. Wake up." He snapped his fingers. "It was never your magick that made you who you are. It was this." He tapped my temple with one of his blunt fingers that I instantly swatted away.

But not to be deterred, he pressed on. "It was always this." Then he stepped back, leaving my hands dangling in midair before shaking his head. "I don't have time to play this game with you, either. It's not just your life on the line. It's mine too. Now you be my partner in this and we get the fuck out of here with good old fashioned detecting, or you go weep in a corner and hope that some godsdamned fairy godmother will come and save your ass for you. What's it gonna be?"

I gaped at him. His moods were so mercurial they made my head spin. One second, I'd been sure he might have even tried to kiss me—the air between us had felt so charged with tension—and now he was looking at me like he was close to making me lunch, and not in the good way.

"Feck you," I snapped, dropping my hands and balling them into tight fists by my sides.

He chuckled. "Good to have you back, Detective."

I wanted to stay mad at him, but dammit, I couldn't. Because he was right. I closed my eyes and rubbed at my temples. "You're never easy to be around, Agent. You know that?"

"So I've heard, Detective. So I've heard. Now, you've seen he lives. So let's get our asses out to that garden before the song starts without us. Shall we?"

Thinning my lips, wishing I could look down at Hook one last time, I knew again that my temporary partner was right. There was still a chance that I could prove that it wasn't me who had caused Aquata's death. If I could do that, then I might actually stand a chance of walking out of tribunal place in one piece.

"Fine. Let's go." Crowley turned, but I glanced back at the peep-hole one final time, feeling torn, as though I was walking away from my heart. Still, I knew following him was the only way out of here. For all of us.

"Let's go," I whispered to myself, more as a pep talk than anything else. It was time to blow this Popsicle stand by hook or crook. Even if I didn't have magick, I could do it. The bastard was right. I'd done it before, countless times.

I was enough. With or without magick, I was enough.

I jogged to catch up with Crowley's rapidly retreating form.

CHAPTER 10
ELLE

HE'D BEEN RIGHT, of course. We were the only ones in this part of the gardens. Everyone was packed like sardines into the spot where Aquata had been found, hoping to chance a glance at her spirit one last time.

It wasn't because they cared for her or even liked her a little bit. It was mostly for sport. Death brought out the worst in people, even sirens. We liked to believe ourselves so superior to the leggers above us, but I'd seen enough of the hearts of men to know that no matter the species, deep down, we were all the same heartless, careless fecks as all the rest of them.

The sea moon was nearly at its zenith. I sniffed and rubbed my arms.

"You ready?" Crowley asked.

I stared at him. He was dressed in the ceremonial garb of the dead. In the above, black was the color of death, but in the below, it was a blue so deep that it was nearly violet.

His hair was brushed back. He looked different tonight—I couldn't quite place how, but he looked, I don't know, lame as it sounded, relaxed and contented. We were at a funeral, for the gods sakes, and yet Crowley seemed more at ease than usual.

"Do I even want to know why you look so happy about all of this?" I didn't mean for my words to sound bitter.

"You think I'm happy?"

"You're acting funny."

He frowned and scrubbed a hand down his jaw. "Fuck me, Elle. I'm growling, and you say I have problems. I try to be on my best behavior, and you still find fault with me. How about maybe I'm trying to put whatever shit aside for the sake of your feelings right now? How 'bout that?"

I swallowed hard. I didn't play well with others and never really had, apart from Hook, and even he had been on the wrong end of one of my legendary temper tantrums from time to time.

Even Hatter had had a rough go of it with me in the beginning. I thought of our countless spats and realized that I still gave him a hard time about a lot of things. I was raised in a world where trusting anyone was a bad idea, where court intrigue could literally get one killed. Only the strongest survived.

But he was a shifter, a wolf. Their tempers were far from tame. I'd been around packs before. Their familial dynamic could be just as screwed up as my own had been.

I squeezed my eyes shut.

"Gods, you fucking fish are gorgeous, but you give me damned headaches. The lot of you." He growled as he rubbed at his temples.

Licking my front teeth, I glanced to the side. Already, I could sense the urgency in the air, the heightening of ancestral magick. One of our fallen would soon return to us.

I wasn't good at apologies, and I wasn't even sure that one was warranted. Maybe it was—I wasn't sure. But I did know this: at the bare minimum, I could call a cease fire.

Crowley was my only real ally anymore, sad as that was to admit. Walking toward him, I didn't overthink things. Instead, I grabbed his hand and slid my fingers through his.

I felt his curious glance and sensed his continued aggravation with me, but I was good at ignoring what I didn't like. Fixing a tight smile on my face, I nodded toward the hedge and the house, which was still undisturbed, thinking that we might finally discover what lay hidden behind that tiny door. "This magick works best if we all sing," I said by way of explanation.

Looking down at our joined hands, I watched his furrowed brows shifting and imagined countless thoughts exploding in his head. I wished I could read them and could know what he was thinking.

I doubted he wanted to sing, but he did want to solve the case—that much I knew, especially when I tried to release his hand but his suddenly squeezed my fingers, holding me tightly to him.

"You're not my favorite person. You never were," he said, finally looking up at me. But his words weren't harsh or rough—they were soft. And there was a tone in there that I couldn't quite make sense of. It felt as if he wanted to believe what he was saying, but he wasn't sure it was true anymore and it confused the hells out of him.

Well, welcome to the club.

Sad as it was, I knew it was his way of extending an olive branch. I chuckled lightly. "Touché, Agent Crowley." I shrugged.

"Why did you save me?" he asked me yet again, for what felt like the hundredth time. "Why didn't you just let that witch have me, Elle? Why?"

I was starting to understand that when Crowley felt deeply, he stopped calling me Fish or Detective and called me Elle. He was openly being vulnerable with me. "It was the right thing to do, Crowley," I finally whispered with a gentle shrug. If he wanted a deeper answer, I hated to disappoint him, but I didn't have one. All I had was the truth. I hadn't liked him, either, but that hadn't mattered because he'd been in need, and I would have liked to believe that if the roles had been reversed, he would have done the same for me. But the way his eyes looked suddenly dark and haunted had me wondering whether he would have cut his losses and run.

I pressed my lips together, not liking the way that thought suddenly made me feel hot and jittery.

"It's Edward," he said so quietly it was almost nonexistent.

My ear perked and I frowned as I turned to him. "What?"

"My name, its Edward Crowley."

I stared agape at him, realizing, maybe for the first time, that in all the years I'd known him I'd never actually known his true name. He'd always just been Agent arsehole or Crowley to me.

His nostrils flared and he gave his head a slight shake, a look of regret already started to bleed over his features. Now it was my turn to clench tight to his fingers.

"Edward," I said it softly, tasting the vowels on my tongue and realizing that while I'd never have pegged him as an Edward, it oddly fit. It was an old name that harkened back to a different era, much like the man himself.

He licked his left canine and dipped his head.

I might have said more, but the magick had grown to its highest level, and it was time to sing.

I wasn't sure I could access the ancient siren's magick—I wasn't a siren anymore. But I opened my mouth, and I sang. To my great shock, Crowley joined me just a few beats later. His voice was robust and not altogether unpleasant, at least for a legger.

The song was low and haunting. All around us, the voices joined in unison, calling the spirit to us and pulling her away from the great watery grave one last time. I could feel the chill of the water around us and sense the heightening tension of a spirit coming.

Ethereal and full of dancing lights, like a school of silvery fish flashing its scales in sunlight, it moved toward us. No one else would know yet that Aquata had come already. They believed that her soul would return to where it had been found. And eventually, it would. But my sister came to us first.

My heart lurched as I was finally confronted by the sight of her, tall and willowy, as sirens tended to be. Her hair was a radiant reddish brown, almost like polished cherrywood. Her skin was as fair as porcelain, and her eyes were a haunting electric blue that glowed like krill in the night. I shook, looking at her as she looked at me.

Spirits could not speak, and although they had some memory of who they had once been, the strong spark of the living flame was long gone from them. I thought back to the spirit who'd infected me during my first case with Hatter and how she'd been instrumental in leading us to finding her lost child. We'd saved him only because she'd inhabited my body and given me the means to finding him. So I knew there was something of the old in them, but I also knew it had to be something powerful enough to make them bother fighting through the unyielding barrier that separated us.

The song died on my tongue, but enough of us were singing that she stayed tethered. Even Crowley was still humming. I wasn't sure if his singing helped, or if it was just the siren's nature that drew the dead to us. But the fact that he would do it with me touched me more than I cared to admit.

I pursed my lips and drank her in, wishing I could hold her and hug her. But I knew my arms would slide right through her. I could not join Aquata where she was, not yet. Maybe someday, but not today, not just now.

"Sister," I said softly, still scanning her form for any sign of foul play. If she'd been stabbed or had her neck broken or died by some other unnatural means, her spirit form would have had some record of it. I would be able see a bullet wound or a bloody stain upon her gown.

But she was glowing and healthy looking and so, so beautiful.

My lower lip trembled, and I fisted my hands, squeezing so tightly that the nails of my left hand dug into the back of Crowley's hand. He didn't even flinch, only held mine tighter.

An invisible current lifted my sister's hair so that it undulated like a sail behind her. The robes she'd been wearing when she'd died were still on her, pristine and white. She'd always loved white, a fact I'd teased her for mercilessly—we all had. In a world where color and pomp was the norm, Aquata had always been different from the rest of us. We'd called her dull and boring, likening her to vanilla. They'd been the taunts of little children, silly and harmless in their own way, but said with an edge of malice that only a child could pull off.

I swallowed hard, telling myself that it was not the time to fall down that rabbit hole. I needed to focus and remember why we were there. I'd barely had time to think about Aquata's death or about what it really meant that she was gone. In the very literal sense of the word, it was not a banishment that separated me from her, not any longer. It was far more permanent.

She just looked at me with a sadness upon her face that made my knees feel weak. I rubbed the fingers of my free hand across my lower stomach, feeling queasy and sick, telling myself I didn't have the luxury to mourn her. *Not now. Not yet. Definitely not here.*

Crowley squeezed my fingers again, still humming in that surprisingly deep baritone voice of his. I could sense that he was silently urging me to remember what we'd come for and why we were here. I needed to get my shite together. A ghost of a smile passed over my lips —I'd almost heard his commanding growl in my head.

Glancing over my shoulder, assuring myself that we were in fact truly alone, I took a deep breath to settle my nerves. "Aquata, I love you. I will always love you, I will miss your hugs and your beautiful smiles until the day I die, but I've not come here to mourn with you. I..." I hiccupped then shuddered as I swallowed down the ball of heat burning the back of my throat. "I've come because I fear it wasn't my returning that caused your death."

She cocked her head, her sleek hair looking like charmed sea snakes in the way they danced in independent locks around her head.

Is it my imagination, or is she now glowing a little brighter? I frowned. My heart raced just a tiny bit harder. "I-I don't know if you can hear any of what I'm saying. And I know this isn't why you've come back. But, Sister, the council means to kill me for your death. They mean to make me jump into the endless hole because of what's been done to you and Father. Aquata, I need you. We... need you." I jerked my thumb toward Crowley.

Do the dead care for the living at all anymore?

Aquata had been the sweetest, softest, and kindest of us. Once, she would have cared. Once, she would have found a way to overcome her terrible fear and shyness to help me, a sister who'd never really been any good to her, simply because the bonds of family had been sacred to her.

Shame filled my soul. I'd been a selfish creature all my life.

Aquata hadn't deserved her fate, but I had. Anahita had. All the rest of us had. I looked down at my feet, feeling as though the shame might swallow me whole. I hated myself for my selfishness and my inability to put anyone else's needs before my own.

Father had been right when he'd called me a selfish bitch. I'd been so consumed with my love of Hook that I hadn't cared a whit for any of the rest of them. Even those I'd claimed to love, I hadn't loved enough to change my behavior.

I'd hurt them all, and I'd killed my baby sister for it too. Of course it had happened because of my return. The odds weren't in my favor—there was little chance that just as the Sea Witch was released, an actual murderer was plotting the demise of both my sister and my father, the king.

Father's attempted assassination made sense, but not Aquata's. She wouldn't have hurt a sea flea—that's how softhearted she was. She couldn't have—

"Elle, look," Crowley whispered hotly in the shell of my ear.

My pulse jumped as I looked up, and I sucked in a sharp breath as I watched my sister's spirit drift toward the magicked house in the garden's hedgerow.

She did not look back as she knelt. She did not say a word as her fingers reached deep into the hedges. Then I heard a loud whirring click, as if something mechanical had disengaged itself.

The door to the house had swung open, and there was a soft glow coming from it.

Dropping Crowley's hand, I rushed toward my sister's side and knelt right beside her. I stared at her profile, silently begging her to look up at me.

When she finally did, I was once again amazed by the look upon her face, one of determination and hope, but most of all, fierce, blazing, undeniable love. It burned through her bright-blue eyes like the hottest heat of a candle's flame.

I planted a fist against my breast, feeling my heart beat as powerfully as a ghostly echo. There was so much burning the tip of my tongue, words I wanted to say, things I wanted to tell her, and things I wanted to apologize for, like never coming back to see her while she still lived. I'd never apologized for calling her dull and vanilla and said that she would never find a love like I'd had with Hook. I'd said she would live alone and die alone, even when all my sister had wanted to do was hold onto me and hug me tightly after Hook had been so savagely taken away from me. I'd taken my hatred of Father out on

Aquata. She hadn't deserved it, and I'd never gotten the chance to tell her how unbelievably ashamed and sorry I was for it.

But I could see the colors of my sister's light starting to fade, and I knew that soon, she would leave me to join the circle of the other mourners drawing her to them.

So I said the only thing I could say, the only thing there was left to say. "I love you, my sister. And I am sorry. I am so, so sorry for everything. For not loving you as I should have. For not coming back to see you while you still—" A strangled cry slipped off my tongue, and I shivered, trembling furiously as the weight of how final the whole scene was suddenly impressing itself upon me. "Aquata," I squeaked out, "my baby sister. My sister. I'm sorry. I'm sor—"

But she was gone, forever taken away from me.

All the pain suddenly came crashing down on me. I was no longer able to pretend away her loss or focus on anything other than her death, and I lost it.

My wails were a terrible thing to hear, ugly in their truthfulness. An emptiness I'd rarely felt before overtook me. It consumed me, threatening to drown me in waves of tears and regret.

Strong arms held me tightly, and I clung to Crowley's body with every bit of my flagging strength. He didn't let me go for what felt like an eternity.

He didn't offer me pointless platitudes of "it's going to be okay" or "you'll be alright. You'll be okay. You'll be stronger for this." He didn't say anything, and I was so damned grateful. Because it wasn't okay. It wasn't alright. And I was pretty sure I would never ever be stronger for her loss.

I might not have seen my sister in decades, but that didn't make it any better. If anything, my regret only made my grief so much worse.

I cried until there was nothing left. I cried until I'd been washed clean. And when there were no more tears, I simply sat and quietly shuddered, feeling as though the pain might literally kill me.

Still, he said nothing. He only rubbed my back and held me tight.

Night was fully at its zenith when I finally managed to regain some sense of control. My soul still ached, and I felt like I was trapped in a strange world of numbness, but I could think again. I could reason.

With one last squeeze, I gently disengaged from him, smoothing my hands down my hair and using my forearm to scrub the last of the tears away. "I've shamed myself," I whispered a moment later. "I'm sor—"

"Apologize, and I swear to hells that I'll put your ass in cuffs and throw you back in that cell," he said roughly.

I was shocked at first, but then I grinned. It wasn't a big one, but it was there.

His nostrils flared as his own lips twitched, and he shoved a hand through his hair and glanced off to the left, looking slightly embarrassed. "She opened the door, Detective," he said, a gentle reminder of why we'd actually gone there in the first place.

I jerked, wondering how it was possible that I could have forgotten that. "Yes. Yes, she did."

We were sitting right next to it.

Scrambling to my knees, I shifted over toward the spot where she'd been. My sister was dead, but she'd left me a last gift. I wasn't sure whether she'd understood me at all. The tribunal meant to see me dead for a crime they believed I'd committed, but she'd opened the door.

Holding my breath, I lowered myself onto my hands and knees and peeked inside. Then I gasped.

CHAPTER 11
HATTER

I GRIPPED the Tinkerer's token in my hand as I slowly made my way up the steps of the precinct.

Bo was going to be furious with me for doing what I'd done. She'd placed me on mandatory leave, but when she discovered what I'd just done, she might take me off the case completely. I would be damned if I allowed that.

Wetting my lips, I spotted the small striped awning of Georgie's coffee kiosk. It'd been days since I'd seen him last, and I wondered if I should talk with him, see if he had any news for me, like he almost always did for Elle. But I couldn't bribe him with baubles, and besides, Undine was a closed realm. What news did come out of there wasn't usually the most reliable.

I was stalling, and I knew it. Fisting the token tightly, I pulled open the door of the precinct.

The familiar hustle and bustle was a welcome sound. Eight hours away, and already I felt like I'd been going crazy.

Róta was the first to spot me—the Valkyrie was always watching. She frowned, her brows forming a tight scowl line. "Detective, what are you doing he—"

I wasn't in the mood to be lectured by anyone, so I shook my head to let her know I wasn't answering any questions. "Where's the Captain?"

She pursed her full lips. Her hair, which was usually a shade of deep gold, was lighter, almost white, and though she had it tied up in a thick bun, it made her somehow look both prettier and more menacing than usual. Róta would have made a good detective. She had the same killer instinct as Elle. My chest squeezed as I thought about my partner.

She glanced at the large timepiece on her wrist. I knew what she was doing, which let me know that Bo had warned her at least that I was not to return before eight hours had passed. Which I hadn't. Just barely, anyway.

I huffed. "Tell me, or I swear by the one-eyed all father, I'll tear through this place like holy hells." My voice grew into a growl as my impatience grew.

She narrowed her eyes. The Valkyrie was a formidable foe and not afraid of much—not even a thing like me, though she definitely should be. If she had known the truth of me, I doubted she wouldn't tremble a little.

"She's out with the Commissioner Marcel. They should be back soon," she snapped tersely, and I felt regret at my actions, but if pushed, I would do it again, if it meant getting the answers I wanted.

"Then I'm going to her office."

"She's not going to like this, Maddox," Róta spoke to my back.

I shook my head. She didn't need to like it, she just needed to hear me out.

"Fine, your funeral," she snapped, her voice fading into the busy chattering background of the precinct.

I frowned as I shoved open the door to Bo's office and took a seat, tapping a nervous finger against my pant leg, wondering how much longer they would be out in the field.

Thank the gods that I didn't have much longer to wait. Bo flung her door open just a few minutes later. "Get me some coffee and head medicinals. Now!" she yelled behind her before slamming the door and groaning.

I stood.

She startled and planted a hand against her heaving chest. "Gods-dammit, Maddox, what in the hells are you doing here?"

I wet my lips, the token in my hand feeling as though it might burn a hole through my flesh. "What I'm about to tell you, you're really not going to like."

She rolled her eyes, frowning hard and glaring at me even harder. "Damn you. You did something, and I should threw your ass in irons for disobeying a direct order."

I held up a finger, shaking my head. "Listen to my story before you reach a verdict, Captain."

Her laughter dripped with irony. "And here, I always thought it was Elle that was the giant pain my arse. I see she's rubbed off on you." Her voice was tight and she winced—it was barely there.

But I caught it. She'd been doing that a lot lately, and I had to wonder what in the devil was going on with the captain to make her as stressed as she was.

She plopped into her seat and groaned softly beneath her breath as she reached for her bottomless drawer of tricks and pulled out a flagon of clear fluid and two tumblers. "Sit. Share a drink with me. It's been a long godsdamned day."

She didn't wait for me to agree but uncorked the bottle, and even from where I stood I could smell the alcohol content, which was strong enough that it felt like a kick in the arse, and I'd only sucked in fumes. "What is that?" I covered my nose with my wrist.

"My backup plan, and don't say shit about it. Now drink." She finished pouring before nudging the cup my way.

In Wonderland, most deals were finalized with drink. The harder the drink, the better. I'd never much been a drinker, but I accepted the gift with a grateful nod. Then, tipping my head back, I chugged it down.

The stuff burned the hide off the back of my throat and made my fires pulse in heated waves. "Holy hells." I huffed, blinking back the heat in my eyes.

She grinned around her own mugful. "Meant to be sipped, not slurped down like a drunken troll would do it. And I'd have expected you of all creatures to be able to handle its potency. All things considered," she said with lifted brow and a knowing smirk.

Much as it tasted like a demon's wet backside going down, there was a pleasant aftertaste of black cherry and oak.

She shook the flask, silently asking me if I wanted another.

"No. One will do me fine."

"Good. Now that you've relaxed a little, mind explaining to me why it is that you're already back in my office and being a pushy dick?"

I snorted, feeling less tense than I had seconds before. I knew it had something to do with her homemade shine.

She leaned back in her seat. The door opened just a second later, and a new temp with short brown hair and dark-green skin, clearly troll in origin, scurried in. He dropped the water and head medicinals down on the desk without looking at either one of us before scurrying out like a frightened mouse.

She glared at the closed door and softly shook her head. "That has to be the world's most terrified troll. I swear to the gods, Marcel is gonna owe me big for this one." She said the words beneath her breath, not trying to hide them from me but also not bothering to explain what she meant.

I shifted in my seat, and her hard, implacable gaze found mine as she popped the willow tree bark and tossed them back with shine instead of water. "Go on, Maddox. I'm listening," she said a beat later.

A part of me thought that maybe whatever Marcel and Bo were doing had everything to do with Elle's imprisonment in the below, but I couldn't be sure.

Still, I trusted Bo, and so had Elle. It wasn't in my nature to trust, yet I'd done it with Elle, and my efforts had been rewarded. Elle trusted Bo, and I saw no reason not to trust my partner's judgment.

Opening my sweat-slicked hand, I gently set the timepiece down upon Bo's desk then leaned back.

She frowned, glaring at the little golden timepiece with curiosity and questions in her eyes. "What is that?"

I shook my head. "Not sure. It was given to me by someone named the Tinkerer."

"Who?" She reached forward, snatching up the golden piece and bringing it close to her eyes. The staff-shaped pendant around her neck began to burn as bright-blue as the hottest part of a flame when the timepiece passed over it. She sniffed. "Now that is interesting."

It was my turn to frown. I'd seen Bo do some strange things with her staff, but hearing her sound so surprised by what it was doing had me asking, "What's interesting?"

Pursing her lips, she crushed her staff in her hand and looked at me. "I have my secrets, Maddox, just as you have yours."

Her eyes were knowing. Of everyone, only Bo knew my true origins. I'd been forced to reveal my heritage in my now-sealed records. She never acted any differently with me than she did with others, but every so often, I could sense her nerves.

It had been over two hundred years since I'd last snapped and done something so monumentally catastrophic that all of Grimm had felt the repercussions. But I'd changed since then, for various reasons, and I would be damned if I ever became that thing again. "I'm on your side, Bo."

She laughed. "You work here, and that's good enough. But don't expect me to just forget what it was you did, Detective, because that can never be."

I inhaled deeply, curling my hands into fists. She and I rarely spoke of my past. It was always business as usual between us, but something seemed to have rattled her enough tonight to help loosen her tongue.

"Then at least trust that I am on her side. I have always been on her side."

"So the commissioner says. Don't worry, Hatter. So long as Marcel vouches for you, you're not going anywhere." She snorted indelicately, and I knew the drink was loosening her tongue. But liquor didn't make people lie—in fact, it usually caused the opposite to happen. She was unburdening a truth to me that I'd never even been aware of.

I'd always liked Bo. She didn't attempt to deceive people, but instead said what she meant and meant what she said. But it was the first time I was aware of just how much she didn't actually seem to want me here.

"I won't do that again, Captain. You have my word."

"And what does that mean coming from something like you?"

Ouch. I flinched. Still, she wasn't running away in terror or fright. She'd known for close to a year who I really was. I couldn't say what she'd first thought of me when she was told I would be coming, but she'd always treated me with respect.

"Ah," she said, sighing. "Godsdamned shine." She held up her almost empty second cup. "Melanie would shit a brick if she knew how I was acting right now." Reaching for her tie, she loosened it and downed the last bit of her glass before scooping up both our cups and the bottle of shine then locking it away once more. "Tell me what you've learned, Maddox." She pushed the token back toward me.

I shrugged. "Little about that, other than it's a timepiece."

"That much is obvious," she muttered. "And who's the Tinkerer? Moreover, how did you find this woman?"

"Crowley."

"Excuse me?" She leaned forward, looking as mentally acute as ever even after two glassfuls of shine. "As in Agent Crowley?"

"Aye." I nodded, rubbing my hands together. "He contacted me early this morning."

"How? He's still in Undine, isn't he? Scout told me the city is in mourning for their lost princess. Tonight is her last song. I doubt they'd go through the bother of releasing a lone agent, considering how ceremonial a royal song is."

My heart ached at the thought of what Elle must be enduring. I knew she wasn't close to her family, but I knew she loved her sisters. I hoped she wasn't alone. I flexed a fist on my thigh, feeling the ineptitude of my being where I was while she was elsewhere on an almost visceral level. I could taste the stench of my failure like acrid smoke on the back of my tongue.

"As far as I know"—I nodded—"he is still in Undine, yes. That's where he reached out to me."

"Agent Crowley?"

I blinked. "Why do you sound so disbelieving?"

She spread her hands and made a sound in the back of her throat. "Well, I don't claim to have any true knowledge of the agent, but he has no magick. And considering he and Elle are both captive prisoners of the realm, I doubt they'd give him access to a mage to pass along such a message."

I narrowed my eyes. "Are you questioning my veracity?"

She cocked her head, her gaze raking and assessing me. Then, after a minute, she said, "No. No, I'm not. I trust you. But that doesn't change the fact that it doesn't make sense."

"It was him." I paused, frowning, thinking back on my talk with him.

"What? What is it?" she asked.

I shook my head, scattering the thoughts like marbles. "I was just thinking about our conversation, it was... strange."

"Strange? How so?"

"He sounded weird. Different."

"How well do you know the agent?"

"Not at all."

She shrugged. "So it's possible, I guess, that he acts strangely under stress. Marcel and I have been meeting for some days now, as you know, trying to figure out how we can safely get to our guys. We have to negotiate terms with the Queen of Undine."

"Elle's father is still in a coma?"

She nodded. "So far as we know, yes. And rumor has it that tomorrow or the next day the tribunal will convene to decide their fate."

I swallowed hard, feeling my stomach twist up in knots. "Surely, they wouldn't try to hang her for this. Elle could no more control what the Sea Witch chose to do than I could the weather."

"They can, and they will try. Mark my words, Maddox. You might not know all of Elle's past, but I do. She is not wholly innocent, and they have wanted nothing more than to find that golden opportunity to make her pay for all that she's done. What is this thing, and can it help us?"

I shrugged. "I told you, I don't know what it is, other than a time-piece of great value. Crowley sent me to the Persiannous district to find the Tinkerer. She gave me this. When he found me earlier in the day, he told me the Tinkerer would ensure Elle's freedom. That's all I know."

A strange look crossed her face. "He said that it would ensure Elle's freedom? That doesn't sound like Crowley at all. That man wants nothing more than to see Elle burn. He's never been her friend. I don't trust this." She glanced down at her staff, which still glowed an ethereal blue.

"Neither do I." I shook my head. "But it's all I have to go on. She has to come back, Captain. She has to."

Bo swallowed hard, and she stared at me harder. "Tell me the truth, Maddox. You and Elle?"

I knew the policy in Grimm. So did Elle. Many had been terminated already for breaking the rules. Bo could report me if I told the truth, but there was something about her that made it impossible for me not to be honest. Though it went against my very nature to expose myself this way, I sighed and nodded. "You already know it, Captain."

"And Elle?"

I flinched and shook my head.

She released a pent-up breath and nodded. "Good. That's good. She should know everything, Maddox. You hear me? You tell her everything first, or you leave her the hells alone. No funny business, or I swear to the all-gods that I'll make it my mission in life to break you."

From anyone else, the threat would be a laughable one. But Bo had a way about her that made me believe in every word she said. She knew I was more powerful. In fact, I was more powerful than anything that existed in this realm. There was little I feared, but Bo knew my one weakness, and I knew that if it came down to it, she would ruthlessly expose it and me before turning me out to face the wrath of those around me I'd once counted as friends.

When Alice had learned my true nature, she'd left me. And regardless of how powerful I was, I'd not been there to save Mariposa. I might have been powerful, but those I cared for, those few that I loved, were not. And that made me weak.

I squeezed my eyes shut. "All I want to do is bring Elle home, Captain. That's it. She's my partner, and I want her back."

"Don't you fucking get attached like that again, Maddox. I swear, don't you do it."

I stood and looked down her, giving her a weak grin. "I won't."

Her nostrils flared, and I wondered if she smelled the lie. Because the truth was, I already had, a long, long time before now. It was far too late for me. "We'll handle it from here," Bo said.

I reached the door and I knew I'd been taken off the case for good. I clenched my jaw and turned.

Her eyes glittered with hard determination. "You're too deep in this, and I won't have this happen on my watch."

I snorted and reached into my pocket. "Fine. Makes this a whole lot easier, then." I pulled out my badge and gently placed it on her desk.

She looked at it coldly for several long seconds. "Don't do this, Maddox. You know that's not what this is. You're a solid detective."

"But you don't trust me."

Bo gave a harsh laugh. "I don't trust anybody."

I shook my head. "Then you should know that I'm going for her. Now that I don't work here anymore, I see no need to try and work through the proper channels."

"Don't do this," she repeated. "You're just too close to this one. I should have done this a while ago. And I should never have let Elle go down to Never."

I heard the regret in her voice, but I felt freer than I had in a long time. "I hope you figure out what Crowley wanted that thing for," I said, pointing at the timepiece. "But I'm going. And now you can't stop me."

"I could always have you arrested."

I smirked. "And we both know how that would go. All I'm going to do, Captain, is bring her back by whatever means necessary."

She leaned back. "Don't tell me anything else. I don't know want to know."

She was giving me an out, but like the wise woman she was, she was making sure to cover her own arse in the process.

I turned to go and reached for the doorknob.

"And we're talking about this little stunt when you get back. And you will get back. Or I'll kill you myself. Also, I'm going to be standing up in a minute and walking over toward that"—she pointed to a filing cabinet in the corner—"cabinet. If something should vanish from my desk in the interim, it will be like it was never there."

Her face was a stoic mask as she stood and did just that. I gaped at her backside, all the cogs in my head turning as realization finally dawned. What had just gone down was suddenly crystal in my mind. She'd goaded me into doing just what I'd done, into turning in my badge and circumventing the law. It had been Bo's plan from the beginning.

Master strategist that she was, I'd fallen right into her trap. My lips twitched. I might be something she didn't trust entirely, but I was also something she trusted just enough to go and retrieve her best detective. I didn't say thank you. I didn't even acknowledge her win.

I looked down at the desk and noticed that not only did the timepiece rest where I'd placed it, but somehow she'd even slipped a golden travel key card beside it. Confirming to me that she'd intended this to be the likely outcome all along. I glanced back up at her briefly. Her spine was ramrod straight, but she wouldn't turn. I sniffed, retrieved the trinket and key card and quickly pocketed it. She still didn't turn, and likely wouldn't until I left. With a silent nod in her direction, I turned on my heel, opened the door, and walked out.

If Bo had played that hand, then it must have meant that she knew Marcel would not come through after all. Crowley and Elle were likely on their own, and me helping was the only chance they had of making it out of there.

Someone called my name, but I didn't stop. I ran as quickly as I could back toward my flat.

There were a few things I needed to do, and then I had to hit the underground. There would be no legal waystations for me to travel through—I wasn't a lawman anymore.

But I knew things. People. Places. I knew how to get what needed getting.

I was getting her back.

Elle was coming home. No matter what I had to do, she was coming back. I picked up my pace.

CHAPTER 12
ELLE

DROPPING TO MY KNEES, I looked at the little creature. A fur seal pup lay on its side, dead for days. Even in the darkness, I could see that his little tail had been badly damaged, and bits of gore and fat had necrotized days before and reeked of hot death. But because he'd been trapped behind an enchanted doorway, no smell had given away his location until now.

I closed my eyes.

I knew it had to have been Aquata's pet. Clearly, whatever had gotten my sister had gotten him or her too.

The nauseating smell made my stomach heave, and I had to clamp down on my back teeth and force myself to take small, deep breaths to work through the need to vomit up the meager remains of my only meal that day.

Crowley knelt beside me.

I glanced at his stern profile. I wasn't sure how a dead sea pup would be of any help to us in the investigation. The witch had been thorough in her dealings.

"Move," he commanded, but his words, while blunt, weren't harsh or angry, but rather, distracted. So I did move over an iota. I was so heartsick by seeing my sister that all the fight had been taken out of me.

If Crowley still wanted to pretend that we had clues to prove anything other the obvious—that the Sea Witch and no one else had committed the crime—then he could by all means be my guest. But I no longer had hope of any other outcome.

While it was terrible to see Aquata's pet as he was, it had been a dead end, a complete waste of our time.

I rubbed my aching forehead, wondering when the guards would come for us. Now that Aquata's song was over, they could come as early as tomorrow morning.

Crowley reached into the doorway.

"Hey, what are you doing?" I snapped, reaching for his arm. "It's dead, Crowley. Let the little beast rest now. There is nothing more. Nothing more to s—" I clamped my lips shut when I saw him wrestle something from out of the tightly curled hands of the pup. It was a triangle of thinly hammered gold. On its front was an intricate scroll-work design that felt vaguely familiar, though I wasn't sure why.

"You were saying?" he asked in his usual gruff tone as he held the object up for my inspection.

I cocked my head. "What in the hells is that?" I gasped, reaching for it.

He dropped it into my palm. It was light as a feather, and I brought it up to my nose and sniffed before locking my eyes onto his bright-red ones. "No scent. Nothing. Not even the smell of this poor pup's decay. What the hell is this?"

Crowley grinned. "Proof, Detective. That's proof. Tell me, was the Sea Witch wearing any jewels whatsoever?"

I blinked, flashing back instantly to the day of the battle. She'd been covered in scars, and her skin looked cracked, like millennia-old parchment. Her dress had been moth riddled, and her hair lank and thin. The one thing I never noted was any ornamentation on her at all. Not that there couldn't have been, but it hadn't been in the least bit obvious.

"What are you implying?" I finally asked him.

He cocked his head. "I believe that in that last battle against you, you wounded her gravely."

"You think she's dead?"

He shook his head. "I never said that. I think we'd be fools to think her threat is gone. But I don't think she had the stamina or strength for this." He gestured with his arm to take in our surroundings. "Any of this."

Jacamoe had so much as said the same.

"You... So what?" I shrugged. "Are you saying that you think someone else has done this? An inside man on her behalf?"

"Or woman." He pouted his lips. "Yeah, I do. I think someone capitalized on our situation. But I don't think he or she is working with the witch. I think the witch is the fall guy for this one. Whoever did this did it for themselves."

"But how would they know to do it? How could they, even when I didn't know until that day that I would be battling the witch for our lives?"

"Opportunity." He shrugged. "It would have had to have been someone quick enough on their feet to make an instant pivot. But think about it for a second, Detective. Whether anyone here wants to own it or not, you're still a princess. Who would it behoove to keep tabs on you?"

"My father." My answer was automatic.

"And anyone else who was in his inner circle, yes." He growled. "Someone knew where you were at all times. They knew you were in Never. They knew." He said it a third time with such certainty that I could not doubt it. "Make no bones about that. And now they're trying their damnedest to frame you for their crime."

I almost asked why, but I didn't need to. The answer would be the same one I'd have given anyone else who would have investigated back on Grimm: because they could. I'd given them their perfect chance.

If Crowley was right, then it would have had to have been someone used to adaptation. Someone capable of shifting on a literal dime. I only knew one person. I swallowed hard.

"I know what you're thinking. I'm thinking it too," he said quietly, stepping close to me. My gaze shot like an arrow to his. His dark eyes were roving my face, and his lips were set into a heavy line.

I shook my head and took a step back. "You don't know that. You're not a god. You can't just jump to these ridiculous conclusions with no evidence to back you up," I hissed, furious at him for even daring suggest it. I'd just lost one sister, and he was trying to poison me against another. It was bullshite.

He grinned cockily, but there was disappointment in his eyes, and my blood boiled in my veins. My hands clenched.

"I thought you were smarter than this, Detective. You don't know her anymore. Why defend her now?"

That cocky arrogance of his, the way his upper lip curled up into a snarl of distaste as he looked at me... It was all too much. All I saw was red. I didn't think. I just acted.

I shoved him, hard—Crowley riled me up like no one else could—but I barely moved the bastard an inch. His body had swelled before my very eyes, and I heard a deep and harsh growl vibrating through his chest.

It was a warning. But I didn't give a rat's arse. "Screw you," I hissed as my chest rose and fell with my swift breaths.

He chuckled, and I wanted to do worse than push him. I wanted to smack that infuriating smirk right off his face.

"Yeah, okay. Deny it. Gods, I was so wrong about you. So fucking wrong. I thought you were better than this." He spat next to his foot, the implied insult very clear.

It was my turn to laugh, and it came out as a low and menacing sound. I felt my markings flaring and saw their glow in my peripheral vision. My dark hair was caught up in a stiff current, flying around my face like a dark shroud. I roughly shoved it back. "You're talking about my sister." I whipped one of my hands up and pointed a finger in the air, wishing I could do a whole hells of a lot more than point at him.

Even though I hadn't touched him, he stiffened, acting as though I'd given him a direct challenge. "You have no proof. No godsdamned proof."

"Why was she there"—he jerked a free hand in the direction of the castle—"with Hook? Why was she there, Elle? Huh? Tell me, since you're so fucking smart. Tell me!"

I jerked at the vehemence in his tone, but not from fear. His anger had only riled up my own. For days, I'd been stuck in this hellhole with only him and the ghosts that sucked me dry for company. I'd had enough of him, the situation, and everyone else. I'd been gunning for the fight, and I wasn't backing down.

I stepped into him, shoving my breasts right into his chest and straining my neck so that I stood as tall as I possibly could. "Back off," I growled tersely, muscle memory causing me to reach for my piece, but it was no longer there.

I felt each of his heavy breaths move against me. Electricity snapped and sparked between us. My glow was so bright that it completely illuminated the gardens in a hazy blue light, adding deepening shadows to the hollows of his throat and cheekbones, making him seem formidable and dangerous.

My lips parted. Just a second, for half an instant, I thought I saw him sway toward me. But it must only have been a trick of the light, because the next thing I knew, he had moved back—way back.

He'd moved so fast that I lost track of him. His glare was openly hostile, but there was something else burning in his eyes too.

We stood there just glaring at each other for what felt like an eternity. The hate-filled tension was palpable, but there was much more below the surface of it too. I wet my lips, and I knew it wasn't a trick of the light when I saw him shudder and glance away.

"You should go," he finally said. "Go. I'll figure this shit out myself."

I shook my head. "So now you're gonna freeze me out?"

"Godsdamn it, Elle!" he growled and stabbed at his chest with a long, blunt finger. "I tried here, okay? This isn't on me."

"You're too damned closed-minded. You're like a fucking dog with a bone. I can see that. I can see that your mind is set." I crossed my arms.

He scoffed.

"You think it's my sister. But it's not. I know it's not."

"Why? Because she's too good? Because she *loves* you?" He finger quoted as he pulled his upper lip back.

I bit down on my front teeth so hard they ached. "Screw you. What would you know about love anyway? Nothing, I'd wager, considering that you could trivialize it that way."

"You don't know shit."

I snorted, realizing I was getting under his skin. Some twisted part of me relished it. "You're a miserable old man. And you're gonna die alone."

Harsh laughter spilled through the night. "You say that as if I care. I don't. You're the one who's too godsdamned weak to see the truth. You hide behind this bullshit curtain and tell me that I'm the one in denial. Whatever, Detective Fish. This partnership"—he gestured between us—"is done. It's over, you hear me? I don't have time for games, and I certainly don't have time for you. You wanna swing for this shit, then by all means, be my guest. I'm through saving your ass. Save it yourself." He turned on his heel and began marching away.

Fury that I'd rarely felt in my life lit me. "You're such a fucking baby!" I snapped at his back.

His only response was to flip me the bird.

His footsteps were so silent that even watching him, I didn't hear him leave, but once he'd gone, all the fight suddenly evaporated from out of me.

I stared straight ahead, seeing nothing but feeling the golden triangle in my palm and what felt like a blade through my chest. *What the hells have I done?*

I'd known I was overreacting even as I was doing it, but his arrogance and cocky disdain had stoked the embers of my rage to an uncontrollable degree. I'd lost my shite—any and all ability to reason or think had gone out the window.

Crowley brought out the worst in me. Being with him for any amount of time was nightmare fuel. And though I could easily work my way up to a level of rage again just thinking about how full of shite he sometimes was, I also knew I'd screwed the pooch big-time.

"Oh my gods," I mumbled as I dropped my head into my hands and silently shuddered. *What the hells have I done?* I thought again.

He had been my only real ally in the whole place, the only one actually trying to help me solve this crime. I hadn't doubted his sincerity then, and I still didn't, even after all that had happened.

Is he right?

Am I refusing to see the truth because of my love for my sister? Was she really capable of staging all of this? She's Father's right-hand man, groomed to be the queen when his reign ends. Had she been impatient? Had she been looking for the perfect opportunity to double-cross him?

Anahita had always been hungry for power, but I'd never seen her step outside the bounds of right and wrong to attain it. Everyone knew she thirsted to rule—she'd often openly contradicted Father in the courts when she'd felt passionately enough. She was as strong as he.

But she was also fiercely loyal, clueing him into uprisings and coups before they ever even got a chance to get off the ground. Even when I'd lived in Undine, there'd been a small but growing contingent of disenfranchised Undinians calling for Father to step down so that Anahita could step up. But it'd always been her and not Father who'd quelled those hungry cries for change, saying that laws existed for the good of the whole and not simply to please the will of the few.

And unless that Anahita had become someone I didn't know in the time since I'd been outcast, I simply couldn't believe it. Yes, she would have been the obvious choice—on that, Crowley was right. In fact, she was too obvious. She was the perfect cover. Everyone who knew my sister would know all that I did about her. The logical assumption would have been that she had done something sinister, should someone have leapt to the same conclusion as Crowley had, that none of what had happened were the workings of the Sea Witch.

It could only mean one thing. If Crowley was right, and it wasn't the Sea Witch's doing, then it was someone else's. That someone was powerful, so powerful that she or he could literally hide in plain sight.

I stood and straightened my hair. The guards would be coming for me soon. The tribunal would convene tomorrow or the next day, I was certain. But I had to bite the bullet. I had to see him, now.

I had to see Father.

"ANAHITA, OPEN UP!" I BANGED LOUDLY ON THE DOOR TO HER study, demanding entrance. I knew she was in there. I'd seen her shadow moving. "I swear to the primordial gods," I snapped, "if you don't let me in, I will kil—"

The door was suddenly flung open, and my sister's scowling face met mine. One of her brows was raised in a high arch. "Who, Elle? Who will you kill?"

I opened my mouth, ready to say something stupid when I caught sight of Ebonia looking disheveled and rumpled. I gasped, realizing why my sister hadn't opened the door right away. I cringed and did a hasty bow in Ebonia's direction.

She merely dipped her head in acknowledgement. "I'll see you later," she whispered intimately before leaning over and tenderly kissing my sister's cheek to say goodbye. Ebonia spared me a withering glance as she swam by, shutting the door behind her.

I bit my front teeth together, grimacing in my sister's direction. "Sock on the door would have helped. And what the hells, sis? We just buried our sister. I mean, the least you could have done was wait a—"

"What, Elle? Huh!" she snapped, violently angry. "What the hells would you know of love, anyway?" she asked, echoing the same sentiment I'd screamed at Crowley only minutes before.

I winced at being on the receiving end of that insult.

"Where were you all these years? Gone! You don't give two shites about us, and now you have the nerve to come down here and chastise me for trying to forget for just two godsdamned minutes!"

Her words were slurred and her movements jerky as she grabbed a bottle of Father's favorite sherry and poured a generous amount into her crystal tumbler. She was drunk. My straitlaced sister was ten sheets to the wind, and I should have realized it immediately, but I'd been trying to joke around with her, being so much my old, stupid, selfish self that it had never even crossed my mind to imagine that she might be grieving the loss of our favorite sister.

Her words were a terrible wound to my soul, though, because she didn't have a clue how much I hurt or how desperately I was trying to think about anything other than the fact that my beloved Aquata was really and truly gone. But as I looked at her, I couldn't believe how much of a selfish dumbass I'd been to not have noticed.

Her face paint was streaked, and her hair was disheveled, and not the good kind that came from a lusty tussle in a bed, but the kind that looked as though she had been grabbing and pulling, trying to yank the damn things out by the roots with fury.

Her warrior's garb was half on and half off with no rhyme or reason for it. Her collar was on, while her chest plate was dangling by a single thin strap. She slammed back her drink, and I saw her shudder.

She squeezed her eyes shut and groaned. "I'm the one who found her." Her words were soft but haunted. Her tone was monotone, as though she was recounting something other than our sister's death. "Facedown with a sliver of sea cheese clenched tightly in her fist for that damned pet of hers. Father told her not to keep that mangy creature. He said to let it live or die as it would. But she would not hear of it. Her and her bloody, soft heart." When Anahita turned her eyes to me, they were shockingly red, and tears streaked down her cheeks. She didn't bother trying to hide them from me.

"She always loved her pets. They were her only true companions," I whispered into the thick and heavy silence stretching between us.

At first, Anahita's glare was hard and set, but when I said nothing more, I saw the cracks start to appear. Finally, she lowered her shoulders, and her face turned red with regret and shame. "She should never have been there."

I watched my sister even as I took a seat, keeping an eye on her like one might on an enraged but confused predatory creature. "Where should she have been, Anahita?" I whispered softly.

She tossed back another tumbler full of father's personal stock. The stuff could add hair to one's tongue and strip the flesh right off the back of a throat when swallowed. She was mainlining the stuff like it was sweet nectar. I watched as she slammed back yet another cupful.

"Ana, go easy on that," I said, leaning forward, ready to gently pry the vessel away from her.

She roared, moving so quickly that it made my head spin. Within the span of a second, she had a trident in hand, and in one lithe movement, she jumped over the desk. Somehow, I was pinned to the edge of it, and she was looming over me like some psychotic version of the reaper himself.

Her teeth were sharp and pointy. She breathed heavily. She stank of liquor. She was so wasted that I was starting to feel almost as if I had a contact buzz just from breathing in the fumes, but I didn't take my eyes off of her.

She'd always been the best fighter of us all. It was partly why Father had chosen her as his successor. Anahita was scary when she wanted to be. Her eyes burned like blue fire. I didn't even blink. I didn't move a muscle or breathe too heavily. I merely kept eye contact with her, nodding slowly and speaking to her in soothing, gentle tones. "It's okay, my sister. It's okay. I won't hurt you."

At that, she laughed. "I hold this blade to your throat, and yet you say you will not hurt me. I should gut you for the insult."

Beneath the growls and the violence of her threat, I knew that she was hurting and that it was the pain that caused her to do as she was doing. Anahita had always been loyal to Father and to the kingdom, but especially to me.

And I'd betrayed that trust long before, when I'd chosen a man over my own blood. "I'm here now."

She scoffed, but the tears were running down her cheeks in thick torrents. Her hands were starting to shake just a little too.

"I'm here now, Ana. I'm here now."

I wasn't sure how long she held the trident to my carotid, but from one second to the next, she threw the weapon aside with a wild cry then nearly fell on her arse. I had to reach down to wrap her up in my arms, and she clung to me like a baby otter, curling her hands into my back, digging in so hard that I felt my flesh opening up beneath her sharpened claws. Her tail wrapped around my legs, and she sobbed like a broken child.

Each tear was a blade to my soul, and I held her even as my own eyes filled with heat. But I didn't cry, because it was my turn to be strong for her and to let her be weak. Anahita was always so brave, so stoic. I couldn't even begin to imagine how much pain she had to be in to be so openly weak before me.

I didn't view it as weakness, not any longer. Being in the above had taught me a thing or two about just how strong one had to be to allow another to so openly view their vulnerability. But I didn't tell her any of that. I simply held her. I rocked her and whispered over and over that I was there for her, for as long as she needed me to be.

Finally, after what felt like an eternity, she scrubbed at her cheeks and shuddered delicately. "Gods, I'm mortified. You should not have seen that, Elle. I—"

I silenced her with my hand over her mouth. "Don't. Don't say it. Don't think it. Just don't. She was my sister too."

"And yet you do not shed a tear for her." She shook her head and pulled out of my arms. Already, I could see her putting her armor back on. But I didn't feel that wall between us now, not like before.

She cast a furtive glance in my direction. "Why have you come?"

I knew what she was really asking, but I didn't know what to say to that.

"If you were powerful enough to summon me or to banish the Sea Witch from our world"—she let the rest of that thought dangle, but I heard it loud and clear: *to banish the Sea Witch from our world but let her maim Father and take my sister from me*—"tell me, Elle, why didn't you just leave? You are strong enough. You had to know that coming here would not save you. You know how our kingdom runs and that we would have no choice but to try you for treason. Why did you come?"

My thoughts were stuck on what she hadn't said. My sister still believed that the Sea Witch had killed Aquata and nearly killed Father. Crowley and I hadn't figured out yet who it really was, but we at least knew it hadn't been the witch. *So if Anahita really believed that, was she innocent of all of this? Was she just another pawn in this game? Same as me?*

Crowley didn't think so, but I knew my sister. Even through all the years that separated us, I knew her.

"I came because of you," I finally said, letting her hear the full truth in those words. "I'm sorry, Ana, for the way things ended, for the choices I made. For butchering Anders—"

She hissed. "Don't say his name. Don't you ever say that monster's name in front of me. I believed you then. I believe you now. I know what he did to you, Elle, even if Father refused to accept it. You had every right to do as you did, every right. No male, no matter how noble of blood, gets to do that to a woman against her will. Of course you did it, and if you hadn't, I would have. I always had your back. I always believed in you. Always."

I heard the betrayal and the pain again. I'd chosen the above over her. She'd chosen me, and I'd chosen Grimm.

My lips parted, and I stared at her with my heart feeling as though it was literally trapped in my throat. This time, a lone tear slid down my right cheek, and I scrubbed at it violently with my wrist before swallowing hard.

"The tribunal," I said, letting the rest of my thought dangle. I knew she would know what I was asking without being forced to say the words.

Looking weary and suddenly defeated, she sat on the edge of Father's desk, hanging her head as she once more reached over for the empty tumbler of crystal that'd fallen on its side in our tussle.

Taking a deep breath, she poured another finger full. But this time, she didn't slam it back. She merely sipped. "They want to skin your hide and leave your meat out for the sharks."

I squeezed my eyes shut, shaking my head softly. "Ana, I didn't do that to Aquata. Or to Father."

"But your actions led the Sea Witch right to us. I don't know if I can sto—"

"What if I didn't?" I pinned her with my glare. "What if it wasn't the Sea Witch at all who did this?"

She flinched, and her hand shook a little. Some of the liquor sloshed up the side and onto a knuckle. "What? What are you saying?"

Crowley would kill me for telling her—he'd warned me that it had to stay between us. But we were quickly running out of time. Ana loved me, even if some part of her hated me too. She was still my Anahita, my protective sister who was more a mother to me than my own could ever have been. "The other male I came down here with," I said, stomach trembling as I knew I was getting ready to cross Crowley's direct order. "His name is—"

"Agent Crowley, I know who he is," she said, her voice full of grit, roughened by too much scotch. "What of him?"

Taking a deep breath to steel my nerves, I rushed to say it before I chickened out. "We don't think it was the Sea Witch who did it, Ana."

"What?" She scoffed, downing the rest of the glass before pouring another. Our metabolisms being what they were, Anahita wouldn't die of alcohol poisoning, but she might wish she had in the morning when the skull crushing migraine set in. Father's stash wasn't for the faint of heart. "How can you be so sure?"

I tapped my nose. "His nose. Crowley is a wolf shifter. He's the one who's been gleaning most of the clues down here. Since I was stripped of my siren's charms, I—"

She snorted and lifted her refilled glass toward me in a jerky manner, sloshing even more over its rim. I winced to see such fine stuff being treated in such a wasteful manner, but I wouldn't say anything about that again, not after the trident she'd pulled on me before.

"You can't be stripped of your siren nature." She guffawed as if it was the silliest thing she'd ever heard in her life.

"I was," I corrected, pointing to my hair and eyes. "Don't you see me? Look at me. That bitch twisted me into something I don't even recognize anymore."

She rolled her eyes theatrically and chortled, "My dear sister, you never were one for learning, were you? A siren's nature is inherent to us. It is what we are."

"She stole it, Anahita, forced me to give it to her so that I would activate my witch—"

"Duh." She giggled, and I was stunned to see her acting in such an indecorous manner. "But like a seedling shoved into the ground, ever will we rise." She hiccupped before taking another gulp.

I frowned. "Wait. What?"

"You can't lose what it means to be you," she said then laughed annoyingly. "Gods, this stuff is strong. Finally, right? I've only had three bottles."

"Three bottles," I hissed, automatically attempting to steal the nearly empty third bottle.

"Touch it and die." She snarled before snatching it up and hugging it close to her breast.

Once again, I held up my hands. She was going to hate herself in the morning. But I'd tried. "Are you saying that I'm... healing?"

She rolled her eyes again before leaning back and placing all her weight on her right hand. She was swaying dangerously. Soon, Anahita would be passed out cold on the floor, which I had no doubt was the point.

My sister couldn't process any of what had happened tonight, at least not right now. The mantle she wore was a heavy burden. I did not envy her. If she needed to get lit to make it through the night, far be it from me to take that away from her.

She hiccupped. "Yup. Soon, you'll be stronger even than Daddy. He knew, you know. Me too."

My fingertips felt numb. "Knew what?"

"That your momma was a witch. *The witch*." She laughed. "Father was such a fecking bastard, slept around on momma all the time. I caught him with her." Her laughter was deep and rolling, and she was making strange noises in the back of her throat.

I felt like I couldn't breathe. The witch had told me as much. She'd said I was hers. I was a witch, too, so of course, I was hers. But it still stung to hear my sister say it so matter-of-factly, to know that she had lied to my face for so long. No wonder I'd never felt like I'd really fit in with any of them. I wasn't one of them.

"He's a bad man, Elle. I tried to deny it. But deep down, I knew. You know why I stayed? Why I didn't run away with you like I wanted to?"

She'd wanted to run away with me? My eyes widened, and I felt cold all over. My heart hammered violently in the cage of my chest. *She'd wanted to leave with me?* I could not doubt her words, for drink was the great truth serum. I'd learned through my years on the force that drink loosened the tongue and could shine new light on reality. But I'd never known that my straitlaced sister had wanted to leave when I had. I'd simply never known.

"To keep him in line. He was ruthless. Bloodthirsty. He's a bad, bad man. He wanted to toss you into the hole. I convinced him to banish you. That curse was never true. You didn't change. You didn't change...

She lied. She lied to us all." She laughed, the sound drunken and light, but I could hear the raw pain in her voice.

I clutched at my breast.

"Said it was a far worse punishment to cut you off that way. And it was. It was." She started sobbing again. "But I wanted you alive. I wanted you to live. Even if it meant I could never be with you again. I hate you for leaving me here alone with him. I hate you, Elle. I hate you so much. I hate that I still love you."

Then she broke down for the second time. When I went to her and wrapped my hand around the full tumbler, she didn't fight me. She simply sobbed, sounding so broken and small.

I was able to half drag her to the tufted ivory chaise lounge in the corner. She fell into it with a plop. I had to heave and strain to roll her securely into the center so that she didn't fall and hurt herself.

One word had resonated in my skull: *curse*. She'd said "curse." My sister didn't look like she was coherent at all anymore—she was muttering, mumbling nonsense to herself, and giggling intermittently.

It pained me to see her that way, but I had to know. "What curse, Ana? Being banished to the—"

She snorted before staring at me with one bleary eye. "Love. Love would change you. Would twist you. Would make you something far too powerful to contain."

I frowned. "What?"

She giggled even harder then pouted, reaching ineffectively for the drink still on the desk before giving up with a lengthy sigh. "That your love would make you a monster. A villain. That he would turn you, and you would hurt us." She laughed harder. "Hurt us! But we hurt him first. Hook can never have you. *Hahahaha*..." On and on, she giggled, tossing a hand over her eyes. "Daddy said that meant you would kill him. And now he almost is, that sick feck." She hiccupped. "He almost is. But we killed Hook first, so in the end it all was for naught. I think I like that part best."

I shook my head, my pulse hammering in my ears. My mouth was dry as cotton. "I'll never change, Ana. You know that. No man will ever again force me to do anything other than what I wish. Never again. I'll gut him first."

"I love you, Ellie," she murmured drowsily. "*Lwubuuuu*," she slurred then snored.

She was already passed out when I pulled away, her mouth parted and her skin an unpleasant shade of green. I doubted she would remember anything when she woke up.

But I didn't think I could ever forget it. *What if drink wasn't really truth serum? What if that had simply been the ramblings of a depressed mind?* There was no way that I'd been cursed like that, no way that Ana had known why Father had tried to kill Hook, and no way my sister would have kept something like that from me for all these years. No way.

But even as I denied it, I felt the coldness of truth flood through me. It ticked off all the boxes, that crazy explanation of hers. It explained why Father had become so enraged when he'd found me with Hook, why Father had hunted my Hook down like a dog, all of it.

My hands shook. I didn't know what to do with myself. If the words she'd spoken had all been true, then it all made sense, but it also meant that my sister had betrayed my trust in the worst possible way. She'd kept that dark family secret from me. She'd let Father hunt him down. She'd let it all happen.

I blinked several times to rid the backs of my eyes from the heat building there. Walking over toward the door, I decided to try to find Father on my own. I wasn't sure what it would accomplish, especially if he was still comatose, but I had to see him.

I opened the door and wasn't surprised to find that Ebonia had never gone farther than the waiting room.

She flicked her tail, swimming gracefully over toward me. Her braided hair was down and loose. Her cheekbones were razorblade sharp, and her jaw more squared than rounded. Her skin gleamed like a black pearl. She was a striking woman made of harsh and soft lines all at once.

"Now you know," was all she said in the elegant tones of her house. Her eyes were the color of a golden dawn and burned fiercely with both pride and devotion to my sister. Theirs was a romance that had spanned several decades. If it wasn't love, then I didn't know what love was.

"Take care of her, Ebonia."

"So long as I am able, I will always be here for Anahita."

"Damn the rules," I growled, grabbing her wrist tightly. "Make her yours, Ebonia. Make her yours and bring my sister some measure of happiness in this miserable life that's been thrust upon her."

"So long as your father lives, you know we cannot. But I will always watch over her. That I promise you."

It pained me to know she was right. I turned to go.

"She never stopped loving you, Arielle. Never. You have been the greatest source of pain in her life. The tribunal will convene tomorrow, she has already told me. But trust in her. Even if she doesn't say it while sober, Anahita will raze all of Undine to see you safe. She will do whatever it takes, for love of you. I just thought you should know that."

I thought of a million different things I could—should—say to her, but none of them made it past my lips. I simply nodded and turned into the hallway. It was time to find Father, and then... then it was time to face the tribunal's wrath. Crowley and I had run out of time.

We'd run out of time.

CHAPTER 13
ELLE

I WASN'T sure how it was so easy to find where they kept Father, but on the other hand, I didn't think they were intentionally attempting to keep him hidden from me—not like with Hook.

I clenched my molars even as I stared down the set of guards positioned in front of the infirmary.

They wore the razor-bladed helmets of my father's elite unit, and their eyes glowed electric-eel blue. They were his deadliest fighters, which only made sense, considering who he was.

I stopped walking and planted my hands on my hips.

I recognized the guard on the left as Barathanous Aenon, brother of the noble Anders. I flicked my chin and glowered at him directly. Barathanous seethed with obvious cold hate, but he didn't so much as flinch.

"Move." I said only the single word. The following day, Barathanous and those like him would get their pound of flesh out of me, but I was still a princess of that realm until then.

He grinned. "No." He too only spoke one word, but it echoed with the promise of violence.

I smirked and jutted out a hip. "I could always make you. You know who I am and what I can do."

Grinning from ear to ear in a manner that made my flesh crawl, he grunted. "I'll not move. Especially not for you. And you're no longer one of us. Haven't been for a long time, *Princess*."

I laughed, doing whatever I could to hide the fact that my blood felt like electrical currents coursing through me. "You would defy the orders of your princess?" My voice was silky but with an undercurrent of promised retribution for his arrogance.

He didn't so much as bat an eyelash. I lifted my hand.

"Stop! Stop this at once. Princess Arielle, of course you can enter." It was Jacamoe, bursting through the door, glaring hostilely in Barathanous's direction before turning his soft, dark eyes upon me. "I was tending to your father and heard the disturbance. I apologize for the delay." He stepped back from the door, ushering me inside solicitously.

Barathanous's jaw muscle twitched several times, and I knew he was likely grinding his molars down to dust at the slight I'd given his ego. But Jacamoe was the King's personal attendant, and his word was nearly as powerful as Anahita's when it came to such matters.

I made a point of smirking as I sidled by Barathanous. But only once I was safely behind the door did I release my pent-up breath and wilt against the back wall. My knees lost all strength for half a second. "Thank you," I whispered sincerely to Jacamoe's back.

He'd turned and was to attending to my father, who was suspended in air in the way Hook had been. And just like Hook, he was tied to what seemed like dozens of miles worth of tubing and machines.

"You should not challenge them that way, Little Fish. You wound a man's pride too often, and he'll bite." He glanced up at me, his lips turned down in a thoughtful but sincere expression.

I sighed, wincing at the gentle chastisement even though I knew he was right. "I know. I know." I shoved off the wall and moved over to a couch in the corner. The cushions had an imprint of a body in them, and I assumed Anahita had been spending most nights at his bedside.

I still couldn't look at his face. But I saw his body. He looked as though he simply rested. He was big and intimidating, even in a coma.

Blue light pulsed around Jacamoe's hands as he ran them down my father's head and chest over and over again.

"Has he woken?" I asked gently.

"No. Not even once."

"How is he?"

His dark eyes flicked to mine. "The same."

"Tell me truth, Jacamoe. Will he rise?"

He clenched his jaw. "I-I couldn't say, Princess. It is still too uncer—"

"Cut the bullshite and tell me truth now, dammit," I snapped, gripping my hands into tight fists, my knuckles turning white from the pressure on them.

His look was as serious and penetrating as anything I'd ever seen from him. "No, Arielle, he will not."

I waited for his words to wound me, waited to feel the pain, to feel flayed alive by them. I'd lain my sweet sister to rest tonight, and I was still reeling from her death. But with Father, there was just... nothing. I was cold inside. "Oh," I said softly.

"I am sorry if I—"

I looked at him, holding his gaze steadily. "I'm not," I whispered honestly.

His brows dipped.

I shook my head forcefully. "I'm not. Really. And this isn't me trying to be strong."

"He did love you, Arielle. In his own way."

I shrugged. "He had a funny way of showing it. To me. To mother. To my sisters. To all those who knew him," I said it so softly, it was practically a whisper, but I knew Jacamoe heard it by the soft flinch he gave. "He was a hard man. His only true legacy was in creating a powerful kingdom to leave behind for his daughter to tend, so no, I will not miss him."

"You never got to say goodbye to him."

I pursed my lips. "Do you honestly think he would have cared? I don't. And I'm pretty sure you know I'm right." I watched as father's chest rose and fell, thinking of what my sister had drunkenly confessed to me.

With anyone else, I might have thought that the actions Father had taken to see Hook dead had come from a place of caring or even love. If he believed the curse, that my true love would turn me into a monster, it might almost have been forgivable. But I was convinced he'd done it for no other reason than to make certain I never grew strong enough to eventually overthrow him.

Funny thing was, he might not have been wrong.

Undine was divided into two camps, those who wanted change at all costs and those who felt better with the devil they knew than the one they didn't. But on one thing, all of Undine could agree: none truly wanted to live under Father's totalitarian grip any longer. The only ones who'd benefited were his generals and lackeys, but even they would have jumped at the chance for a coup if any one of them had thought the odds of success attainable.

With father out as he was, a vacuum would be created. And with Anahita set to ascend, a target would be placed on her back. My sister would be given the throne, but she would have to earn the hearts and minds of her subjects in order to keep it. Her position was as precarious as tap dancing on thin ice. I clenched my fists and got up, moving over to where Father floated peacefully and steeling my nerves to look at him.

Rumors of his infidelity had followed him for years, but those hadn't been the worst, growing up. The worst had been the ones saying Mother hadn't died of a mysterious illness. It was no secret that Father had never truly loved her. Theirs had been a political alliance, the merging of two great houses, and once he'd exploited her power and money for his own, he'd been through with her.

But whether he was so wicked that he could have justified her murder was another question. I thought of his vendetta against Hook and me and thought that maybe a man capable of that would have been capable of so much more.

"How much longer does he have?" I asked into the sudden and deep silence that hung between us.

"There is no way of saying." He paused, and I knew he wanted to say more. I could practically hear his thoughts. So I waited him out.

"If I might be so bold as to say, Princess," he finally said, asking if I would allow him to speak honestly before me.

I nodded. I knew that whatever he would say would not be pretty.

And in most other places, in most other times, he could get into a heap of trouble for it. But he was safe with me, as I'd always been with him.

"He is not worth your tears. The only true legacy your father leaves behind is his ability to make good men turn bad. He was the pied piper and led them all down to the gates of the twin hells with his forked tongue."

I'd always known Jacamoe had despised my father, but I'd never known just how much. I did not chastise him for stating the truth. "That is enough, Jacamoe," I whispered into the silence. That was all I said. I didn't care that he'd said it, as it had only been the truth, but walls had ears, especially in this place.

I turned. He had thrust his jaw out, and his gaze was turned toward the shadow. A dusky rose had crept into his cheeks, but whether it was from shame or mortification, I wasn't sure. It didn't matter. Jacamoe was my friend, but he took too many liberties, even against someone who actually deserved it.

"Did you find Hook?" I finally asked.

He startled, guiltily looking up at me. I bit my lower lip before nodding. "I know you did. I also know you lied to me. Why? Why wouldn't you take me to him as you promised?"

"I"—his frown grew deep and hard—"he will not make it either, Princess. I didn't wish to give you false hope."

I laughed. The sound was manic and high-pitched, nearly frantic. "So what else is new? I lost him once. I knew I would never get to keep him. He is cursed to me. Always has been." With that, I turned on my heel and left.

I'd never even looked at Father's face. I'd not even said a word to him. There was no point.

If he'd been conscious, mine would have been the last face he would have wanted to see, anyway. He probably wouldn't even have bothered having a tribunal. He just would have cast me into the eternal pit without a word of fanfare.

Live by the sword, die by the sword. Father had never made friends. Not even his own family would mourn him.

I closed the door behind me, ignoring Barathanous's glare and walking without hurry back to my room.

When I opened my door, I saw Crowley sitting on the edge of my bed. His bloodshot eyes were full of questions.

We'd failed, he and I, and we both knew it. We'd been around the block enough times to know when a case could not be solved. We'd learned some truths, but not nearly enough of them.

He might live tomorrow. But I would die. That was as sure as the rising of the sun.

I nodded slowly, telling him he could stay. That he *should* stay. We'd fought like cats and dogs earlier, but that's just what he and I did. We were past the point of taking things personally anymore.

Funny how death threw things into perspective.

He held his arms out to me as I toed off my uncomfortable slippers.

I didn't say a word to him as I crawled into the giant four-poster bed and into his arms. We positioned ourselves in the middle, he with his arms wrapped around me and me with my head on his chest, listening to the steady rhythm of his heartbeat.

"My father is not going to make it, Crowley. Possibly not even through the night. Neither is Hook, or so I'm told."

"*Shh*," he said, squeezing me tightly.

My lips twitched, but I wasn't done. "I will die tomorrow too. They got their chance at me, Crowley. They got what they always want—"

"*Shh*. Stop. Just stop." Then he kissed my forehead, and I let him, stunned by his honest touch but also yearning for even more human contact. I looked up at him with my lips parted, giving him every chance, every sign that I was willing.

My body yielded against his.

He wasn't my truest love. I wasn't even sure he was a love. But he was there, in that moment with me. We were in it together, and it might have been my last chance to feel love, lust, whatever it was. I splayed my hand on his chest, leaning up ever so slightly and pressing my breasts fully against his hard-as-stone muscles.

His eyes glittered with animal hunger, and his jaw muscles flexed and relaxed as he clenched and unclenched them. He wanted me. I knew it. I also knew he wouldn't take my offer.

"Don't be noble, Crowley. Don't be noble. It won't matter tomorrow. I'll be gone and—"

With a hungry groan he rolled up, taking my lips for his own. He was lightning in a bottle, magnificent and powerful. I was his willing and pliant partner in every way, consumed by the ferocity of his hunger for me. Neither of us said a word, but we spoke with tongues, touches, sighs, and with lingering caresses that turned the blood in my veins to fire.

His movements were raw and honest. I didn't know how it happened but soon we were both naked. His body, all hard lines and planes, felt like it'd been made to fit perfectly against my own. And when he thrust deep in me, I hissed. The pleasure so good that I almost cried.

Our heated moans filled the room. He kissed and nipped at me, biting me gently, and then sometimes not so gently. I ran my hands all over his body, marveling at how he'd been made. The sinewy strength of his body had me hungry for more and more of him. We came together once, twice, and then more times. Moving as though on autopilot needing more and more of each other. Our bodies sweaty and our touches more intimate as time passed. He whispered things to me I knew couldn't be true, but must feel true in that moment. Like how he'd always wanted me. Always hungered for me. And I started saying some of those things back to him. That the rage and fire between us was more than just hate, that somewhere deep down I'd felt him as a kindred to the very depths of my soul. Then I said that I saved him because I could never be without him. Those words seemed to unleash something in him, a fervor of passion that made my own rise to the fore. I didn't know if those words were entirely true, but I wasn't ashamed of saying them either. Somewhere deep down I thought that maybe they weren't such a lie after all. Apart from Hook, Crowley proved to be one of the best lovers I'd ever known and it was a shame that this was to be my only experience knowing him. Or him me.

And when it was done, we simply held each other. His hands were gentle in my hair, and I smirked.

"What?" he asked in that deeply accented growl of his, his tone faintly amused, his body languid and loose and completely at ease.

I snorted and shook my head, even as I swirled my fingers through his groomed chest hair. "Only that if I wasn't one hundred percent certain that tomorrow would be my last day on this Earth, I'd have said we've changed our dynamic forever. You can't hate me now, Crowley. No matter how much you want to, you can't."

"You're ridiculous. Go to sleep," he said warmly, his hands still gently massaging my backside. It felt good. So much better than I ever thought it could have been with him.

I chuckled. "You're gonna miss me when I'm gone," I whispered, my voice quivering a little as the truth of those words really sank in.

There wasn't a damned thing I could do to fight the tribunal, and no matter how much Anahita loved me, her position in the under was too precarious for her to publicly stand for me. I laughed at the irony of it all. I'd left because I'd known staying would eventually get me killed, and I'd been right.

He growled. "Shut the fuck up, Elle."

My spine stiffened, but then I got it, what he was doing. So I laughed even harder, wrapping my arm around his waist and squeezing tightly until my laugh turned into something else.

He just held me.

And I was so damned grateful that it was him with me. For the first time in my life, I was grateful Crowley was the one I'd been lost with.

"Thank you," I whispered.

His only answer was to kiss my temple once more and run his nose through my hair.

And that was enough.

⚜

Hatter

I GRIPPED THE CHARM TIGHTLY IN MY FIST, STARING AT THE doorway that would guide me into the very heart of Undine.

I'd visited a witch so that I could breathe below water once the doorway opened. I'd paid in copper and dragons' claws.

After I'd successfully freed Buttons from the hangman's noose, he'd gifted me two of his hind claws. Claws were literally worth their weight in gold, as they were imbued with powerful magick. I'd not had cause to use them before but was glad that I had them to buy the spell.

I stared at the algae disk in the palm of my hand. The blind witch had assured me that all I had to do was swallow it, and I would be able to breathe below the waves for eight hours. After that, I would lose the ability, and if I didn't gain access to more air, I would drown.

But I wasn't planning on spending more time in the below than I needed to. Getting to an underground waystation hadn't been difficult, though I'd gotten more than my fair share of dirty looks from people scurrying out, trying to hide from the law. But Georgie had vouched for me with one of his dwarf brothers, and in exchange for one of Elle's stashed sapphires, I'd made the impossible possible.

I glanced at my watch. I knew from our PD contacts that the fallen princess's song had been the night before, which meant if they were going to move on Elle at any point, it would be very, very soon.

Time was a commodity I no longer had an abundance of. My plan was simple: run in, find her, and steal her back if I had to.

But Undine was an entire nation beneath the waves, and I doubted my plan would go off so simply, which was why I'd gotten one of the level-ten witches back at the precinct to set a tracer on the charm.

When Crowley came for it, I would be able to trace him right back to her, or so I hoped. That was if he was indeed working as her ally, which I had serious doubts about.

I took a deep fortifying breath. I'd done all I could to try and plan for all eventualities, but something was bound to go wrong—it always did. I just hoped that when it did, I would be ready and able to weather the storm.

Glancing down at the trinket, I wet my lips and rubbed my thumb over the face of it. *How am I supposed to summon Crowley?* The witch had never said, or if he had, I'd been too distracted by his even being there that I'd completely forgotten.

I glanced over my shoulder. The waystation was located in the one of the most derelict spots of Grimm, tucked away in one of the hundreds of abandoned and rotting buildings that housed little more than rats and the occasional transient looking for a semi-warm place to escape the rain and cold.

The floorboards in the room I was in were split and riddled with weak spots—one misstep, and I could fall twenty floors to my death. It was a death trap, and yet the spot where the doorway was placed had recently been renovated. The flooring had been reinforced with a fresh batch of wood, and where there were mounds of dust throughout empty room, the section around the gateway was dust free. It was definitely a well-used doorway.

I pressed my lips together, thinking of the countless crimes that had been committed by using this door. I should have blown it up, but it was my only way to gain access to Elle.

"Dammit," I spat. Swallowing my own hypocrisy with a shake of my head, I turned and walked out of the room, making sure to keep on the newly renovated bridge section. Once outside the small room, I closed the door behind me then called for Crowley: "Agent Crowley, I'm here. I've retrieved your device. Show yourself to me."

I wasn't sure if it would do a damned thing. So far as I knew, Crowley had no inherent magick, and yet he'd somehow reached out to me. I waited in the cold, empty hallway, watching a lone bulb flicker at the end of a nest of exposed wires. The place was a firetrap in the making.

On my walk there, I'd passed several muck-faced children playing in the filthy alleyways. I swallowed hard and balled my fists.

"Listen, you bastard," I snarled, my own impotence and impatience leaking through my usually calm façade, "you called out to me. So if you're there, you need to answer me. Now!" I snarled at the empty space before me.

My plan could not work if I couldn't set the tracker on Crowley. The Undine was too vast a place for me to have any hope of locating Elle or her castle on my own. For all I knew, the doorway could toss me out into one of the deepest trenches of the deep, forcing me to walk for miles in every direction just to find the breadcrumb that would eventually lead me to her castle, thus using all my reserves of air before I ever even reached her. That could not happen.

"I found your bloody trink—" Before I could finish the sentence, I felt the air shift, turn colder, and coalesce with paint streaks of color.

And then, there he was, staring at me with his cold, red eyes. He stood before an unusually shaped stone archway, with a blue radiance gleaming at his back. "You have found the trinket? Let me see it?"

No greeting or anything else—he was all business, and I sensed an urgency in him far more potent than the one I'd sensed even the other day. His movements were frantic, and whatever he was doing was just outside my field of vision.

I held up the trinket. For a second, his shoulders stiffened, and then a flash of relief scrawled across his tight features. "Hand it to me. The tribunal meets in mere moments. There is no time left to spare."

I clenched my jaw. "How will this keep her or you safe? What is this thing? You never did say."

He grinned, showing nothing but teeth even as he hastily began to jerk golden fabric on over his arms. "No, I did not."

I cocked my head, waiting for him to say more. But he didn't. "How do I know you're not deceiving me?"

His smile was ruthless. "You do not. But I did not lie to you. She will be kept safe."

"Where are you? Where is she?" I had to try anything to help narrow my own search.

He shook his head. "It matters not. You could not come to where we are, anyway. Good day, Detective."

Then the image vanished, and I was standing in an empty hallway, staring into the yawning blackness with a curious frown gathering my brows. I stared at my palm. I'd never handed it to him, but I knew before I looked that it would not be there anymore. Somehow, some-way, he'd called it to him.

I was right. My palm was empty.

But it was not the device that caused me such consternation. Last time, I'd been too emotional to realize that when he'd spoken to me, he'd done so in a manner that was not at all reminiscent of the detective. His words had been far too eloquent, learned, scholarly. He'd spoken without the use of a single contraction.

I thought of Crowley, the real Crowley. He was gruff and hard, and he spoke in the style of the streets.

My heart raced as I scanned the empty floorboard before me, seeing not the dust streaked everywhere but rather hearing the Tinkerer's voice, her caution that the agent was evil and not to be trusted. I'd assumed that she'd meant Crowley—I'd had no reason not to. *What if the agent isn't Crowley at all, rather a mage in disguise? It has to be, right?* Crowley had no magick. I'd known that all along.

I doubted B.S. had access to the kind of magick that had literally pulled the timepiece from my palm through a magickal ley line directly to him. I knew enough of witches and wizards to know that what I'd just seen was high-level craft.

The Sea Witch hadn't been caught.

Ichabod had assured us that the battle between Elle and the Sea Witch had to have weakened her enough so that she was not a threat for the time being and that she would be forced to lay low to recover before she could engage us further. He'd said that she was a null piece on the board. But he could have been wrong. *What if she'd merely been biding her time? What if the Sea Witch had been down there with Elle the entire time?*

My pulse jerked, and before I knew what I was doing I was racing for the waystation. Running as fast as I could, reaching into my inner jacket pocket at the same time and swiped the card through the keypad just a moment later.

The door thrust open, and the water world beckoned to me. Sea kelp wrapped like living vines out the watery doorway. A blue phosphorescence like the one that'd been at Crowley's back glowed from within.

I waited to feel the first faint pulse of the targeting magick Layla had slyly embedded within the timepiece itself. I hadn't worried about Crowley finding the tracker because he was not a mage. But I no longer believed I was dealing with Crowley, and if I wasn't, that meant whoever had taken the charm from me was powerful enough to spot the tracker.

I waited and waited, but no telltale pulse came to me.

"No," I whispered, shaking my head forcefully. "No. Elle... Arielle, where are you?"

I gripped the doorway with both hands, bracing my legs and craning my neck as far as I could, hoping and praying against all odds that I just needed to be more patient. But nothing happened.

My fires began to roil within me. The sizzle of water meeting flame created steam that began to billow around my ankles and up to my knees.

I could find her another way.

I wet my lips.

I'd sworn to the agency that I would never use my powers in that way, that I would never step outside the carefully governed bounds of what I was allowed to do.

A thing—a creature like me letting loose could be a dangerous thing. But it was Elle, my Elle, and I would be damned if I would let anything happen to her.

I chuckled. "You're already damned anyway, Maddox. Not like you have any more to lose."

That wasn't entirely true. I had a lot to lose. I had everything to lose.

I squeezed my eyes shut. If I let myself do what I was about to do, the hunger to be as I was born to be would rise in me again. I'd spent a lifetime quelling that madness, and I hated to think what would happen if I wasn't strong enough to put that genie back in the bottle when it was all said and done.

Steam hissed all around me as I clenched tighter onto the doorway.

There was no other choice. I had to find her. I would not lose her too. If I did, I would go truly mad, and no one in the twin hells or on Grimm would be safe from my wrath.

"Not this time," I growled. I slammed back the algae tablet, and with a quick prayer, I stepped through the doorway.

CHAPTER 14
ELLE

W HEN I AWOKE the next morning, I knew before there'd even been a knock on my door that they would be coming for me.

So I'd gotten dressed and waited for them. My hair was in disarray —I'd never bothered to unpin it before bed. I was still wearing the funeral dress from the night before.

I glanced over to where Crowley should have been, but all that was left was his imprint. I touched the edge of his pillow, frowning as I stared at the wrinkles in it.

He was already gone, probably back to his room before the summons. I wasn't sure why he'd left me without a word, not that it mattered. Last night hadn't meant anything. It'd just been a way for both of us to release the tension and anxiety looming over both our heads.

The knock sounded again, more forcefully this time.

I sighed and got up.

When I opened the door, I was met by the royal guard. Barathanous was in the lead, a wicked grin tipping the corner of his lips. "Arielle, disgraced *Princess*"—his voice dripped with contempt at that bit—"of the Undine. You have been summoned by a jury of your peers to see to—"

"Yeah, yeah, yeah," I muttered angrily, glowering at him. "Just get on with it already, dick for brains."

I probably shouldn't have said that part, but I was pissed. I was surly, and I didn't think right when I didn't get my morning cup of java.

Rough hands latched onto my shoulders, turning me so forcefully that I stumbled, and then my arms were yanked behind me in a punishing grip before even more iron was clamped to my wrists.

I snarled. But I'd asked for it too, so I didn't say anything else—it would only be worse for me if I did. He merely had to summon me to the tribunal. There was nothing saying I had to arrive in any shape other than still breathing.

I bit my tongue as he jerked my bonds and force me ahead of the vanguard. The way I saw it, I had two options. I could hang my head in shame and let those gathering like a small school of fish around me gossip and whisper and say whatever the hells they pleased while I pathetically just accepted it all. Or I could let them gossip and whisper as I stared cold, defiant death at all of them. I went for option two.

The walk seemed to take forever, and as I went, the citizens began to throw things at me: first fruit, then spoiled fruit, then more painful things, such as pointed coral and sharp-edged rocks. I bit my lip, saying nothing. I would let them take their pound of flesh out of me, enduring the injustice of allowing them to touch me, slap me, kick at me. To take my gown into their hands and rip it off of me, exposing my legs to them.

Their vitriol became more heated after that. I wasn't one of them any longer. That point could not have been made clearer.

My nostrils flared, and heat stung my eyes.

I endured the labyrinth of shame that I was forced to walk with whatever scraps of pride I still had left. I'd known how it would go down because I'd been forced to suffer it once before.

But the first time it hadn't been so hateful, so personal.

It didn't matter that I didn't physically kill my sister or gravely wound my father. In their eyes, I was a traitor, and I always had been.

Then a young boy swam in front of my eyes, and I saw his beautiful, perfect face with those electric-purple eyes so like Anders's that my heart skittered in my chest.

He threw a tiny projectile at me with such force that when it struck my temple, my head swam and stars danced in front of my eyes. I felt the warm slick of blood sliding down my cheek when I finally became lucid again. It must have been Anders's grandson—I'd known it the first second I'd seen him. Beautiful just like his devil of a grandsire had been.

I'm sure in those stories, I was the monster, but the boy would never know how Anders had raped me, how he'd held me down as he heaped one humiliation after another upon my body.

In fact, no one other than Anahita and Father had known. Father had told me to just accept it and make my peace with it. Anders came from a vaunted and respected line, and if I knew what was good for me, I would shut up and play the game.

Anahita had wanted to kill him. She'd wanted to torture him. Her rage had been such that she would have torched his entire house to make it right again, so I'd killed him instead. I'd saved my sister's reputation. And I'd gotten my own revenge. First, I'd cut off his cock and balls. Then I'd forced him to watch as I'd fed them to the eels. After that, I'd sunk my blade into the soft meat of his belly and had played with his organs until the light was extinguished from his beautiful, cold eyes.

I'd been found half mad with bloodlust, covered in his gore. I'd been labeled a monster then and banished for my crime, but not before I'd taken down the first wave of guards who'd come to take me in. I'd butchered them all, singing them into enough of a stupor that it'd been so, so easy to carve them up too.

I swallowed hard.

I had gone mad with grief and shame and horror at the bloody awful things I'd been able to do. And after I'd been banished, the killings hadn't stopped. I'd hunted down all the dogs who'd ever wronged my Hook. That's how Crowley had known me once. I had been the monster of the sea, the mistress of the dark. He hadn't lied when he'd said it.

The young boy had tears streaming down his cheeks, and his hand was open. A tiny seahorse carved of pewter rested in his palm. He must have thrown one of his toys at me, landing a once in a lifetime hit that'd bled me like a stuck pig.

I blinked hard, wishing I could look away from his agonized glare but knowing that I had to take it. I had to see it, and I had to remember it. Because though his grandsire was the spawn of the devil, that boy had clearly never heard that. I'd been in a dark place then, a very, very dark place. That didn't make it right, but it made it understandable. I could never slide like that again. The things I'd done to myself, to others... I could never be that again. So I let him direct his hate at me. I gave him a target because sometimes that's what people needed so that they didn't spiral like I had.

Barathanous growled in my ear. "He is Anders's grandson. All our boys are raised knowing what kind of a monster you truly are. You deserve that and more, Arielle. So you live with it. C'mon." He shoved me between the shoulder blades, forcing me to stumble forward.

By the time I arrived at the tribunal, my shame was complete.

I was covered in rotting meats, fruits, and even waste. My dress was torn, my flesh shredded.

My sister's eyes flinched from her central spot at the council table. But she said nothing, only breathed slowly and deeply.

I caught sight of Crowley shackled to the wall from my periphery. His look was hard, almost angry. But I couldn't look back at him. I couldn't take his censure or his pity, and I didn't care to figure out which one it would be.

I glanced at the four males sitting arrogantly on the dais just below my sister's, openly and hostilely glaring down at me. The five noble houses were represented, and I knew I was in deep shite when I saw who they'd sent as their delegates: members from the families of males I'd killed.

I huffed beneath my breath. It was never going to be fair, and I'd known it all along, so seeing the evidence of that truth shouldn't have affected me at all, but it did. My knees felt weak, and it actually hurt to breathe, though I knew my sister hadn't taken her favor off of me yet.

Jacamoe stood, dressed in the ceremonial golden garb of court. He held up a decree before him and spoke in a loud, authoritarian voice, "Arielle, princess of Seren and the Undine, has been charged with the death of Princess Aquata and the grievous injury to her father, King Triton. How does the defendant plea?"

I could feel the glide of displaced water and, the amphitheater filled with more and more sirens come to see my trial. *Why does this feel so rushed? Why aren't they waiting for the courtroom to be gated and sealed?* There were rumblings amongst the tribunal, and even Anahita was openly glaring at Jacamoe. I clearly wasn't the only one wondering at the rush.

I swallowed.

"How do you plead?" He pressed harder with a sharper edge to his words that had me cocking my head in curiosity. *Why is Jacamoe acting this way?* It went beyond the bounds of decorum.

I'd known the day was coming since the moment I'd arrived in Undine, but I still felt overwhelmed and unprepared for the events.

I glanced over to where Crowley was chained. His look was cold, hard. But he wasn't staring at me. He was glaring daggers at Jacamoe. There was a look in his eyes that I recognized, and it shook me.

He was looking at Jacamoe as he'd looked at me when he'd been on my scent and I'd been insane with vengeance and grief. He was looking at Jacamoe as though *he* was guilty.

A cold chill ran down my spine.

"How do you plead?" Jacamoe raised his voice, causing me to startle and twitch.

"Jacamoe! That is enough!" Anahita lifted her hand in an imperious manner, glaring at him sternly. "Have you lost your senses? Since when do we—"

That was all she got out before all hells broke loose.

"Not guilty," he growled, and then lifting his hands, he held up his unshackled wrists, and I knew. Dear gods in the above and below, I knew everything.

And I wasn't the only one. The crowd gasped, murmurs beginning to roll through them. I saw the high elders at the table, looking at one another with wide panicked eyes. They knew it too, the truth that Crowley had clearly already reached.

The one we'd been looking for had been under our noses all along. Jacamoe was a Djinn, one in a very unique position. He was bound to a man in a comatose state who could not stop him from enacting his planned retribution. And if Father didn't check him, no one else could.

Is that why he'd done what he'd done to Father? To get him out of the way? As father's Djinn, Jacamoe could not actually harm him. But what if Father had been the one accidentally slammed by the Sea Witch's magic and not Aquata, as I'd first thought?

What if Jacamoe had been present for it, had seen what had been done, and in a split second had acted upon his sudden reversal of fate? What if my sister had seen it too, and she'd tried to stop him?

I stared at Jacamoe's robe, and my breath caught in my throat. Upon his neck, he wore a hammered golden necklace with gold triangles that were nearly identical to the ones that Crowley had found, and that I had seen in the palm of Aquata's little sea otter.

I trembled as the puzzle pieces fitted together more swiftly. She'd been found in the gardens, which meant that Jacamoe would likely have tossed her pet off of him with such force that he'd instantly killed the little beast, who, in his death grip, had never released the hammered bit of gold. He could have stopped it then.

He hadn't needed to proceed with this ill-thought plan of his. Rather than admitting he'd not actually injured Father but had merely planned to twist the circumstances to his advantage, he'd taken his first real step over the line.

He'd killed her. Snapped her the small bone in her neck, leaving virtually no outward sign of damage to her body that her spirit would look fully intact. But he'd still been cuffed, which meant he would have done it at great personal cost to himself. That explained why his limp was profoundly worse than it had ever been before. The lack of scent at the scene still baffled me, but I knew I had figured out most of the timeline. It all fit. It was right. And in my gut, I knew that was how it had to have happened.

The Sea Witch would have had to travel through there, but she was severely weakened from her battle with me. Maybe she was still in Undine, though I doubted it. If I were her and as magically depleted as she must be, especially after slamming what dregs remained of her into Father, I would have chosen to get far away as quickly as I was able.

"Jacamoe, stand down," my sister said slowly, softly, unmoving and unblinking as she looked upon my father's advisor. Behind her, Ebonia suddenly appeared, holding onto a glowing staff, pointed at the tip. Her look was hard, formidable. Around me, I saw a contingency of soldiers began to slowly rise and creep toward Anahita, encircling her, shielding her from Jacamoe's reach. Sealing him off from her, their queen.

To the layman, it should have looked as though Jacamoe had nowhere to go, but I'd witnessed the ease and strength of his magick and knew in my soul that it was far too little, too late.

His full lips curled into a smirk. "No."

All the color leeched from my sister's face. She swallowed forcefully and shook her head. "You do not want this. You do not want to do this."

There was a long, fraught pause, and stupidly, I hoped that the male whom I'd once thought of as my only friend would listen and stop. But Jacamoe was like a dog that'd been poked one too many times. Whatever kindness he'd once had—and I knew in my soul it had been there—had slowly eroded until all that remained were spines and thorny barbs of hate.

"Oh, but I think I do, my *Queen*," he spat the title like poison from his mouth. "I really, really think I do. For too long, I have been forced do endure the brutality and anathema of this dictatorship in silence. I've had to sit back and watch as Triton bullied, belittled, and destroyed anything that stood in his path to glory and complete domination of all of Undine. No more."

Before I could blink, he was looking at me, and there was magma burning in his dark eyes. "I'm sorry," was all he mouthed before I was suddenly caught up by an invisible force and tossed with such force that I wondered how every bone in my body hadn't snapped.

He couldn't do magick. He was cuffed. Same as me. He couldn't do this, but he had. He had done it.

"Elle!" Crowley roared. "*Noooo!*"

That was all I heard. I screamed as I fell. And fell. And fell. It dawned on me that I should have crashed into the ground or slammed against a wall. But there was nothing but cold, rushing, arctic air.

That was when the panic gripped me in its fist, and my screams turned to howls of desperation. He'd tossed me into the endless pit, an eternal fall that would end with my eventual painful, slow demise.

Blinking, my eyes tearing from the rush of air all around me, I fought the panic beating in my chest and forced myself to think. The fall wouldn't kill me. No, the lack of food and water would eventually do that. That meant I had time to think.

What do I know of the pit?

It was endless. Eternal. But it was a hole, which meant there was a side to it.

It was dark as the void in here, and there was no sound other than my own breathing and the whistle of air shrieking past my ears—very few sensory details to help me see my way out.

I wet my lips, and my stomach dove down into my knees. *If I can't see and I can't hear and there are no smells, then how the devil am I to get out of here?*

I started to shake as adrenaline coursed like a geyser through me. "Stop, Elle. Think. Think. Thi—"

I gasped then gripped my wrists with opposite hands. I held them close to my eyes, but the darkness was complete and impossible to see through. But I sensed the lack of their weight upon me. The golden cuffs that immobilized my powers were gone. *Had Jacamoe meant for that to happen when he'd tossed me? Had he intended to give me a fighting chance here? Why had he said "I'm sorry"? Was it not me that he wanted to hurt? What is he doing to them now? To my sister? To my Hook? To Crowley?*

I clutched at my chest and shook my head. Going down that path would make me freeze up again, and I couldn't afford to do that. I had to get out of there, and there was no one else to help me. *But what can I do?*

My gown had flipped up from the heavy rush of displaced air around me. I wish I had light or protection to stop the whistling shriek so that I could think. So that I could—

I blinked.

You are a detective of the realm, Arielle. You must learn this spell. It could save your life one day...

He'd said that to me during one of our few sessions together. My skin went cold all over, and my hands turned numb. There was a loud ringing in my ears, and my stomach heaved violently. I'd laughed at him for wanting to teach me such a ridiculous spell: how to create a bubble.

What a silly thing to learn in the two hours we'd been given. How to summon my familiar had been great, but I wondered what good a bubble was. Yet, he'd been so insistent that I learn how to say the words precisely.

He had meant for me to survive. "Oh my gods," I whispered, shaking my head softly. He'd been teaching me what to do to get out of the void when the time came.

The words that had seemed so foreign to me the first time I'd said them rolled easily off my tongue: "*Videre lucem caeli, et usque ad internicinem.*"

I'd struggled so hard for hours after my battle with the Sea Witch, fearing all was lost. But this time, the power surged out of me like a tide. I felt strong, powerful, and able.

My familiar, who had ignored me just the day before exploded from my hands, filling the pit with light, and a completely formed bubble encased me. My downward fall was completely halted.

For the first time, maybe ever for any citizen of Undine, I looked at the eternal pit. It was nothing but hollowed out limestone. It wasn't filled with the souls of the damned. There was no boogeyman in there to grab me. It was just a pit. There was nothing special about it.

Jacamoe had saved me, and he'd done it intentionally.

I looked above me. The sea otter rested just above my head, burning like the sun in the thick darkness that surrounded us.

I didn't know what I was doing. I was a novice spellcrafter. I'd not learned much of any use. I'd barely started. I wasn't falling anymore, and that was good, but I didn't know how to get back up. I did know that I was running out of time. Whatever Jacamoe had planned, he was doing.

My family depended on my getting back up there. I didn't give a damn about my father, but I wasn't heartless. If he didn't have to die, I didn't want him to. And my sister... Ebonia was more than an able warrior, but even she was no match for a Djinn as powerful as Jacamoe.

I could easily imagine the slaughter taking place above me, and my hands started to shake.

"Go up. Move!" I yelled, but the bubble just floated where it was.

My nostrils flared, and I clenched my fists. It was bullshite. He gave me the means to not fall, but I didn't know what I was doing. *What am I supposed to do now? Just wait around for him to pull me out of here?*

The second I thought it, I realized that as likely to be the case. If I had been up there, I would have been doing everything in my power to stop him, and he'd known it. But he didn't want me dead. Jacamoe really had loved me.

That meant that I was one of his few and only weaknesses. If I could get up there, I could exploit that. But just that thought made my insides tremble and heat flood my eyes, because I loved him too. Even after all of it. He was so wrong for all he'd done, but dammit, I understood why he'd snapped, why he'd lost his shite that way. No one could be treated like an animal and not eventually break, no matter how good, honorable, or kind. We all had a breaking point.

Maybe he hadn't meant to kill Aquata, but he held no love for Anahita, and she had none for him.

My heart squeezed, and I growled. He would kill her.

I had to stop him at any cost.

The bubble wouldn't move at all, at least not with magick. But when I swung my arms, I did feel a tremor of movement, sort of like swimming through mud. It wasn't fast, but it was something. If I stroked upward, I would tire quickly. I'd fallen for far too long to even attempt it.

But... I glanced toward my left, at the limestone wall of the pit. There were natural crevices in the pit itself, places where I could find finger- and toeholds. *Maybe I could climb out.*

But to do that, I would have had to drop my bubble, leaving me in a precarious position with no safety net below me. I would fall again, and I wasn't all that confident I'd be able to get the bubble to appear a second time. My magick wasn't always the most reliable.

I looked back up at the endless, yawning darkness above my familiar's light and shook my head. "Impossible."

Don't be a bitch, Elle, and climb!

I jerked, looking up, swearing I'd just heard Crowley's angry growl, but there was no one above me, no moving shadow, nothing. And yet, it was as if he'd been standing over my shoulder.

Move your ass, Fish!

I snorted, but my lips twitched. I was seriously losing my marbles if I heard him. And yet, I did move.

I used a swimming motion to move the bubble in excruciatingly slow increments. Sweat was pouring down my brows and into my eyes as I doggy paddled, even kicking my legs as I heaved and grunted my way over toward the side of the pit's wall.

By the time I reached it, I resembled a drowned rat—the effort had been so straining that my muscles quivered from the effort. I would have to drop the only protection I had down here and hope that I timed my jump just right, or I would fall again, and the gods only knew if I could stop myself a second time.

I swallowed hard. I could give in to the fear and the paranoia and all the what ifs, or I could just turn off my thoughts and move my ass.

I looked at the wall, studying it for any weaknesses or places where I could easily and sturdily hang on. I'd gone years without a tail, which meant I'd developed my leg muscles enough that I hoped I would be able to bear my weight. One way or another, I was about to find out.

"Okay, okay, here goes nothing," I muttered after locating a spot where I was sure my toes could fit.

I maneuvered the bubble just inches away from it then took a deep and fortifying breath, shoving down the terror and panic as best I could.

And then I released myself from the bubble and I jumped. "*Ahh!*" I screamed. I couldn't help it.

My cheek crashed against wet limestone, and I gasped, my arms trembling. My fingers had found the wrong holes, and I was just barely holding on, but my toes were curved like claws into the recess. I looked up again.

"Elle! Elle! Damn you, bitch, you'd better not die on me. Or I swear I'll kill you myself! Answer me, Fish! Holy hells!"

My eyes widened, and I craned my chin upward, trying as hard as I could to peer through the darkness. I hadn't imagined it. That was

Crowley's voice. The echo of his desperation was a tangible and palpable thing.

"Crowley. Crowley, how... are you?" And I saw him, a moving shadow. He was moving like a panther down the wall with a graceful ease that made me jealous.

His face moved into the light, and I couldn't help the smile that stretched from one corner of my mouth to the other.

When he saw me, he stopped moving, and the look on his face was one I knew I would never forget. It was shock, hope, relief, and most of all... joy.

"Oh, fuck you," he murmured before resting his forehead against the wall. He was on the opposite side of me, and I could see tremors work through his back muscles.

I might have been offended, except I knew that "fuck you" hadn't meant that at all. Crowley didn't know how to handle his emotions, and it was as close to his saying "thank the gods" as anything could be.

"What's happening up there?"

He swallowed once, wiping some sweat out of his eyes as he shook his head. "It's a godsdamned shitstorm. Jacamoe has gone apeshit. Dead bodies are everywhere. And—" He stopped, staring at me with open hunger and pain. He didn't want to tell me whatever he'd been about to say.

"What?"

There was a pause. "I-I know what he was planning with Anihita. About Hook. He's controlling him. Like... like the witch did. He's soulless, Elle. He can't be stopped."

He didn't have to tell me what Hook couldn't be stopped from doing, because I already knew. If he was being controlled in the same way the Sea Witch had, it meant he was killing—he was Jacamoe's puppet, doing the dirty work. And without a soul, he was basically an immortal shell, like a golem. He was a monster on a string, nearly inde-structible and incapable of feeling pain, empathy, anything.

I sucked in a sharp breath. "I gotta get back up there. I have to stop... I have to stop him."

I wasn't even sure who the "him" was. "Why did you come for me?" I suddenly asked.

"Because you wouldn't leave me," he whispered. "Now, hurry the hells up." Without looking back at me, he began to scale back up the wall with the ease of a monkey, moving out of sight of my familiar in seconds.

Crowley was so much more than I'd ever known. And if he could do it, then so could I.

No longer fearful, I began to climb, forcing my muscles to work beyond the point of endurance. I was practically screaming from the agony of the climb when I finally began to near the top and no longer needed the light of my familiar to find my way.

I was gasping and panting for breath when a hand suddenly reached down into the darkness for me. It was strong and powerful, and I instantly recognized it. With a cry, I latched on. When he pulled me up, I instantly wrapped my arms around him. My body was nothing but pain. I could barely stand.

But I clung to Hatter's jacket with fingers that could barely feel. "How... When... How?"

His hands were on my face. Crowley stood just behind him, a hard gleam in his eyes, before he turned and scanned our surroundings.

Where there'd been an amphitheater full of sirens earlier, there was nothing but bodies piled on top of broken, bleeding, dying, and dead bodies. There was smoke and rubble everywhere.

"Oh my gods," I said, once it clicked in my head.

"It's bad, Elle," Hatter whispered. "It's really bad."

My gaze shot to his. "How did you find me?"

He grinned softly. "I'll always find you. But now we have to go. We have to go, and we have to stop him."

As if to punctuate his statement a scream rang in the air, and my soul clenched. "That's Anahita. She's in trouble. I have to—"

"I'll go," Crowley growled, and then he was loping off, moving as though he had energy to burn for days. It was as if he hadn't just crawled down and back up from a tunnel leading straight to the bowels of the twin hells themselves.

I tried to move as he did, but everything screamed. My toes were cramped, and my legs, which never enjoyed carrying that kind of weight, nearly buckled under me.

Hatter's hands were on my waist in an instant. "Hang on," he said with a grunt, and then he was moving. I rested most of my weight on him as I tried to run beside him.

When we exited the theater, there were yet more bodies and what looked to be an army of the dead slashing and hacking at anyone running away.

My jaw dropped. "Oh my god."

What had once been a bustling and active castle had been transformed into a living hell.

I spotted Crowley. He was spectacular as he fought, half transformed into his beast mode, plowing through the undead without a care as he received one brutal slash after another from swinging swords.

Anahita was flanked on all sides by Ebonia's own guards. She had a terrible gash on her cheek and was holding the flap of skin together with her hands. Her eyes were wild and dazed.

Hook was leering before her. Part of his nose was gone, along with a chunk of his left cheek and his good hand, yet he still moved on them. A spectacular warrior in his own right, he fought like the devil himself, his aim obviously to get to her.

Crowley was just steps behind, but he was slowing from his countless injuries.

"Hook's going to kill her, and he's a golem. He can't be stopped. He can't be stopped."

No sooner did I say it, then I saw it. Just as Hook reached for Anahita, Crowley reached him. He dug his claws into Hook's back, ripping him away from her.

But Hook twisted and in a move I never expected to see, he lifted his hooked hand and swung it down with such brutal and terrifying force that he ripped a hole directly over Crowley's heart.

Everything stopped for me.

I saw Crowley look down, a quizzical expression on his brow, as if he couldn't quite believe it himself.

"No," I whimpered even as I saw the first spot of scarlet bloom. "No," I said more forcefully as he fell to his knees.

"*Noooo!*" I screamed when Hook pulled out a sword from his scabbard and in one smooth move severed Crowley's head from his body.

Horror pierced my soul. Hook's distraction helped Ebonia to whisk Anahita away, and they raced into the church, slamming the doors behind them. But Hook was already on the scent, moving toward it with determined strides, covered in Crowley's blood. He stared sightlessly ahead.

"I've got to go get them. I've got to help them," I heard Hatter saying, but it sounded far away and as if he was speaking through a long tunnel.

I whipped around on him and like a feral cat, I shoved hard, not even sure what I was doing anymore. "Go away! Go back home! Leave! Leave now!"

His brows dropped. Pandemonium was all around, with people screaming and infants crying. Jacamoe had won. Hook couldn't be stopped.

I would try, but I would be damned if I saw Hatter die too.

The bastard wasn't leaving. "I'm staying," he said, voice cracking.

I shoved him again, hard enough to make him stumble. Panic was making me crazed and frenzied. "I don't need you! I don't want you here. You go. You leave! Go now! Why are you still here? Go." But when he still didn't move, I went apeshite. "I said go! I don't need you. I don't need you to fight my battles for me! Why are you still here?" I pushed him hard enough that he should have fallen, but he grabbed my wrists, locking his heels in place, causing us both to sway and nearly lose our balance.

He growled, cocking his head. The fight had suddenly left me, and the only thing I could say was, "You saw what he did to the others. To Crowley. Why are you still here?" I choked on the sob stuck in the back of my throat.

"Because, godsdammit," he snapped tersely, his body glowing with the heat from his fire, "I need you. I need you." And with those words, he pulled me in tight, kissing me so brutally that his sharp teeth pricked my bottom lip, making me bleed.

But the pain was good. The pain made me feel alive, wanted, and full for the first time in a long time. I kissed him with everything I had, with all of me. I was his, and I had been for a long time.

"Hatter," I said breathlessly when we finally managed to pull away from each other. His forehead rested against mine. His breathing was harsh and ragged, but his heartbeat was a steady rhythm under my palm.

The rustling snap of moving branches caused us both to become alert at the same time. I looked at him frantically, lost and terrified of losing him, too, just as I'd once lost my Hook.

Hook: my greatest love and my worst pain, a golem sent to destroy us, feeling nothing and only existing to kill. The way he'd driven his hook through Crowley's chest and ripped into his heart was a sight I knew I would never be able to purge from my mind.

I'd loved Hook with all my heart and soul, but I wasn't sure I'd ever be able to forget the horrors I'd witnessed today. He was an unstoppable monster. But his maker wasn't. *Kill Doctor Frankenstein and kill the beast.* "I know what to do."

Hatter looked at me. "We take down Hook. We—"

"It's not possible. Not yet."

"So what do we—"

"We kill the head of the beast. We have to find Jacamoe. We have to find him, and we have to stop him."

CHAPTER 15
ELLE

I COULD BARELY WALK. Hatter never let me go.

"I don't know where he is," I admitted, trying like hells to focus on the fact that a man I'd once loved as well as any girl could love a father figure had turned into a complete madman. My heart hurt for all the deaths and for the fact that Crowley had died alone. If Hook ever woke up from his programming, he would hate himself—I knew it because I knew him.

"Where did you see him last?"

I shook my head. "He was at my hearing, reading off the charges to me. But he wasn't there anymore."

"You know him best, Elle," he said as he gingerly helped me over a pile of rubble. The level of violence that'd befallen the king's realm spoke of deep-seated rage and hatred. It wasn't merely about toppling my father's legacy. It was more than that. It was about obliterating that legacy to the point that it had never existed at all.

We entered the castle proper, which I'd expected to be in as much disrepair as the grounds, but it was still mostly intact. I could hear the screams and groans of those trapped inside. The ringing of steel on steel let me know the undead had made their way in here too.

What's his plan? To destroy it all? Or to take it over and reshape this place to suit his needs? I was confused. "How the hells did he get his magick back? That's what I'd like to know." We were making out way up the stairwell and toward the private quarters. "He'd been cuffed. There's no way in hells that he should have been able to—"

"I think I might know the answer to that, Elle. I'm sorry, but I think it was he who contacted me in the above and requested that I retrieve a charm for him. I thought it was Crowley who'd contacted me, but I think now that whatever that charm was granted him the ability to do all th—"

We were just rounding the bend when an explosion of steel on stone sounded. "Watch out!" I cried.

An undead siren with a face and body badly decomposed so that I couldn't tell if it was male or female, lifted its bony arms to strike us down.

Hatter shoved me away, and my breath rushed from my lungs when my back hit the wall. He then grabbed the soldier by its arms and, using a rush of fire, obliterated the limbs to dust in seconds. I winced at the heat billowing off him as steam rose up around us, obscuring us in its foggy folds.

The undead didn't die because it wasn't alive to begin with. Though it had no arms left with which to strike at us, it attempted to do so with its jaws, smacking its decayed and rotting teeth together as it lunged violently in my direction. I threw my hands out, too tired even to conjure up my familiar.

But Hatter grabbed it from behind and roughly pulled it off of me. It smelled of viscera and spoiled meat sitting out in the sun too long. I gagged and watched with tears in my eyes as he once more placed his hands on the nightmare's head and reduced that to ashes as well. Finally, the threat had been neutralized.

"Buggers aren't easy to kill," he grunted as he slipped his arm around my waist once more.

"I'm fine, Maddox," I whispered. "You should go. You should go now."

He glowered down at me. "I already told you, I'm not leaving."

My lips turned down. "Y-You could die here too. I won't watch that happen, Hatter. I can't—"

"C'mon," he groused, picking up our pace and making certain to keep us deeper in shadow. It soon became impossible to remain hidden. There were just too many of them loitering about, with arms dangling down at their sides and weapons gripped loosely in their bony hands. The undead were everywhere, but they were no longer battling. There merely stood around like macabre statues. It seemed as though they could jump into action at any moment but had temporarily been shut down or immobilized.

They didn't say a word, but I felt their eyes on us. My skin crawled, and breathing was difficult to do. My eyes stung from the rotten smell, my stomach heaved, and I had to swallow back my body's natural instinct to gag.

The wall of them grew thicker and thicker as we moved down the walkway. They hovered deepest around the door to Father's chambers, where I'd seen him just the day before.

Jacamoe could not harm Father, not while Father owned his mark. And even with him in a comatose state, the magick recognized Father as the Djinn's sovereign. He was probably the safest of everyone and ironically the entire reason for why Jacamoe had snapped as he had.

Hatter looked toward me, and I nodded. We had to go inside.

Stepping out of Hatter's arm, I lifted my chin. I felt stronger than I had earlier. *I can do this. I have to do this.*

I gently pushed open the door. It groaned on its hinges, making me automatically cringe and reach for my weapon, which wasn't on me and hadn't been the entire time I'd been trapped in Undine.

Father was still lying as he'd been before, but Jacamoe looked up at me with bleary eyes. And behind him hovered a body. A form that I'd recognize anywhere. It was the Sea Witch herself. Comatose, just as father was. But I couldn't understand how she'd shown up here now, when she'd not been here before.

But I saw the power, the dark black shadow curling and winding like cobras from her body, flowing through Jacamoe's form and somehow I knew that he'd used her powers for his own.

He'd amplified his already not so insignificant magick with hers. The Witch had literally been under our noses the whole time.

"Oh my gods," I whispered, as the full scope and horror of just how deep this plan had gone went.

Weariness was etched into thick grooves around Jacamoe's eyes and upon his forehead. "I knew you would find me," he said in a soft, scratchy tone.

I stared at the man whom I'd loved with all my heart as a child and even as an adult. Even though I knew the horrors he'd committed, that damned love was still there.

I knew what it was to snap, to still be a good person but to do the most heinous and awful things to others because of a pain so terrible that it twisted you from the inside.

He was sitting beside Father with an expectant look upon his face. The Witch was as harmless as a child behind him.

"The day I saw you," he said, and I frowned, wondering what he was doing, "I do not know, Arielle, but I felt... a bond. An instant bond. You were the daughter to me that I could never have. And you treated me as a father. I loved you well. With all my heart. I was never going to allow them to hurt you."

I trembled. Silence filled my bones, a type of silence that could only be born from a dawning horror of realization.

"Your father made me watch for you. I had to report everything back to him. When I saw you with your mother, the witch, I knew what would happen because I knew you."

I gasped, mouth gaping. A thousand thoughts rolled through my mind. "What are you saying, Jacamoe?"

He was quiet for so long that I thought perhaps he meant not to answer, but he finally let out a long-suffering sigh. "I lured your sister into the gardens. And when the witch's soul tore through our Kingdom, I captured her. I managed to siphon off just enough of the witch's power to enhance my own magick so that the cuffs could not hinder me. Just long enough to make it look authentic. But your father swam into the blast I had directed at Aquata, and...I...I..." He shrugged. "I was not supposed to be able to harm him, maybe because it was not purposeful, but he is stronger than Aquata, and he survived what she could not, though the blow took its toll on him. After that, I panicked. And I got you mixed up in this, and I am sorry, daughter of my heart. I am sorry. I only wanted to be free of this place. Of these people."

I didn't realize how hard I was shaking until I nearly fell. Hatter's arms around me once more kept me standing. That strange numbing silence in me grew. "You did this. You did all of this. You killed my family. My friend. This wasn't a small deed you did, Jacamoe. You hurt people. A lot of people. You need help. And I need to take you in."

He shook his head. "It is over for me now, anyway. When the Council of Djinn discovers my perfidy, they will sentence me to a life-time of purgatory. The tortures I will endure there will be worse than your imagined nightmares of it." His smile was stiff and grim. "No, there is no other choice. I have to die. I will not allow them to take me in."

"Are you asking me to kill you?" I shook my head. That wasn't happening. I knew what he did, but I would not allow it. He could still be saved.

He frowned. "I see your thoughts, Little Fish, but they are no use. I will kill myself. I have done wrong. I see that now. It all slipped through my hands. I never meant for any of this to happen. I just didn't know how to stop it. When I am dead, the undead will cease moving. But not Hook. Anahita wanted me to place a charm on him, allowing her to control him."

"What?"

He shrugged. "She meant well, I think. It is your curse. She thought she could thwart it by being able to control any future actions on his part."

I shook my head. "There is no curse on me, Jacamoe. I don't believe it. Father had to have lied about that too. Hook died. I never changed."

He sniffed, ruffling bloody fingers through his salt-and-pepper hair. "Mayhap. Your father, I fear, was an enigma to us all. Perhaps he did lie. But it is no matter now. What does matter is that Hook has no soul. It was easy to turn him into a golem because he could not fight me off. And without his soul, he can never be saved. Once I am dead, you will need to put a spear through his temple then cut off his head and all his limbs. Bury them separately. Without a soul, he will simply come back together and rampage again unless you do. Bury him as far as the East is from the West. It is imperative you do so, Arielle."

"You keep saying that you will kill yourself"—I held up a hand, inching closer to him—"but you don't need to. Let me speak to the council of Djinn. Not everyone who is lost is unworthy. I was once too. And I came back. You can come back."

He grinned. "No, princess. I can never come back. Because I will kill your father."

My father was not a good man, but I would never allow that. "No, you won't. You won't stain your hands that way. You won't do this, Jac. He will answer for his crimes, but you must stop this. Now."

His smile was soft, and full of pain. "I love you. I always have. He is a bad man, Arielle, who has done many, many bad things. He has hurt countless others. His tyranny is unlike any I have ever known before. I know you want to save everyone, but some people are not worth saving."

"No." I shook my head and took a step closer. "No, Jacamoe. No. You will not hurt him. I cannot allow it."

Then, finding strength I'd not known I had, I ran toward my father. Hatter wasn't far behind. Using myself as a living shield, I widened my stance and held up a restraining hand.

I expected for him to try and fight his way to me, but he still sat, staring at me with an overwhelming radiance of love bursting through his eyes. "So you did not know. It is okay, my dear. I always wondered. But you have given me a gift this day. Your love was always uncondi-tional, I see that now. I wondered with the others. But I always hoped you did not know."

I frowned. "What?"

"Long ago, when he captured me, he forced me to tether my soul to his, binding my life force to his and lengthening his years exponentially. The only true way he can die is if I do. You see, that blast should have killed him. He cannot come back from it, Arielle. Not unless I will it, and I do not. The Djinn are notoriously difficult to kill. But there are ways."

Suddenly he held an obsidian blade.

My eyes grew wide. "Stop! Don't!"

"It is okay, Little Fish. It will not last long. Just look away. Look away."

"Jacamoe, stop!" Hatter roared, racing for him, but time slowed to a standstill, and I screamed as I watched him raise his arm and pierce his carotid with the knife. A geyser of red pumped thickly into the water.

I feel to my knees. "No! No!" I reached for Jacamoe, my heart shattering in my chest. What he'd done had been monstrous, but he'd been my father in every sense of the word.

My blood father's body began to convulse and twitch violently. He was dying too. Jacamoe hadn't lied—Father really had leeched off of Jacamoe's life energy.

It was neither as painless or as quick as Jacamoe had said.

"Elle," Hatter squeezed out, and then he was racing toward me. What was happening, neither of us could stop it. But I could not look away either. I held onto my blood father, but it was Jacamoe that I watched with tears and love burning in my eyes.

When it was over there was nothing but silence. The witch remained unmoved. Her powers returned to her now withered and near skeletal body. My mother. My true mother. What a fecked up world I lived in. I felt myself sinking into a quagmire of pain and thousands of thoughts and what ifs.

Hatter's hands were on me, and I felt a violent shaking. "Get up. Stop. You must come back to me. We have to reach Hook before he gets to your sister. Don't forget why we're here. Come back to me, Elle. Come back."

Tears and snot ran down my cheeks and nose, but his words snapped me out of the yawning darkness of agony. I clutched at his arms. "Hook. Yes. We have to save him. Hatter, I can't—"

"You won't lose him. I vow it. Now. Get. Up!"

I did. Somehow, I found the will. I got up, and we went to find Hook.

I'll be damned if I let him die. No more death. Not today.

WE FOUND HIM ONLY MINUTES LATER, STILL BANGING ON THE church doors protecting my sister and her last few guards.

Jacamoe said I needed to kill him, but I would be damned. He said he was unsaveable without a soul. But I did have his soul. His soul was in me, keeping me sane. But it was not mine to keep, not anymore.

I just had to figure out a way to return it to him without completely losing myself in the process and going batshite crazy on Hatter when I was without a soul.

Taking my hand in his, Hatter led me toward another trail, one we'd already walked through. He made sure to keep our steps precisely where they'd been before so that we didn't leave a new trail.

Once we no longer heard any rustling, he stopped and crouched, pulling me down with him. "I know what we need to do. I know what to do, Elle. Do you trust me?"

"With all my heart and whatever's left of my soul." I breathed the truth to life, deciding that I could open myself fully to him. I could let go of the armor I'd carved for myself so long ago. I could be weak with him, because being with him wasn't actually a weakness. It never had been. Being with Hatter made me stronger. And I made him stronger too. Together, we were whole.

He framed my face with his large palm. His words were low and hushed, but I heard them just fine. "Then I need you to let me carve Hook's soul out of you."

"What?" I frowned. "Y-You can't do that. Only a—"

He closed his eyes. "You've known for a long time that I'm not human, Elle." When next he looked at me, the fire that sometimes danced around his skin burned brightly in his eyes.

I swallowed hard, realizing that I was finally about to learn who Hatter really was. And for the first time, I was ready. "Angel?" I guessed. All those times I'd seen him around demons, how they reacted to him, the fire that burned brightly around him like holy flame made me think he had to be an angel.

He snorted. "I wish. I'm no angel, Elle. What I am is high caste."

I sucked in a shaky breath. Instinct had me snatching my hand from out of his, staring at him in wide-eyed wonder. "How high caste?" My voice wavered for just a second.

His jaw stiffened, and I caught sight of his fists clenching.

"How high, Maddox!"

"All the way," he barked back. "I'm a king." He flinched, casting his eyes to the side. Shame and regret were so prominent on his face that it almost hurt me to look at him.

Vertigo stole over me, and I had to slam my hand against the hedgerow beside me to brace myself.

He was a king. There were only two Kings of Hells—one ruled Hel and the other Hell. They were brothers, and with tempers so bad that rumor had it they'd once been responsible for the ruination and subsequent destruction of one of our most ancient peoples of Grimm for nothing other than petty jealousy and spite.

I knew very little of the kings because no one sane traveled through either of the hells at all, unless under very specific circumstances, like Midas' ball. I gasped, my gaze finding his. "Which kingdom is yours?" I asked, trying to prove my hunch correct. "One L or two?"

He glanced off to the side, frowning as he scanned the horizon for any sight of Hook. "This isn't the time for this, Elle."

I slashed my hand through the air, shutting him up. "I know it's not. And yet, when is it ever the time for us, Maddox? You drop a bomb on me and expect me not to have questions? Well, I have them. And lots of them. Which hell?"

He growled low. "One L. And before you ask, yes, I granted Midas use of it for his ridiculous ball."

"That's why that demon acted so strange around you. Isn't it? Because you're his king? But if you're his king, why did you almost die? You're immortal. You're a god. You're death. I don't understand how—"

He squeezed his eyes shut, and I knew our time was running out and that I should shut down my line of questioning and try to save us rather than interrogate him. But for so long, I'd had questions he'd always refused to answer.

"I have been transformed!" He growled angrily beneath his breath, inching in toward me. And though he was a demon king and I would do well to run away in fright from him and brand him an enemy as surely as Jacamoe had become to me, I couldn't. Because though I was confused and angry about his continued deceptions, I would have liked to think I was generally a good judge of character. And I'd seen his heart countless times—I'd seen him with me and with others, how desperately he fought to help those in need, and how badly he felt at the death of innocent life.

"By whom?"

"My brother, of course. Who else?"

I bit my lip, worrying it. Time was running out. It was just not the time for this discussion. But gods, I had a thousand questions. *Why is the angel tattooed on his arm? Why is he cursed in the first place? And when will he return? Because if he is the King of Hel, he'll have to return to rule eventually. Won't he?*

I thought suddenly about his golden soul and how godlike it had felt. That had been my first real clue that whatever Maddox was, it'd been far greater than I'd ever imagined.

There had been so many times I'd likened his face to the beauty of a demon lord, little knowing that he was the father of many of them. And then I thought about his child, his Mariposa, and the terrible pain I heard in his voice whenever he spoke of her.

Finding out my partner was literally a beautiful monster crawled out from the bowels of Hel had been shocking. But as the dust settled, I knew for certain that I'd always been safe with Maddox before, and his nature hadn't changed. Knowing who he was didn't have to change things between us unless I made it that way.

"I have a hundred questions," I whispered.

He shuddered. "Elle, I—"

I held up my hand, because if he showed me a shred of kindness in this moment, I might actually have broken. After everything I'd been through down here, I was just barely hanging on. "Don't," I whispered. "Just don't. Not right now."

He wrapped his large hand around my delicate wrist. So big. So strong. So much power lived and breathed within that man, a man I'd held, a man I'd been falling in love with—did love. I mentally corrected myself. There was no sense in lying about it anymore.

"Later? I need you to answer all my questions later. Can you do that? Can you trust me enough to do that?"

He flinched, and his dark eyes looked haunted. I wondered if he'd ever had the conversation with Alice. Maybe things hadn't worked out for them because she'd allowed her fear of his true nature to overcome the love she'd once had for him.

Loving a being like him was a doomed effort. At least, that's what I might have thought before, but I'd suspected for a long time that Hatter was much more than what he'd first appeared to be. His powers and his looks hinted at that.

If I was being honest with myself, on some level I'd known. *How often had I thought of him as a demon? How often had I subconsciously made those comparisons? Constantly.* Of course, I'd known.

Be brave. I placed my palm against his whiskered cheek. His mouth formed a tiny O, and his nostrils flared. Hope burned like a flame in his dark eyes.

I didn't understand how any of it was possible. I knew I played with fire. The man wasn't just godlike—he truly was one of them. So I couldn't figure out why he was here and why he couldn't just snap his fingers and make all of it end, immediately.

His free hand curved over mine, trapping my hand against his cheek. "Elle." He breathed my name like a benediction.

Finally, I heard the approaching footsteps of Hook's shuffling gait. He'd been shot to hells and stabbed, and one arm had been torn off. Nothing had stopped him. Still, he came, a cursed soldier who knew no pain and no fear, nothing other than his insatiable thirst to kill.

My sisters were all safe indoors. My power, which had felt depleted earlier, was a spark in my chest once more. If I made it through, the first thing I would do when I got back to Grimm was study. Hard.

"Do you trust me?" he whispered with a note of hope and longing in his voice.

The answer was simple. Since the shock was gone, I knew the answer to that question. I'd always known it—I'd just been scared to completely let go again. I'd let go once, and the loss of Hook had nearly driven me mad.

But life couldn't be lived in fear. Because then that was no life at all.

So I answered him truthfully, but not with words. I leaned forward and kissed him. It was just a whisper of lips on lips, just a touch of our two souls, but I hoped he would recognize it for what it truly was.

His arm wrapped tightly around my waist, and he trembled.

A demon king, trembling in my arms. The beast of all beasts, and he seemed undone by one simple kiss. I pressed our foreheads together and breathed him in, as he did me.

"I can take out his soul, Elle, with my claw. But it will hurt like hells."

I squeezed my eyes shut. "Hook needs his soul back if we're to wake him from his golem state. I understand, Maddox." It was my turn to shake. Without a soul, I would become the monster. "You have to promise me," I whispered, "that when I... turn, you won't hesitate. You're a demon king, so I probably can't kill you—"

"I can be killed in this form, Elle. You almost saw it happen once."

He was referring to the time, of course, when Hook had stabbed him with a poison-tipped blade. He'd said "this form," and I wondered what his true form—his true face—was. Gods, I had so many questions.

I shook my head. It wasn't the time for that. "Don't let me hurt anyone. Promise me, Hatter."

"You're a witch now too, Elle. You may not need a soul."

"I'll become my mother!" I hissed in a violent whisper, even as the shuffling feet drew closer and closer. "Just because witches can survive without them doesn't mean they're better for it. You'll kill me. Promise."

"No." His jaw tightened. "No. Never. I won't lose you. I told you, I will always find you. Because you are mine. You are my promise. You are the hope I've waited for all of my eternal life. I love you, Elle. Where you go. I go. Trust me. That's all you need to do. Let me handle the rest this time."

The shuffling drew closer and closer, and then I saw his shadow before he turned the corner. He was a terrible and macabre sight. Crowley had done a number on him, ripping off one arm, mangling the toes of his opposite foot. His guts were out and trailing behind him, leaving long bloody smears in his wake.

His face, once so beautiful, was deformed, missing its nose and part of his lower lip. I knew that if we could just get him topside to the fae doctors of Grimm Central, he could be saved. Maybe he would never be whole again, but he could be saved. Hook was a survivor, no matter what curveballs were thrown at him. Like a cat, he always seemed to land on his feet.

And yet, I had my doubts. I rubbed at my chest. No matter what we threw at his golem form, he could manipulate it and throw it back to us tenfold. Fighting him was no longer an option if I had any hope of him and us surviving the night.

I looked at Hatter and smiled softly even as a heated tear gathered in the corner of my right eye. I had a giant lump in my throat as he reached up and wiped the tear away with the pad of his thumb.

"You ready?"

I didn't need to ask him how much it would hurt, because I knew it would. "Always," I whispered.

He sniffed then set his jaw with grim determination, and I felt the scrap of an elongated black talon curve along the side of my cheekbone, where'd he'd just wiped the tear away.

"I love you, Elle," he whispered hoarsely. "So damn much."

Then he reared back, and I stiffened my spine, but no amount of bracing could have saved me from the fiery torture of having his bladed fingers tear through the soft meat of my stomach.

I screamed, no longer bothering for stealth. Fire poured down my throat. Screams sounded in my ears. Dry bones raked at my flesh. I was being flayed alive by the very demons he ruled.

And then I began to convulse. The colors of night began to fade away. I spasmed, feeling myself starting to choke on my own bile, seizing violently as those sharpened talons moved up, up, up, sliding against my organs. I screamed, but nothing came out. The veins in my neck were stretched to their bursting point.

I heard Hook drawing ever and ever closer.

"Hang on, dark heart." Hatter's whispers were harsh and demanding, but they sounded so far away, as if I heard them through water. I knew what that meant. I was losing my grip on reality, and I would pass out soon. And if I did that, if I lost control of who I was, I didn't know what I would become.

"Just hang on," he commanded, "just a little bit more. You're doing so good. So good, Elle. I'm so proud of you." Hatter whispered a running litany that sounded like a dirge in my ears.

Blood was pouring out of my nose and the sides of my mouth. My eyes were starting to roll. And then I finally felt it, the soft tug and pull of Hook's soul.

The scream that came out of me then was like that of an animal being brutally tortured. It was raw and visceral and real. The waters rolled. The earth beneath our feet heaved.

I felt the flood of siren's magick rise up. The witch had told me she'd stolen it all from me, but she'd only wounded me. She hadn't stripped me completely. I felt it, a dark and twisted violence that wanted to consume everything and everyone in its path.

My own fingers grew talons. My skin rippled, turning a ghastly bluish-black. The bottomless wellspring of a siren's unnatural hunger rose up like a flood in me.

I sank my claws into Hatter's shoulders, dug them in deeply, chortling as I scented his gods blood.

"I love you, Elle," was the last thing I remembered before he pulled Hook's soul out of me.

The world turned black, and I remembered no more.

۞

Hatter

SHE WAS A TRUE MONSTER. HER FLESH WAS BLACK, AND SHE HAD scales running down her legs. Elle had become a twisted amalgamation of two different species. I gently ran my blood-soaked hand along the sharpened curve of her cheek. Her breathing was shallow. She wouldn't last much longer.

I'd felt her latent siren magick as I'd searched for Hook's soul. She was right to fear losing her soul completely, as she was a creature that would put even my own demons to shame.

I heard the grunt, and I shot quickly to my feet, forced to release my hold on her. She would rise as a monster once the shock wore off, but I wouldn't allow it. Elle's suffering was at an end.

I turned, looking at the battered face of the male who'd come before me. His eyes were nothing but empty sockets, and his soul orb rested in the palm of my hand, but it was different than a normal human soul should be. There was power trapped in it, time itself. His soul hadn't seemed to alter Elle, maybe because she was more powerful than even she realized. I wondered what it would it do to a human like Hook, but I had no way of knowing and no time to figure it out.

Hook reached for me. He would never stop. That's what Jacamoe did to him. He'd stripped him of all autonomy and made him little more than a machine that existed solely to kill, just as had been done by his previous mistress.

A part of me knew that I should hate Hook, because he still owned Elle's heart, no matter how much her words and actions tried to deny it. But I didn't. All I felt for him was pity. He'd been used for ill ever since his first death. My only hope was that by returning him his soul, all that torture might finally come to an end. And whatever happened from there, Elle would undoubtedly figure it out. My job would be to support her decision, no matter which way she chose to go with things.

I could let Hook die, and she would not blame me for it. It would be too easy to believe that he'd been so far gone that there was no coming back for him this time. But I could not do that.

And it wasn't for me, for I'd done worse in my time. I'd learned a lesson by being with Alice, though: no relationship could survive without truth between us. So I did not do the thing for me, but rather for Elle's soft heart.

No matter what she told me, I knew that Elle would always love him. He would always come first, and I was okay with that. I needed her, but that didn't mean I needed every part of her, not unless she wished to give it to me.

I'd seen the devastation in her eyes when Crowley had fallen, and I wondered if she even knew how she felt for him. How I'd suspected for some time that she'd truly felt for him. They'd been trapped together in Undine, with only each other to lean on for support. I knew their dynamic had shifted, and possibly for good. But those were bridges that would be crossed later. Much later.

I pressed my lips into a thin line. "For her," I whispered, and then I struck, shoving my fist through a ready-made cavity in Hook's chest.

I wasn't sure if returning Hook's soul would snap him out of his rage killing, but it was his last chance. If it didn't stop him, then I would do what I had to do. At least then I could honestly say I'd tried everything I could to save him. I would be damned before I let him kill her. Death could not have her. Ever.

"Awake!" I roared, thrusting my powers into that command. The blue mortal light washed through him, casting out a glow that made him seem to burn like fire.

In the next second, he gave a hard grunt then collapsed, and black smoke curled out of him, gathering and coalescing into a fiery whole. It wailed like the souls of ten thousand damned were trapped within it. The shadow ball throbbed with power, pulsing harder and harder and harder until it exploded in a shower of ebony sparks.

The last of Jacamoe's magick was finally extinguished. Hook landed with a heavy thud on the ground, his broken body oozing and seeping blood and gore from the countless exposed wounds.

I knew his reign of terror was finally at an end. I turned and looked at Elle, beautiful even in her monstrous form. My heart was full with longing and with sadness for what I had to do.

She twitched, her lips softly smacking as the thirst for destruction began to rise up in her like one of Jacamoe's undead.

I shuddered.

I'd come to Grimm to find the one thing I'd always wanted but could never find in Hel, my partner. My queen.

The mantle was a heavy one, being queen of Hel, and one few would ever wish upon themselves. My brother had mocked and scorned me for doing so. Bhex had always found me weak and my fascination with finding my queen pathetic at best.

I thought I'd found it in Alice. We'd even had a child together. But having Mariposa had changed me in ways I could never have imagined and made me a different man, one who was no longer so sure about his way or his reasons for doing as he'd done for so long.

Elle twitched, her groaning growing louder. The hunger to consume souls would soon become a ravenous thing in her. I remembered the only other time I'd seen her turn—she'd almost been too much for me in the puny mortal shell I wore.

What will she think when she learns the full truth of me? Will she still touch me? Want me? Will she still trust me? Alice hadn't, not when she'd learned everything.

I blinked. If I didn't do it now, I would never get another chance again. I'd asked her to trust me, and she said that she did. I hoped for the gods' sakes that she'd meant it.

Kneeling beside her, I gently but firmly placed a hand upon her chest, keeping her locked where she was. Then without another thought or a second's hesitation, I did to myself as I'd done to her just a couple of minutes ago.

Blackness swirled around me as the world spun. My claws trembled as I latched onto the edge of my golden soul.

I could only do it once. If she didn't accept me—if she didn't truly accept me—the soul would turn to dust inside of her. She would reanimate as a monster that would need putting down, and I would kill the whole world before I allowed that.

"Please, Elle, please," I whispered around the blood that smeared my own lips as I violently yanked and tore my soul in two.

The birth of a queen of Hel was a violent one steeped in darkness and in blood. Nothing about my world was simple or easy.

Licking the blood from off my lips, I yanked my hand out from the cavity in my chest and looked at her. Her eyes were fully black, her face a mask of fury and raw, primal rage. Gods, she was a beauty.

"Forgive me, my queen," I whispered before thrusting my fist through the wound I'd inflicted when I'd forcefully torn Hook's soul out of her. She screamed, hooking her clawed hands into my back, driving them deep like spears and bleeding me like a stuck pig on a hook.

My fires began to rise up, bathing me in flame, and her too, meeting the water of her own form and turning instantly to heated steam. It was literally a baptism by water and fire, a cleansing and a test to see if she was worthy to walk beside the King of Hel.

Her unholy screams filled the night, and I shuddered as I landed in a heap on my arse, bringing her body to my chest and holding her tightly. Her skin was peeling off from the steam, blistering up in other places. My fires were consuming both of us. My hands were nothing but bone now.

Alice hadn't wanted that life. She hadn't wanted the burden I'd thrust upon Elle. Alice hadn't wanted me. Nobody did, not when they knew the reality and burden of what it meant to be with something—someone like me. Bhex had warned me, told me I would find nothing but disappointment in the human world. I was too soft and too stupid to not seek companionship amongst my own kind, those born to endure the same hardship.

I cradled her bones to my bones, bending my head over hers, whispering words to her that came from my own heart. I'd always known I was different, that I was flawed, that I was not what a true demon king ought to be.

"Sleep now, Arielle. I'll be here when you awake."

CHAPTER

ELLE

I knew something was wrong the moment my conscious mind began flooding back in.

I felt every tear in my flesh, the ache of my wounds throbbing and burning, and hands holding me. I heard the rushed murmurs of a male's voice. Slowly, everything came back to me: Jacamoe's betrayal. My pathetic attempts at matching his magick with my own. Watching as Hook had risen like a zombie from its dirt cradle. The emptiness in his eyes as he'd stared at me. Father's death...

I trembled.

Anahita's inability to stop Jacamoe had been breathtakingly brutal. I didn't even know if my sister lived or if I would be burying not just a parent, but another sibling.

Jacamoe's revenge had been so well played that he'd nearly won. He'd nearly succeeded in bringing them all down. Crowley and I had fought like twin devils to stop him, but he'd tossed Hook at Crowley, effectively separating us.

If Maddox hadn't shown up when he had—my nostrils flared and sickness rose up the back of my throat—I would have been dead. I almost didn't make it out of that fight alive.

My mentor, my friend had betrayed me, betrayed us all.

I frowned. I felt different. *Why?*

It took me a second to realize that suddenly nothing hurt anymore. *Wait, how am I thinking so rationally? So reasonably? Shouldn't I be the monster of the deep again, the one who'd very nearly toppled all the great houses of Undine in her destructive and violent path once before?*

My eyes snapped open. I wasn't sure what I expected to see.

But it was just Maddox. His skin gleamed like molten metal. He had no cuts and no bruises—he was completely healed somehow. Yet somehow, he looked different too. Same hair. Same eyes. Same everything. But... I sat up.

He instantly released me. I cocked my head. "How..." My fingers curved over my chest, and I noticed that my skin was also healed. The cuts and bruises were all gone.

In fact—I flexed my toes, stretched my calf muscles, and there was no pain whatsoever.

I looked back at him. His lips were set in a straight but tense line. I knew that look. He'd been my partner long enough that I knew when something wasn't quite right.

"What did you do? Why am I not insane with bloodlust?" The second I asked it, I felt the glow of a soul burning brightly within me. But it wasn't a normal burn. It wasn't like my own had been, or even Hook's.

The new soul burn was brighter even than the sun and so incredibly powerful that I literally felt as though I could fly if I focused hard enough, which was absolutely ridiculous. I'd never felt so good in my life.

I wet my lips and started to shove strands of hair out of my eyes, and that's when I noticed that it was no longer black, as it was after my battle with the Sea Witch. It was white. Snow white and streaked with blue at the tips. I blinked. "Ha-Hatter? What is—"

"I healed you, Arielle."

The answer was suddenly crystal clear, and I wondered why it'd taken me so long to figure it out. I glanced over toward Hook, who lay prostrate. His chest was barely rising and falling. We had to get him topside soon, to our healers and away from the death trap that was Undine.

All of it needed to wait, and yet... "You shared soul with me." It took me less than a second to understand the ramifications of it all. His soul was golden. He was also a demon king. I shared a soul with an immortal godlike being. But I didn't feel dark or violent or wicked. I didn't feel deranged or like a monster. I only felt like... me, just better.

I swallowed hard. "How much will this change me?"

He sighed deeply and gingerly got to his feet, patiently holding his hand out to me to take it. I stared at his hand, feeling a little as though it was symbolism in some way, like if I took his hand, I was silently accepting what he'd done to me. He was a demon. I knew keeping his soul would not come without ramifications—maybe good ones, and maybe not.

I took his hand.

His breathing stuttered for just a second. He held my hand tightly to his chest.

Who is my partner? Who is he really? I felt in some ways like I was just beginning to explore the truth of that.

He brushed tendrils of hair behind my ears, and his touch was exquisitely gentle, almost tender. And then he spoke in that deeply cultured voice of a Landian male. "I don't know," he finally said. "But what I did was irrevocable. In days or even weeks you will begin to see the truth of your transformation."

My stomach bottomed out and I was terrified to ask him what that meant. Scared to fracture this tenuous feeling of gratitude I still felt. So for now, I didn't want to think about it.

"Why? That's all I want to know right now. Why did you do it?"

"Because I couldn't stand living in a world without the you that I know. I didn't lie when I said I need you, Elle."

"I can't be your hope of salvation," I said without thought, though the words were true. "No one can be that for anyone. It's a fool's errand to even try."

He shook his head. "I don't need you to want me. If you don't, I accept that. I only need you to be."

I squeezed my eyes shut. We had so much to talk about, but as ever with us, there was no time for any of it. "We need to get to Hook and

Crowley. We need to let my sisters and their guards out of their cages. And then when we get back to Grimm—"

"We need to talk. I know," he said, sounding resigned to his fate.

Odd that I wasn't mad at him. Maybe he assumed I would be. Hells, maybe I should have been. He hadn't told me what he planned to do. He'd let me think he would kill me once I turned and became the monster of the deep.

He was a demon. The highest of them, in fact. And of course splitting his soul would come with its own share of consequences. I wasn't stupid. He'd said I would transform and that thought was an ominous one. Just who would I be in two weeks time? Me, or a darker more twisted version of me? Was it just shock keeping me so sane right now? I halfway thought so.

Nodding, I pointed with my chin toward Hook's body. "Can you rush ahead and take him to the hospital. He's finally got his soul back. He might actually survive this."

"Of course, but what will you do?"

I pressed my lips together. "I need to see to my sister. I will also be needed here. Father's song will be in a few days. I was a terrible daughter to him in life, and though the bastard doesn't deserve it I will be here for him in death."

He clenched his jaw. I knew he understood that I was sending him away. But the truth was I needed time to think about everything. I wasn't stupid, but I was done with snapping first and thinking later. He'd done what he'd done to save me, and I didn't see how I could fault him for that. But I'd gone from being the puppet of a witch to... *what?* I didn't even know what I was anymore.

And judging by the look in his eyes, he didn't know either.

"I need time, Hatter. That's all. I'm not mad at you. If you hadn't done what you did, I wouldn't be here now. I wouldn't be me. So thank you. Thank you for doing it. I don't ever want you to think I don't recognize the sacrifice you've made."

He pursed his lips but nodded once. Still, I read the conflict in his eyes, and I knew that on some level, he understood that what he'd done wasn't entirely fair. I'd asked him to kill me. That had been my choice. I knew little of demons, and what I did know wasn't good. But then all I had to do was think of my partner, of all that he'd done for me, for us, and I was conflicted all over again. *What's truth, and what's fiction?* I didn't know, and I no longer had the luxury to find it out, because like it or not, a new world had been thrust upon me.

"But you also didn't give me a choice in this—"

He flinched, and I could see the pain reflected in his eyes. He knew it was true.

"Am I demon now too?"

He swallowed, and for brief moment, I wasn't sure he would answer. "Yes."

I wanted to laugh. I also wanted to cry. Every time I turned around, it seemed like I was losing another part of me. A demon, a siren, and a witch walk into a bar..." I snorted with laughter, but the truth was that I didn't know how I felt about any of it. I sniffed, swallowing the lump in my throat.

"I'm sorry. But there is more, and I would not forgive myself if I didn't tell it to you. You aren't just a demon, Elle. You're mine. My queen. You're now the Queen of Hel."

I turned away, trembling and shaking all over, telling myself not to leave that way. He deserved a pat on the back or an acknowledgement, at the very least.

But I couldn't. I just couldn't. I heard rather than saw him pick up Hook's body. I felt the pulsing power of the travel tunnel at my back, courtesy of the key card.

When he left, I thought that maybe I would feel empty, cold, and dizzy with desire to get him or even Hook back. But I didn't. I was completely numb. I felt myself walking back toward the pathway where Crowley's body lay scattered in pieces.

Hook had really done a number on him. If Crowley actually could heal from something like this, he was gonna have a helluva of headache.

I glanced down at the bits of him scattered along the cobbled floor. He was healing, just as he said he would. I saw new flesh already beginning to form on the stumps that remained.

So if it was true, then it was also true that it was the last time he would heal. Jacamoe had stolen his last and final recharge from him.

When Crowley came back, he would be as mortal as Hook and just as physically weak.

I saw his beating heart in the corner. I almost walked past, but I felt something for the first time since my reawakening, a soft and gentle stirring in my breast, and I marveled that a creature of hells could feel that way. Kneeling, I tenderly reached for the beating organ, bringing it gently to my breast and cooing softly to it.

He'd been there for me when everyone else had abandoned me. Knowing what it would mean for him, Crowley hadn't left me. We might have had our disagreements, and he might even have hated my guts at this point, but he hadn't abandoned me. It had been just us, and he'd stayed.

I kissed the heart, feeling the smear of hot blood upon my lips. I licked it off without thinking and felt a queer sensation coursing through me.

I hadn't hated the taste of it.

Do demons drink blood? And how demon am I, really? As Queen of Hel, will I one day feel the sudden desire to bathe in the blood of my enemies? There wasn't a group in all of Grimm more bloodthirsty than demons. I shivered, only snapping from my thoughts when I felt the heart lurch with a slugging beat in the palm of my hand.

I didn't know if it was true that the epicenter of the soul resided in the heart, but I thought that maybe it did. And if it did, I whispered to it, "When you wake up, I'll be here. Though I'm not the same anymore, I'll always be here for you, just like you were here for me too."

Then, standing, I turned and walked his heart back toward the largest mass of him that remained. I set it down gently, almost reverently, back in the cage of his chestplate.

I had to find my sister. I had to release her and her guards. Then I would stay just long enough to bury my father and wait for Crowley to fully regenerate. After that, I would face what awaited me topside.

I thought that maybe a sane person would hate Maddox, and I wondered at why I didn't. I didn't have a clue what lay in store for me in the future. All I knew was that I wasn't even close to being the same as I'd been just a year before. Then, I'd been a cursed siren.

I had become something altogether different and singularly unique. *Who am I, really? And more to the point, who do I want to be now?*

I needed to know that before I could decide on anything else. I needed a chance to grieve the loss of my kin and to grieve the loss of who I'd once been. I needed to become stronger and better so that this never happened to me again.

When I went back to Grimm, I wouldn't be the same. But I no longer wanted to be.

The End, for a short time...

PLEASE LEAVE A REVIEW! REVIEWS LET ME KNOW WHEN A SERIES IS APPRECIATED AND IT HELPS ME TO PRIORTIZE THE BOOKS I WORK ON NEXT BECAUSE YOU, THE READERS, REALLY WANT MORE OF THEM!

LOVE GRIMM? WANT TO KNOW WHEN BOOK 4, *THE DEVIL'S IN THE DETAILS,* COMES OUT? MAKE SURE THAT YOU FOLLOW ME ON FACEBOOK FOR DETAILS. I'm already hard at work on book 4! I just couldn't stand leaving Hook, Crowley, Hatter, or Elle waiting to find out what happens next! So make sure to sign up for my newsletter!

UNTITLED

More Books!

The Night Series written as Selene Charles

The Complete Night Series Collection, a boxed set of all 4 books!
With over 2000 four star reviews on Goodreads alone!

The Night Series originally written as Marie Hall, I'm now writing as Selene Charles. Fully Completed Series! Written by the USA Today Bestseller of Crimson Night.

NO CLIFFHANGERS

Welcome to the carnival of the damned. I'm one of the seven deadly sins, they call me Lust, but you can just call me Pandora. This is a story of darkness. Redemption. Hope. And betrayal I never saw coming.

UNTITLED

A reaper's found me—deadly to my kind—and though I know I shouldn't be I'm as drawn to him as a moth is to flame. But I don't have time to indulge in my fantasies of stripping him down naked and having my dirty, dirty way with him. Because there's a prophecy going round. Real end of the world type stuff. And somehow this little demon is at the heart of it all. I'm thousands of years old, but I'm starting to feel like my numbers finally come due...

COMPLETED SERIES!!

Tempted Series by Selene Charles YA Urban Fantasy (Spin-off set in the Night Series world)

Welcome to Whispering Bluff, Tennessee. Where the guys are hot. The girls are sweet. And nothing is what it seems...

Forbidden, Book 1
Reckless, Book 2
Possessed, Book 3

COMPLETED SERIES!!

***The Southern Vampire Detective Series written as Selene Charles
(Loose Spin-off set in the Night Universe)***

Meet Scarlett Smith, Southern Vampire Detective...

*Well at least that's what she is today. Not too long ago she was just a regular
Southern Belle in love with her soldier, dreaming of a life full of babies and
white picket fences.*

Then she died...

Whiskey, Vamps, and Thieves, Book 1
Fae Bridge Over Troubled Waters, (short story) 1.5
Me and You and a Ghost Named Boo, Book 2
The Vampire Went Down to Georgia, Book 3

UNTITLED

COMPLETED SERIES !!

Made in the USA
Las Vegas, NV
25 January 2024

84890354R00132